BAILEY THOMAS

Trent's Redemption

MILL CREEK MYSTIQUE
BOOK 1

BTA PUBLISHING

Published by BTA Publishing

Cover Design: Melody Pond

melodyypond.weebly.com

Interior Design: A Fabulous Production

(@afabulousproduction on Instagram)

PAPERBACK ISBN: 978-1-967156-02-3

Third Edition: March 2025

MILL CREEK MYSTIQUE SERIES

A collection of stand alone, small town, romantic suspense novels.
Each book can be read independently but features characters from the
Mill Creek town.

Suggested Reading Order
Trent's Redemption
Hidden Identities
Breaking Point
Kane's Reckoning - Coming Soon
Legally Bound - Coming Soon

Contents

To my wonderful husband: You are
my inspiration, support system, and
happily ever after.

In loving memory of my dad—
a humble miner.

One

T HE RAPID KNOCK AT Trent's front door had him hoping that this unexpected interruption would spare him another lonely evening. Hastening his steps, he twisted the knob and sucked in a sharp breath. Nothing would have prepared him for this sight. His partner's sister, and the woman he had dated. Margaret King's haunted green eyes stared back at him. Her blonde hair was thrown into a loose ponytail. Several strands had escaped and fluttered in the evening breeze. Even disheveled, she was still beautiful.

Dread settled in his gut, anchoring a weight to his chest as Dalton's last words filtered through his mind. *Promise me you'll look after her and keep her safe.*

"Maggie, what brings you here?" Trent's mind raced with possibilities, and none settled the growing dread that rotted in his stomach.

Her eyes widened briefly before she found her voice. "Can I come inside?"

"Of course, sorry," he stammered, moving aside and making a sweeping motion with his arm.

She hesitated for a second, then looked over her shoulder toward the driveway. Turning back, she met his gaze and released a deep breath. Remorse slapped him in the face as she entered his home. The last time he'd seen her was about ten months ago at Dalton's funeral. Not once had Trent reached out to see how she had adjusted to life without her brother. Now, the weight of his mistake stood in his entryway. Guilt riddled his body and his gaze shifted toward the floor because he'd let her down.

The subtle scent of oranges and vanilla floated by him as she passed. The moonlight shining through the open window cast a silvery glow across her pinched face. He clicked the deadbolt then flipped on the light before he sat on the sofa, waiting for her to join him. Her feet didn't budge, but her gaze circled the room.

Maggie raised an eyebrow, her eyes blank. "I'm sorry I didn't call first. I thought this discussion would be best in person. I can't believe I had to search the internet for your address."

"I'm glad you're here, and I should have given you my address. There's no excuse for that..."

The tension in the room increased with every second of silence that followed.

"I-I don't know what to think anymore. You might think I'm crazy or worse, have overreacted to drive all the way here." Her voice sounded like sandpaper on wood.

Trent grabbed her hand and swiped his thumb softly across her knuckles. A rush of emotions flooded his system with that simple touch. He hated the strain emanating from her body. "Are you okay, Maggie?"

He released her hand and patted the spot next to him. The cushions dipped as she sat, her gaze lingering on the room and surroundings. "Why do you have scaffolding outside? Did something happen to your home?"

Trent smiled and shook his head. "No, I just finished renovating the interior and have decided to upgrade my roof. What's going on, Maggie?"

She turned to him, flashing a brief smile. "Good. I'm glad nothing bad happened to you. Could I have a glass of water?"

"You can have anything you'd like." He meant those words and vowed to himself to prove it to her. "But you need to tell me what's upset you. What made you drive all this way to find me?"

The single tear traveling down her cheek gutted him. Her resolve and strength may have had her sitting beside him, holding herself together, but her vulnerability undid him. He tugged her body against his, to feel her warmth and the pulse of her heart as he held her tight. To remind her she wasn't alone in dealing with whatever worried her. Even if his actions these last ten months told a different story.

A niggle of hope bloomed in his chest when she hugged him back just as fiercely. This wouldn't erase his absence from her life since the death of her brother, but maybe she'd see it as an olive branch to reconnect them to days long past. To the days when they were friends and all three of them spent time together.

When she sat back against the cushion, dark circles marred the delicate skin beneath her eyes. Trent's mind whirled with a million questions. Had someone hurt her? Had Maggie been with a man who threatened her? Why was she here? All of them remained unspoken because shame swamped his system. Not only was he a shitty person, but he'd broken a promise to his friend.

Dalton would still be here if I'd taken out the shooter in the rafters. Suffocated by the memories of that horrible day, Trent shot up off the sofa, desperately needing air and space. "I'll get you that water. When I return, how about you start from the beginning and explain why you're here? We'll figure this out together."

"Thanks. You're the one person I knew would understand," she said in a mere whisper.

Jesus, what had she been through that would make her run? The woman he'd known was full of mirth and energy. He hated the mixture of defeat and uncertainty radiating from the depths of her green eyes.

"Here you go, Miss Margaret King." Trent handed her a glass of water.

"Ugh, call me Maggie, you know better. My parents called me Margaret, and that was when I was in trouble." She stared into the distance for a moment. "Maggie Moo was the nickname my brother preferred," she added with a slight wobble.

"Sorry, I miss him so much. I just never thought I'd lose him after my parents died. I figured we'd grow old together. It's been difficult knowing I'm all alone in the world."

Trent's heart was clogged with condemnation. "Never apologize for missing him. Dalton loved you. He would've done anything for you. You were his little sister. Hell, I'd known him since training at Quantico, and I knew then, he'd be the biggest pain in my ass and best friend. His death left a hole in our lives." The words he left unspoken were that he'd abandoned her, too.

A soft giggle escaped her lips. "Yes, he could be a pain. He also tried controlling my life down to who I dated."

Trent nodded in agreement. "Yes, he had firm opinions on who should date you and why."

"If I recall, you did, too, since you cited your job as a complication of our relationship. Anyway, blood or not, you've always been a part of my family, which is why I'm here." She forced a slow steady stream of air into her lungs. "You were both logical and rational men who worked from facts to solve life's problems. I've lost count of how often I've endured a lecture about being observant and always aware of my surroundings."

He interjected, "A smart person assessed their situation and acted accordingly. That coincidences rarely, if ever, exist. Yes, I speak that same dialect."

"You are cut from the same cloth as Dalton, which is why I'm in Mill Creek. I've analyzed my situation, and my findings have shocked me." She gulped the cool liquid. Straightening her spine, she continued, "Dalton made me promise—almost to the point of ritualistic chanting—that if I were ever in trouble and couldn't reach him, I should call you. I always thought he'd meant while he was alive..." Tears streamed down her face. "Someone has been following me because I'm Dalton's sister."

Trent's eyes narrowed. She'd piqued his curiosity with that assessment. He then schooled his features so they'd remain neutral. "Why would you think that?"

"I first noticed a white van parked on the street facing my apartment. It appeared after Dalton's death. The days and times were random, but it was the same van. It disappeared for a while, then returned a few weeks ago. I can't explain it, but I got a strange feeling about it."

Maggie fidgeted, cracking her fingers one by one. He sat quietly while she fidgeted with nervous energy. He didn't want to add to her stress, so he gave her the time to process her thoughts.

"How? What made it seem unusual?"

She lifted her gaze to meet his eyes and shrugged. "I only saw the driver and passenger twice, but I'm pretty sure they were the same men from the first time. This sounds bizarre, and I know it does, which is why I didn't report the van to the police. Those men could have lived in the complex or in the area. What happened the other night changed my mind, but instead of calling the police, I headed straight to you. This is personal, Trent, and it scared me."

"I'm glad you came to me." He gently urged her to continue by nodding and keeping his expression neutral. Deep down, his stomach knotted with apprehension over what came next.

A tiny smile crossed her lips. "God, you remind me of him, fierce and protective. I appreciate that you're not judging me—at least until I'm done."

"You're doing just fine, now, keep going."

"Early Saturday morning, I was working at my computer when the fire alarms went off. When I went outside to check, the adjacent unit had smoke billowing from inside. My neighbor appeared outside with her child, panicked, and talking into the phone about a grease fire and firemen coming. I ducked back inside my place to retrieve my messenger bag, which held everything that mattered to me and waited outside with my neighbor. After the firemen arrived and controlled the scene, I was informed that the fire was out, but it would be a couple of hours before I could return. I decided to head to our local coffee shop to hang out while the chaos passed. When I returned..."

The color drained from her cheeks. She lowered her head to stare at the carpet between her feet. "My front door was ajar, again, which I figured was so the firemen could finish their investigation. I caught a glimpse of that white van pulling away. When I entered, everything seemed fine...until I reached my office. Drawers were opened, and papers and folders were scattered across my desk and floor. Then, I noticed a knife stabbed into my desk holding a note that read, 'What did he know?'"

Trent snapped his brows together, his mouth drawn tight. He couldn't quell his reaction to what he'd just heard. The hairs on his neck bristled. He didn't know how, but he'd find a way to slay every one of her demons...or die trying. He owed Dalton that much.

"Why didn't you call the police? Do you know if anything was taken? Were other rooms searched?" Trent squeezed her hand a few times, bringing her gaze upward.

With her other hand, she reached for the glass and gulped the last few sips before she answered, "In my gut, I know this reaches beyond the police. The only 'he' in my life was my brother. My brain went into survival mode. I had to get out of my apartment and get to you. You'd know what to do. I-I didn't look any further. All I kept thinking was, this can't be good to have a knife stabbed into your desk, especially with how he died. I took my bag, hit the bank, and withdrew as much money as allowed. I left my car at the office and called a car rental company. I decided leaving my car behind was best. I stopped at one truck stop to rest, used only cash, then drove until I pulled into your driveway."

She sat still as if she had waited for him to say something. Processing what he had just heard shredded his insides. The last time they had spoken was at the funeral, and that encounter was strained, not ugly or mean, just distant because of him. This was opposite to how he and Maggie usually interacted. Instead, he struggled with his anger and self-condemnation while nursing the injuries he'd sustained that day alongside Dalton. As a result, Trent's job and assignment changed, which deprived him of retribution. He hated the exhaustion etched across her face. Starting now, he would atone for his wrongs.

"Brave and resilient is what you are." A surge of pride and respect flood his system. "You did damn good with disappearing off the grid and adapting in the face of adversity. You're far from an agent but acted cautiously and logically."

Fatigue, stress, and fear radiated from her, but he also saw a brief glimmer of relief. That was something he would build upon.

"Your brother would be proud. Hell, I'm proud of you. I'm also so damn sorry I haven't reached out before now. I own that. My apology doesn't change anything, but I hope my actions will. *If* you give me that chance. I'd say you read the situation right—a clusterfuck for sure."

Her eyes closed for a moment, and her shoulders dipped as tension seemed to fade from her body. Something deep inside Trent's stomach twisted painfully. Had she thought he might deny her his support and protection? Of course, why wouldn't she? It wasn't his intent, but he'd removed her from his life. Another epic screw-up to add to his list that he needed to fix.

He cupped her chin. "I understand why you weren't sure about coming to me for help, so I'll clarify that misconception now. I will always protect you, Maggie. You have my word."

She shifted her head from his grasp and stabbed him in the chest with a finger. "You hurt my feelings, but I'm not blameless either. You have to promise you won't put yourself in jeopardy in any way. I can't stand the thought of losing another person."

The painful truth behind those words constricted his chest. The vibrant woman he had known seemed to have retreated somewhat. Trent snatched her hand, loving how buttery soft her skin was under his fingertips. "Give me your keys. I think it's best to put your rental in the garage for now."

She stood and dug into her front pocket to retrieve the key ring. "Thanks for allowing me into your home, especially with my trouble in tow."

Trent extended his palm and caught the keys. "You always were trouble. I'll give you the grand tour first and point out the highlights from my renovation."

"I thought you liked living out of boxes. You know, afraid of commitment."

"Smart ass," he lamented. "I'm working on unpacking everything."

He couldn't imagine her thoughts when she arrived but was glad she'd come. He started in his kitchen, explaining how his friend Kane had updated everything to stainless steel and gas.

"This is amazing. I love the gas stovetop. That refrigerator must keep you fed for months. It's huge."

"I've heard that bigger is always better," he deadpanned.

She rolled her eyes and protested, "Seriously? You haven't changed one bit."

He flashed her an exaggerated wink and guided her through the rest of the house. When they reached the master bathroom, he showed her his second favorite feature from the renovation: his walk-in shower with multiple adjusting heads that also produced steam. He owed Kane for this gem, too. Her small whimper when she spied the shower didn't go unnoticed. Trent also hadn't missed how closely she followed him the entire time. He'd do anything to diminish the worry radiating from her body. He ended his tour with the room she'd be using and the bathroom.

At the door to the bathroom, he paused and met her eyes. "Why don't you shower in my bathroom while I move the vehicle? You can give me a woman's perspective on my shower."

She leaned her head against the doorway and sighed. "A shower sounds heavenly, but I'll use the guest bath. Will you grab my bag from the front room and put it on the bed?

"Sure, do you have anything in the car you need?"

Her mouth twisted into a frown. "No, I didn't pack any clothing or even think about bringing my bathroom supplies. In my haste, I went with the less-is-more theory. Do you have a toothbrush and paste? And if I could borrow a few things to wear, that would be super. Walking around naked might be awkward."

He groaned internally as his mind conjured several inappropriate scenarios involving her sans clothing. Built like a goddess, with her curves and creamy skin, he'd love nothing more than to see her naked. He caught her staring at his reflection in the bathroom mirror and knew he'd been nailed. His traitorous cock stirred behind the confines of his pants. This woman still caused his mind and body to want more from her. His cue to leave.

"I'll put a T-shirt and a pair of sweatpants on your bed. Leave your clothes outside the door, I'll wash them for you. We'll go shopping tomorrow to fill in whatever you left behind."

She opened her mouth as if to speak, then clamped her lips together as she moved into the bathroom.

"What's on your mind?" he asked.

"Do you have any cereal or yogurt? Something easy to fix."

He put both hands on his waist and cocked one eyebrow. "You can have whatever you want. When did you eat last?"

Her eyes narrowed, and her mouth gaped. "I-ah, a granola at the truck stop."

He shook his head. "You're my priority. That includes food, sleep, protection, and whatever else I've forgotten to mention. Get that through your thick, stubborn, and beautiful head." Trent punctuated his point by wrapping her in a crushing hug. He wasn't sure what else to do, a move so familiar from all the previous times he and Dalton had visited between assignments or while on break.

He sighed as her curves melded perfectly against his frame and in all the right places. A surge of possessiveness roared to life within him, and not only did it startle him, but it also made him back away, breaking their connection.

"Shower, then kitchen," he said in a tone that encouraged no debate.

He headed down the hall and heard the snick of the door as it closed behind him. Needing to put space between them, he'd take care of her car. This woman in his home was Dalton's sister. The same baby sister his partner proclaimed off limits to any man who worked in a risky profession. Dalton was adamant that Maggie should marry a man with a stable job, allowing him to come home every night. A man whose existence wasn't nestled in danger, with the potential to cause her harm because his job encompassed every aspect of his life. Trent had squashed his attraction to her because he hadn't wanted to ruffle Dalton's feathers. Even though he hadn't been exempt from Dalton's censure, he had to agree with the man. She deserved better. She deserved a marriage where her husband would be around every night, a man whose job wouldn't risk her safety or threaten their lives. A fact of his employment he couldn't offer.

RELIEF WASHED OVER MAGGIE'S body when Trent agreed with her assessment—she hadn't overreacted. She should never have doubted that he'd support her, but hearing it from his lips alleviated her apprehension. The warmth from his embrace grounded her. If she could press the rewind button, she'd rather go back to when Trent held her in his arms. There was a familiarity to it, and she'd missed the simplicity of knowing someone had her back.

She'd gotten to know him when she went to college in Washington, D.C. and had chosen to live in Dalton's place instead of on campus.

Her brother brought Trent home during break when they were both at Quantico. Not only had they become partners but friends. It wasn't like he was home often with his career, but it gave her an excuse to be close to her brother. She and Trent had dated a few times, but he had ended saying he didn't have time for a relationship due to his career. Her brother would never answer her question, but she would put money down on the fact he interfered.

When Trent smiled and flashed the bluest eyes she'd ever seen, it could melt the panties right off a girl. Never in her life had she experienced such a strong reaction to another person. It also didn't hurt that he was devastatingly gorgeous at six feet tall with his athletic build and all those well-defined muscles. His touch still made her girly parts tingle.

She'd cranked the shower tap to the left. When the bathroom mirror fogged over from the steam, she tugged back the curtain, adjusted the heat, then stepped inside. The hot spray pulsed against her tired muscles and sluiced down her body. She visualized removing Trent's shirt off his body to reveal raised pectorals and a ripped abdomen that flowed into a trim waist with sculpted hips. She bit her bottom lip and moaned. Well, that was what happened when one was sex deprived and surrounded by male hotness.

She adjusted the dial until a cold blast of water jolted her system. That daydream would be her little secret. She needed to stop this line of thinking. He probably had a bevy of beautiful women on speed dial. The type who looked perfect even after a torrential rainstorm. The same type her brother had circling him at all times. A girl could dream, couldn't she?

After stepping from the shower, she dried off and slathered on some lotion she found in the cabinet. She finger-combed her hair and mentally added an actual one to her list of things to buy. There was nothing like a shower to make a person feel human again. Towel wrapped around her body, she padded to the bedroom he assigned. As promised, the clothes and items from her car were sitting on her bed. She removed a stuffed animal from her tote and kissed the cow on its nose before putting it back inside. She'd give anything to hear Dalton call her by her nickname again.

She took in his home as she made her way to the kitchen. It had the perfect blend of cabin and modern.

The center of the room had a wooden dining table with four chairs, and in front of one chair sat a grilled cheese sandwich, her absolute favorite. Especially when she was having a crappy day.

Trent looked over his shoulder, holding a spoon. "You look more relaxed. The tomato soup will be ready in a minute. These are my go-to choices when I need comfort food."

Her insides melted like the cheese in the sandwich.

"Mine too," she said. The part she kept to herself, watching a hot man cook for her, did wicked things to her body. Good grief, she needed to get a grip. He was being nice, not offering her a night of decadent sex. Or a life of love, marriage, and children. The fantasy train needed to stop so she could disembark because that destination did not exist.

The last few months had changed her. She had to find a way to survive before her grief and despair consumed her entirely. Being around Trent has created a few sparks in the recesses of her mind, reminding her of the woman she had been and what they had shared.

"Are you for real? A good-looking man who can cook and isn't afraid to admit that grilled cheese and tomato soup have the power to cure most things in life. I think I've died and gone to heaven," she tossed out and took a seat at the table.

He rolled his eyes and huffed dramatically. "I hate to burst your bubble, but men can do many things these days. I can even load the dishwasher and do laundry, but I draw the line at ironing."

Maggie burst out laughing. "Ah, I needed that. It's been a while."

Trent ladled soup into a bowl. "Feel free to laugh anytime. It suits you very nicely. I also happen to appreciate the eye candy comment."

Did he just flirt with her? She took a bite of her sandwich and moaned. "This is delicious."

"The secret is mayonnaise instead of butter. It's how my mom makes them. Tonight, I want you to promise me you'll rest. I don't like seeing those dark circles under your eyes."

"I'll try, but it's hard to get my brain to stop churning over everything." She blew on a spoonful of soup.

"Well, I promise to keep the boogie men away. Hey, one question, though. Something you said earlier confused me. You said you left your car at the office. Do schoolteachers refer to their classrooms as offices now? Are you still teaching?"

She put down her spoon. "No. I quit teaching."

His eyebrows knit together as he processed what she said, but to her relief, he didn't question her any further. She didn't want to get into it tonight. Her love of teaching had died after she buried Dalton. The burden of life's truths wore her down, and she couldn't handle deceiving those precious faces daily.

Trent filled in the prolonged silence. "We can talk about all of this tomorrow after you rest."

"Okay," she said between a spoonful of soup.

"Oh, one more thing. I'm meeting some friends for breakfast tomorrow. I want you to come. Afterward, we'll head to the store to pick up whatever else you need."

Maggie took a big gulp of water. "I don't want to impose."

"I see your listening skills haven't improved," he muttered sardonically. "We're meeting them tomorrow at eight. I'll have your clothes folded and waiting for you outside your door. You'll love the Knotty Pine Tree. The food is delicious, and I want you to meet my friends, Kane and Annika. They're good people; you can trust them. Besides, your smart actions put distance between what happened in Dallas and here. It'll give us some time to figure it all out."

There was a time when meeting new people and being a social butterfly came naturally, but that part of her died when she put Dalton in the ground. She should label her life accordingly now. BD—before Dalton—and AD—after Dalton.

The scaffolding outside the kitchen window reminded her of a skeleton in the moonlight. She hated the nights the most. All her fears and problems grew into large, creepy monsters that caused her constant worry that whoever left the note would find her.

Two

BELLS JINGLED AS TRENT held open the door of the Knotty Pine Tree for Maggie to enter. The delicious scents of bacon, coffee, cinnamon, and freshly baked bread surrounded him. It was slower than usual for a Tuesday morning, but he wasn't going to complain.

Placing his palm on Maggie's back, he guided her toward the rear to his favorite booth in the corner. This table allowed him to sit with his back to the wall with views of the entire restaurant. The two big windows along the side wall gave him a perfect line of sight to Main Street. He waved and nodded to practically every customer in the diner.

She slid into the booth, and then he followed her so they sat side by side. He needed caffeine to jump-start his system. Sleep had evaded him last night. He mulled over every detail she relayed and documented those events, creating a timeline. What she told him last night blew his mind and dredged up memories he preferred to keep buried. After breakfast, he'd call Noah Parker, his friend and FBI analyst, to enlist his help.

"This place is amazing, and everything smells so good. I love all the old license plates and pictures decorating the walls. Is this the history of Mill Creek?" she asked.

"Yes, this diner is one of the original landmarks. The Sullivan family has owned it since the beginning."

"Wow, imagine all the changes they've seen over the years."

He turned to the approaching woman. "Were your ears burning, Sally?"

The older lady waved off Trent's attempt to stand. "Let me guess, you were discussing my good looks and how amazing my food is?"

Her husband hollered through the metal window that separated the front of the restaurant from the back. "Whose good food? Hey, Sheriff, Sally, I've got a question when you're finished."

She winked at Trent, then turned her attention toward Maggie and held out her hand. "I'm Sally. My husband, Peter, and I own this diner. I haven't seen you around here before. Are you planning to take this hot bachelor off the market?"

A lovely shade of pink suffused Maggie's face. He was about to jump in and save her from Sally's noisiness, but she beat him to the punch.

"Oh, I know, right? He's hot, but he's too stubborn. Besides, we're practically family. So, I'm solidly in the friend category. I'm Maggie, by the way. It's nice to meet you."

Not liking that he was the punchline or what she had said, Trent gave Sally and Maggie, who were still laughing, his best annoyed look. "I like her. She's a keeper." Sally winked then announced, "When everyone arrives, I'll circle back to take your orders." She sauntered toward the next table of waiting guests in her section.

Trent couldn't agree more, but that could never happen. Maggie's intelligence, matched with her sense of humor, made her special. Not many could diffuse Sally's interrogation style with such ease and decorum. In the process, Maggie didn't miss a beat and made a new friend. When she spoke, she gestured with her hands. With each move, her body vibrated against his, causing a zing of electricity to pulse through his system. *Friend category, my ass.*

She had the body of a man's dreams. This woman next to him, with her expressive eyes, would test his restraint at every turn. He liked seeing glimpses of the women he knew. Not just the startled and reserved woman who'd shown up on his doorstep. Seeing how she'd dropped her guard a few times gave him hope. Maybe they could help each other work through the gigantic hole Dalton's death had left in their lives. His mind traveled back to that awful morning.

The pulsing vibration of metal against the wood of a nightstand had roused him from sleep.

Snatching his phone off the nightstand, Trent glanced at the display and answered, "Can't even go a weekend without me?"

"It's those blue eyes. They've mesmerized me," Dalton cooed over the line.

Trent glanced at the alarm clock before turning over to see if he'd awakened the woman lying next to him, but she was still asleep. Maybe he could coax another orgasm or two after he ended this call.

"Let me guess," he whispered, "you're bored waiting for your flight from Dallas? Sorry, man, I'm otherwise occupied."

"Oh, you're man-whoring," Dalton drawled.

"Nice try, but the intent and expectations have been defined, so I'd call it a win-win."

"Whatever. Hey, I flew home last night from visiting my sister."

Trent bolted upright then turned to put his feet on the floor. "You left early. What the hell is up? Did you piss off Maggie?"

"Relax, I hadn't seen Maggie-Moo for a while, and I needed to take care of some family business. It's the protector in me. Although, she was just as shocked as you by the visit. Apparently, being unpredictable doesn't come naturally to me."

Trent ran his hand through his hair and smiled at the thought of Maggie giving her brother an earful. Maggie never liked it when her big brother was overbearing and intrusive. Her passion and beauty were a lethal combination that always kept her brother on his toes.

"Besides, if I recall, you're always blathering that I should live outside my comfort zone."

He snickered. "Right. Please remind me to call NASA before the debriefing meeting to report that aliens have abducted you. You sound like Dalton, but that's where the familiarity ends."

"Pull up your skirt, man, and find a damn pair of pants. I have something important to show you. It's big and not something to discuss over the phone. Meet me in the parking lot of the old, abandoned railroad warehouse."

When the bells jingled again, Trent snapped out of his reverie in time to see Kane and Annika enter the diner. He could tell by Kane's wide eyes that Maggie's presence confused him. Trent stood, shook Kane's hand, then hugged Annika. "Kane, Annika, this is Margaret King, Dalton's sister."

Maggie waited to extend her hand until they had taken their seats. "It's nice to meet you both. Please call me Maggie."

"I'm so sorry for your loss," Annika replied in a solemn voice. "Trent loved Dalton like a brother."

Trent tugged Maggie against his side, unable to resist comforting her when tears fell down her cheeks. She leaned into his side before responding wobbly, "Geez, I try not to cry within the first two minutes of meeting people. It's just...talking about him is still hard."

He squeezed her shoulder, showing his support. "It's only been ten months. Besides, I don't think there's a time limit on grief."

Kane flashed a sincere smile before studying the menu, giving Maggie a couple of minutes to compose herself without the newcomers' prying eyes. "How long will you be visiting?" he asked.

Maggie turned to Trent, as if searching for how to respond. He winked, and she returned her attention to Kane. "Well, I seem to have some bad luck following me around lately, and Trent is willing to help me exorcise those monsters."

Kane's gaze shot up from his menu to Trent before sliding to meet Maggie's. "I'm sorry to hear that, but he's the best at exorcisms or other pesky problems. Would it be better to postpone our breakfast? We don't want to interrupt if you need to speak privately."

Trent winced as he removed his arm from Maggie's shoulder, absently rubbing the spot where he'd taken a round. "Nope, we're good. So, did you two pick a wedding date?"

Kane expelled a hearty laugh and nudged Annika. "See, I told you he would want to know dates. He's a planner, sweetheart."

Annika nodded. "How does Labor Day weekend sound? We'd marry on Saturday, in our meadow. Afterward, we'll start construction on our home."

Sally stopped by to take everyone's order and fill their coffee cups.

"Sounds like a great day. Does this mean no monkey suits since we'll be outside?" Trent asked, waggling his eyebrows at Annika.

She pinned him with a stern expression that faded into a devious smile. "I would never pass up the opportunity to see you strutting around in a tuxedo. That alone will make the day special."

"Traitor, and after all I did for you," he grumbled.

Maggie leaned forward and held out her hand to Annika. "Can I see your ring? And, please, you have to send me a picture of him in a tux."

Annika beamed with pride, immediately sticking out her hand. "It's a deal, and if you're still here, consider this your invitation. Then you can see him in person."

Trent shook his head and wrenched his face into his best look of horror at the women's antics.

"Oh my, it's beautiful! Congratulations," Maggie exclaimed, ignoring him.

"Well, that's if your father doesn't kill me, Annika. We still have to tell them what happened," Kane murmured while he nudged her with his shoulder.

Before long, the women chatted while he and Kane discussed his plans for the house he wanted to build for Annika. The conversation stopped when Sally appeared, her arms full of plates and condiments stuffed in her apron pockets. Once she served the food, the only sounds at the table were forks and knives scraping across the plates.

"Oh, my God, this brioche French toast is sinful," Maggie crooned between bites. "Nothing will fit when we go shopping for clothes because I'm going to eat all of this goodness."

Her face softened in pleasure, and her tongue darted out to lick a spot of powder sugar off her bottom lip. A bubble of warmth formed in Trent's stomach as he watched Maggie smile and laugh. It reminded him of lazy Sunday mornings when Dalton and Trent visited Maggie and went out to breakfast before returning to their jobs. This was what he had hoped would happen this morning—normalcy. A reminder of what life was supposed to be like, not the current shitstorm that had enveloped her world. The same sentiment applied to Annika, who had barely survived her own ordeal.

"Trent...Trent?" Maggie elbowed him in the ribs, jarring him from his thoughts.

He turned to look at her, hoping she'd throw him a bone since he'd zoned out and missed a key part of the conversation. At the moment, he couldn't think of one single reason that kept him from checking on Maggie during these last ten months. What the hell had he been thinking?

"Sorry, my mind drifted to the day's tasks. What did I miss?" Trent asked, not missing that everyone stared at him as if they didn't believe a word he'd spoken.

Annika jumped in and saved him from further embarrassment. "I have an idea. I'll take Maggie shopping while you and Kane do whatever you need to do. Could we meet at the sheriff's station in about an hour?"

Trent glanced at Maggie, who seemed comfortable with the idea but also looked at him for input. "Sounds good to me. What do you think, Maggie?"

A smile covered her face. "Sure. I don't want to keep you from work."

Kane pressed a kiss to Annika's temple. "We're making a quick trip to Los Angeles. It's time for me to meet them, and we have much to discuss."

Trent motioned to Sally for the check. "That should make an interesting first impression. What time do you leave?"

Kane palmed his wallet. "Not until we arrive, but we're aiming for two. A perk of owning a jet. I need to pick up the deed to our property. You officially have a neighbor."

Trent glanced at the check as he listened to Annika and Maggie discuss their shopping strategy and which stores they should visit.

"Breakfast is my treat." He slid out of the booth and offered his hand to Maggie. As soon as she stood, he gave her his credit card. "Buy whatever you need, and if there are any problems, tell them to call me at the station."

Maggie nodded her head. "Okay, but I'm paying you back, Sheriff Jacobs. And that's on the record."

He gave her his best attempt at intimidation and then watched as she walked toward the exit. Once she left the restaurant, he gave the cashier the check.

Kane waggled his eyebrows. "I know that look—"

"Zip it, lover boy," Trent shot back. "Today's your lucky day. You get to ride with me. I'll even let you ride in the front. And, before you ask me again, no, you still can't use the siren."

Kane let out a loud whoop as he followed him to his service vehicle. Trent rolled his eyes at his friend's exuberance. This man raised with a silver spoon in his mouth, had missed out on so many boyhood experiences. Maybe, for Christmas, he'd buy Kane one of those toy police cars that had sound. Annika would just love him for that one.

MAGGIE LIKED THE QUAINT old-town style of Mill Creek and how Main Street preserved its charm of days long past when horses and wagons roamed the streets. The stores, restaurants, and hotels were constructed from logs and had tin roofs. A long sidewalk made from wooden planks ran down the length of the storefronts. Some even had hitching posts and watering troughs out front. The well-worn boards were smooth and groaned with each step from years of use. Each store's large picture window displayed items for sale amid seasonal decor.

Annika wrapped her arm around Maggie's and tugged her toward the door. "Rayna's Outpost is amazing. I would call it more of a boutique, but she does have everything from outdoor clothing to sexy lingerie. It's become one of my favorite places. Oh, and I love the lilies she planted outside her store in that big box. Afterward, we'll head to the drug store."

"That's an old feedbox for animals," Maggie answered before removing her sunglasses and opening the big door.

Inside, it resembled a big city department store rather than an outpost, but also had an eclectic blend of clothing. Definitely trendy, but the selections were cool and not pretentious at all. One day, when she wasn't buying the bare necessities, she'd come back and browse. She immediately liked how the clothing was not segregated by size; each rack held all the sizes in one spot. It was inclusive. There were so many cute items she wanted to try on, but now wasn't the time. She took her handful of practical items to the dressing rooms.

Annika rapped on the dressing room door. "Hey, you disappeared quickly. Did you see this dress? It's sexy, and the color makes your eyes pop. I love this shade of orange. Oh, and I found these cute tops and shorts."

Maggie's eyes widened into large saucers at the mound of clothing Annika held in her arms. "Uh, I don't need sexy lingerie. I'll just grab a multi-package of underwear. This is really about getting the basics since I didn't have time to pack."

"You should always have options. Besides, maybe I'm wrong, but it seemed that Trent couldn't keep his eyes off you. If you catch my drift." Annika waggled her eyes.

"I'd call that worrying. We've already dipped our toes into that pool. It didn't work out."

Oh, she'd love nothing more than to seduce him. When he ended things, she'd been crushed, but she didn't want to lose him as a friend. Never had another man's touch made her body ache in all the right places. It was enough to make her brain short-circuit.

She smiled at Annika. "He's beyond awesome, which makes me happy to call him a friend. Plus, I have no doubt he's dating someone or has at least had several women vying for his time and attention. He's never lacked for company, if you know what I mean."

Annika moved closer, held up her elegant hand, then started ticking off items one by one with her fingers. "I had concerns about Kane. He was too wealthy. Too handsome. His parents were mean. I had too much baggage, but here I am."

"Seriously? That's horrible, and you're so nice. Why wouldn't anyone like you? Plus, you're gorgeous."

Annika winked at her. "Thank you, but I'd kill for some of your curves or Marilyn Monroe's. I'm not picky. As for the dating part, I didn't see him with anyone when we stayed with Trent over the summer. It never hurts to have secret weapons at your disposal, just in case you two decide to try again. Here, try these outfits on. If not for Trent, then do it for yourself. You never know when Mr. Tall, Gorgeous, and Single will present himself."

Maggie giggled as she took the pile of clothes into the fitting room and closed the door. She liked Annika, and more importantly, she liked shopping and hanging out with a friend. She'd missed these types of interactions and didn't even realize how much until today. It had been too long since she had a little girl time. "All right, give me a few minutes to see what fits."

When she finished, she came out carrying the stack of clothing she decided to buy.

On her way to the cashier, Annika added a baby-doll nighty to the pile. "What? I'm just making sure you don't have to walk around naked. You know, friends don't let friends be naked, especially when there's something this cute to wear." She batted her eyelashes.

Maggie rolled her eyes and snorted out a laugh. "Oh, you're a funny girl. Thanks for coming with me. This has been fun. It also beats worrying about all of the not-so-fun things."

Annika pulled her into a hug. "I know, but you're in good hands. Trent is one of the main reasons I'm standing here today. He never gave up and kept digging thanks to his gut instincts."

She'd like to sit down and hear Annika's full story someday. It seemed they shared a common bond, and knowing Maggie had someone to talk to helped ease the tension. She'd missed being with her friends and being social, but those indulgences also came with a healthy dose of anxiety. Your happiness could be torn from your grasp in the blink of an eye.

She had to face the fact that some of her hardships from that isolation were self-inflicted. When Dalton died, she'd cut herself off from everyone. She didn't think she could handle losing one more person she loved. It was lonely, and she had kept a tourniquet on her heart.

Maggie gave the saleslady Trent's credit card. "You and Kane remind me of my parents—best friends who were madly in love. They always fought for what they wanted. There was a time when I wanted to have that same type of relationship."

"Then you should keep working toward that goal. Life is too short sometimes, so no time like the present." Annika replied solemnly.

Relieved that the transaction had gone through without a glitch, Maggie collected her bags and followed Annika toward the drug store. As they strolled down First Street, Maggie took in everything Mill

Creek offered, including all the friendly residents who waved or of-fered a greeting along the way.

Annika pointed between two buildings. "See that park? Every Sat-urday night they play a family movie. Practically, everyone in town goes and picnics."

"That's a cool idea and a great use for that space."

"Maybe you two will get the chance to go. I think your visit will be good for Trent. I'm almost certain he blames himself in some capacity for Dalton's death."

Maggie thought about what Annika had said. *Why would Trent blame himself?* "That doesn't make any sense. Did he say anything else about it?"

Annika pushed the door open to the drug store and held it for Maggie. "Not really, but it was the way he said things and acted—or maybe what he didn't say."

Once inside, Maggie found a cart and added everything she needed to it, along with a few extra items she had found along the way, in-cluding her favorite lotion.

While the cashier rang up and bagged her purchases, she turned to Annika and whispered, "Did you share that with me so I can encour-age Trent to talk about Dalton?"

Annika pressed her lips together before she answered, "I think he's struggling with survivor's guilt. It's an educated guess, but I'm pretty confident in my assessment. If you decide to push, don't let him hide. He'll come up with many excuses, so stand strong and push right back."

They strolled back toward the sheriff's office in mutual silence. What Annika said made sense, but Maggie didn't know if Trent would open up to her. After all, he'd chosen to shut her out of his life. "I remember how shaken Trent was at Dalton's funeral. He'd kept to himself and barely said a word to me. I'd chalked it up to grief and that he'd only been released from the hospital a few days before his service. It was an unbearable situation, right down to the fact I wasn't allowed to see my brother's face one last time to say goodbye. I can't imagine how Trent felt."

"Why was his casket closed if that was so important to you?" Annika stopped moving to face her.

"The FBI demanded that his casket be closed. I never asked why. I figured it had something to do with protocol since he was killed in the line of duty."

"Oh, that's horrible." Annika gasped.

Maggie had gone stony. "The day was horrible. Trent could barely stand or walk. He'd remained in the back of the church. The pew reserved for family members had only one occupant, which was me. It was a miracle that he'd survived. One of the bullets nicked a major artery." Her mind returned to his apology last night about not reaching out to her sooner. *More guilt? Maybe Annika has a point.*

They resumed and ascended the concrete steps to the sheriff's office. Eagerness washed over Maggie to see Trent's new domain. The place he'd come to when his life crumbled. The fact that he was the sheriff of Mill Creek County made her smile. It also hit her that she had never really thought about all he'd lost until now. Being overwhelmed by grief didn't excuse her self-centered actions. She'd never reached out to offer him solace or support.

The scent of wood and oil hit her nose the moment she entered the building. The hardwood floors shined but creaked and moaned under her steps. The hand-carved wooden railing separating the waiting area from the main office was beautiful. Squirrels, pinecones, and trees covered the surface. As she moved farther into the building, she saw that the open cubicles and desks had modern computers but really old phones. Flat-screen televisions hung on various walls, displaying local and national news feeds. The space was functional, and she liked the blend of past and present.

Kane stepped out of an office in the back. "Hey, ladies, I see you were successful, given the number of bags. Have fun?"

Annika held up her bags before placing them on an empty desk. "Maybe a little. Did you two finish your chores?"

Kane kissed his fiancée on the forehead. "Yes, it's official, Trent has new neighbors. We own the meadow."

"Yahoo," Annika cheered before a gigantic smile plastered across her face.

A woman with a beautiful mess of auburn hair piled on top of her head, several tendrils framing her face, approached. "Hi, you must be Maggie."

Annika and Kane spoke at the same time before Kane stopped and motioned for Annika to proceed. "This is our friend, Margaret King, and this is Trent's assistant, Aimee Lang."

Aimee extended her hand. "It's so nice to meet you. Trent asked me to keep an eye open for your arrival. Can I get you anything to drink while you wait? He's finishing up a call."

"No, I'm good, thanks," Maggie said and shook Aimee's hand.

Aimee had a beautiful smile that made her hazel eyes sparkle. That, paired with her curvy figure and friendly disposition, made her a total knockout. She motioned to a desk behind her. "I sit right there, so if you change your mind just holler. Kane, Annika, safe travels. I'll see you next time you're in town."

"Are you leaving now?" Maggie whirled around to ask Annika.

"Yes, we're scheduled to leave Boise at four. I had so much fun today. Call me if you need anything." She hugged Maggie first, and then Kane hugged her.

"Thanks. I will, and I had fun, too." Maggie stood motionless as Kane and Annika headed toward the front of the building hand-in-hand and then disappeared through the doorway. She had to admit, she really did have fun today, and what surprised her most was how she forgot about her drama for a while.

Aimee broke the silence and gestured to the closed door. "Trent's ready. You can head on back."

As Maggie headed toward the big office, she noticed the bank of file cabinets along the wall that had recently been delivered since the packaging still clung to each unit. At the sheriff's door, she turned the knob and crossed the threshold. Her insides warmed at the sexy sight that greeted her. He'd rolled his sleeves up to his elbows, exposing his muscular forearms that flexed and bunched as he moved stacks of folders. *Good Lord, this man is still a looker and has handcuffs.*

"Ah, just the woman I wanted to see. It doesn't seem like you encountered any problems using my credit card, although I did have Aimee call ahead to several shops and provide advance authorization."

Maggie took a seat. "Thank you. It would have been embarrassing if someone thought I stole the sheriff's credit card."

He arched an eyebrow and grinned. "Lucky for you, I have a key to the jailhouse."

"Who's this pretty lady?" A tall, lean man dressed in uniform drawled from the doorway.

"A beauty who's off limits to you. Miss Margaret King, this is my deputy, Lance Charles, who has quite the reputation in town with the single women."

Trent's reply made her heart flutter. It sounded like he'd staked his claim on her. *Silly?* Hell yes, because she knew he wasn't being possessive of her. He was being protective. She'd almost forgotten that Trent would have the same reputation. Maybe not serious relationships, but it had always been something her brother teased him about.

Lance extended his hand. "Guilty, but the pleasure's all mine. I can't help it if I'm dashing and charming."

"I've always liked a humble man," Maggie replied.

A smile split his face. "I like this one. She'll keep you in line."

He gave her hand a brisk shake before withdrawing. Then, he proceeded with various updates before heading out on patrol. Once Lance left, she watched Trent type something into his computer.

"Your desk is beautiful." She lightly trailed her fingers over the intricate carvings. "Did the same person who carved this desk do the railings out front?"

"No. This was given to my father when he worked in New York for the Federal Deposit Insurance Corporation. He gifted it to me when I was elected sheriff. I don't know who did the railings."

"Wow, that's special, and I bet he's proud of you."

"I think so, but I also know I've made my parents worry too much. They're both happier with my new career." Trent moved the mouse on his desk, clicking it every so often.

A lump formed in her throat. "I think that comes along with the whole parenting thing and when you love someone."

His smile didn't quite touch his eyes. "Something like that, anyway. Did you get everything you needed, or do we need to make another stop on the way home?"

Home. She liked the sound of that more than she should, even if his context was vastly different from what she wanted it to mean. "No, I'm good for now. How does it feel working in the same building as your grandfather? I like that you've kept a lot of the original charm."

Trent perked up, his smile now touching the corners of his eyes. "It does remind me of my grandfather when he was the sheriff. The only things I've upgraded since my arrival are associated with technology—the security system, jail monitors, the office computers and monitors, and I've even had a few flat-screen televisions installed. I like being able to watch real-time updates from around the world. It was something we had at the Bureau. The old phone system is next. That thing is archaic right down to the tape answering machine."

Maggie giggled. "Can you even buy cassette tapes anymore?"

"Couldn't tell you. My predecessor, who took the position after my grandfather, used his remaining budget on updating the jailhouse before retiring so I can't give him too much grief. He spent his money wisely, but that antiquated phone system had to go. Next, I need to finish evaluating my team and fill in the gaps as needed."

"Are you happy wearing that star?" She studied him intently, looking for signs of distress.

"Being able to help others is who I am and is what I need to do."

Her heart clenched at his declaration. He hadn't answered her question, but what he said spoke volumes. Knowing him the way she did, it was what he hadn't said that bothered her the most.

"Aimee's great," she blurted, switching topics.

"Agreed. I haven't regretted hiring her from the minute she started. She's a great addition to my team and keeps me in line. So, you ready to head out? I've taken care of everything urgent for the time being and thought I'd cut out early to give you a tour of my town before we head home and talk."

"Lead the way." Maggie stood and followed him out the door.

She wanted to hear his assessment and what he'd learned today. She also wanted to bury her head in the sand and delight in this moment. It had been so long since she'd enjoyed the genuine camaraderie of friends. She couldn't believe how easily her old self had risen to the surface. Being around a familiar face with a link to her past melted away the carefully crafted protection she'd erected. What did it hurt to live in the moment because she trusted Trent? She would just have to keep her heart out of it. When she returned to Dallas, she'd transition back into her carefully constructed life of isolation. It was her safe haven.

Trent would keep her safe. She was sure he'd already analyzed her situation to a gnat's ass of detail. Like he said, she put distance between her problems in Dallas by coming to him. This glimpse into her old life made her want to prolong those feelings for just a bit longer.

"WHAT THE HELL DO you mean they can't find her? It's been two days. She's a civilian who lives alone. My order was simple: monitor Margaret King's apartment and report to me. Now that she searched the web on that name, the reason couldn't be more important. We need to find out what she knows." Michael Mason, Falcon's leader, simply known as Talon, exploded. "The two men you assigned were supposed to be highly skilled in surveillance. Their orders were to surveil and bring me information. Now, I have no information or person, so what does that tell me? Nothing! Why is she missing?"

"The bitch must have run. She's not in Dallas, or my team would have found her." Talon's thug whined in defense of his men.

"Don't refer to her as a bitch again. She's a lady who deserves respect. That will serve as your only warning. Now, if you and your men would have done their jobs, this discussion would be moot. I've grown very fond of Miss King and losing her is a big fucking problem," Talon admonished in a tone that remained low, and menacing.

The hired gun, clearly not understanding the dangerous line he was close to crossing, continued to push. "Listen, Talon. These guys are commit—"

"Enough! Here's what will happen," Talon commanded, turning toward his operations manager who sat at the conference table. "The men this idiot assigned were sloppy." He jerked his thumb toward the thug. "If I can't trust them to surveil Miss King, then why would I ask them to bring her to me? She could be hurt, which would disappoint me even more. I won't tolerate this type of disrespect or ineptness within my organization. I need to make an example out of their mistakes."

"You're bat-shit crazy, these men are loyal—"

Talon whirled on the goon. Fists clenched, he punched and punched until his knuckles hurt. A red haze filtered across his vision which carried the coppery scent of blood.

"I'm not crazy, and I'll never tolerate disrespect," he spat while slowly climbing to his feet. He pulled a handkerchief from his pocket and wiped his face and hands clean before tossing the cloth onto the body. "Get rid of that trash, permanently."

"Sure thing, Boss, but next time let me know, and I'll throw down a drop cloth," his operations manager quipped.

Talon's breath sawed in and out of his chest from his exertion as he strode out of the conference room.

A chipper female voice echoed down the hallway behind him. "Talon, I have good news."

He turned to greet his administrative assistant who'd been with him since he formed Falcon. The extent of her knowledge was that he ran a security consulting business.

He forced a smile to his face. "I could use some good news today."

"Your man found the admitting hospital for that poor mother and son who you heard about on the news." She handed him a piece of paper with all pertinent information scrawled on it. "Oh, and I almost forgot, the husband is dead. I shouldn't say this, but I think he got what he deserved."

Another good reason to have a government worker on his payroll. Talon refused the note. "I agree. Please make the necessary arrangements to pay both hospital bills in full. Use the same account as before and use anonymous as the name."

Her smile radiated her happiness and eagerness to deliver some good news to a struggling family. "I'd be delighted, but I don't understand why you don't put your name on it. It's such an extraordinary gesture."

Talon saw his second-in-command walking toward them. "Sometimes it's better to believe in miracles." He dismissed his assistant and turned toward Darren Waltz, who followed him into his office.

Waltzer, as he was known within the Special Forces community and within his team, was a brutally efficient soldier who now pledged his loyalty to Talon via a carefully negotiated contract. His tactical skills and cunning made him a lethal threat to anyone in his sights. It didn't take long to recognize those abilities, which was why he rose to the rank of second-in-command. Since then, Waltzer had formed two tactical teams of mercenary soldiers who operated under his orders. Oh, yes, they were all expensive as hell, but worth every penny.

Talon motioned to the man to take a seat. "Today hasn't gone as I'd have liked..."

"Yeah, I passed by the conference room on the way here. I've asked one of my men to help tidy up the place," Waltzer replied, taking a seat in a chair opposite Talon's desk.

"Get Alpha team ready to roll. I want those men that thug hired hunted down and executed. Before your team pulls the trigger, make sure those thugs know the particulars. Send me the video, I have plans for it. Also, find out what they did to make Miss King run." Talon slapped the man on his back as he moved toward his desk.

"Roger that, I'll instruct my men. Do you want them to take over King's reconnaissance?"

Talon nodded. "Start with her brother's partner."

"One more thing," Waltzer said, "I highly recommend changing protocols since we're unsure about the extent of exposure—"

Talon slammed his hand onto his desk. "This is my organization, and I'll decide how we move forward. Your role: hired help."

A slow smile spread across the man's face. "Understood. But you pay me for my observations too, which is why I'm going to press. This obsession with that woman is becoming a problem. If I feel my men are being put in danger by your decision-making, we're out."

Talon's jaw clenched, but he restrained himself from saying more. He'd love to wipe that smirk from his face, but now wasn't the time. He needed this man and his skills. "Noted. But watch your fucking tone."

Talon waved his hand dismissively, pleased when the big man stood and exited his office. He needed time to think. Letting his anger get the better of him wasn't acceptable. His success had come from being strategic, patient, and diligent. His boss had used those qualities to describe his strengths while in the CIA, alongside his exemplary service record and numerous commendations. Talon understood valor and honor, so he didn't cross that line with Waltzer today when he stood up for his team.

The problem was Talon didn't believe in that philosophy any longer. It died the day the CIA deemed him expendable for the greater good, the day his boss pulled out that weapon, shot him three times, then left him for dead. He vowed on that day, and every grueling day of his recovery afterward, he'd make the government pay for their arrogance and betrayal. Just as his father had.

Talon had monitored Maggie again for less than a month when his IT team informed him she'd performed a search on that snitch's name—Bart Schamko. Nothing had surfaced since Dalton and Schamko's death, so Talon was confident he'd handled the problem. Now the big question in Talon's mind: had Dalton given her this information and instructed her to wait? How much did she know or have?

All good things come to those who wait. His mother's words echoed in the back of his mind.

He slid open a desk drawer and rummaged around until he found her photo, one that had worn edges and yellowed with time. He ran his index finger over his mother's face. His thoughts drifted back to when he was a small boy helping her make chocolate chip cookies.

Ah Mom, I miss those days. Hey, I have some news for you. I know I have told you numerous times that I'd never marry, but I found a woman. And to think she's Dalton's sister—life couldn't get any better.

He rested the picture of the woman over his heart and stared out the window. First, he had to locate Margaret King. Oh, how he loved a good game of cat and mouse.

Three

TRENT EXHALED AS HE pulled into his driveway. The destruction zone, as he referred to it, had grown since this morning. Between the mess and the crew, the timing couldn't be worse.

The reason behind her escape and the long drive to his doorstep worried him. Eighty-percent of his mind and gut told him that Falcon was behind it, but he had to remain objective until he knew for sure. Over the years, he and Dalton had made plenty of enemies.

Scaffolding had now been erected on all sides of Trent's home to assist the roofers. Alongside his driveway, a big dumpster sat for the old roofing materials and debris. Tired of living in a state of chaos, he'd be happy when this project was over. Almost everything he owned was packed in boxes or closets for safekeeping. The process of unpacking and putting the house to rights had stalled. At some point, he needed to prioritize that, but for now, it was Maggie.

She slipped out of the truck and opened the rear door to gather her shopping bags. "Wow, things change quickly around here, including the temperature. We get summertime storms in Dallas, but it doesn't get cold, just more humid."

"The weather out here can change on a dime," he replied, rounding the front of the truck.

"Thanks for the tour. I enjoyed seeing the town through your eyes and appreciate the time you carved out of your schedule."

He loved the twinkle of joy that sparkled in her eyes. "It's a great town. Plus, it's good to have a general idea of what it offers since you'll be here for a bit. I'm going to check out today's progress, then change out of my uniform," he answered, then headed toward the side of the house.

She hollered to be heard over the rustle of leaves. "I'll help with dinner in a minute."

The hard slap of plastic whipping in the wind caught his attention. The crew had secured tarps over most of the pallets, leaving him one to cover. The lone wooden platform sat exposed with the underlayment. The sky transformed from light gray to darker as big black clouds billowed in the distance. A cold gust swirled around him and skittered down his collar. The weather could be unpredictable in the mountains.

Heavy with moisture, the air had him hastening his steps to move fast if he wanted to finish grilling dinner before the rain hit. He found a cover for the pallet in the garage, then stopped to turn on the grill before heading into the bathroom to wash up and change. After slipping into a pair of jeans and a Henley, he left his boots by his bed in exchange for a pair of flip-flops. Afterward, he stored his service weapon in his gun safe.

Cold air pressed against his body as he removed the meat and vegetables from the refrigerator. He carried the platter of food outside to the table next to his grill. Heat warmed his face as he rotated the lid backward. After removing the butcher paper, he added the steaks one by one. The meat sizzled on the hot grates before he sprinkled a liberal amount of seasoning on each.

He thought back to how he reacted when Lance flirted with Maggie. Trent's possessiveness shocked him. The thought of Lance pursuing her bothered Trent. Man, he needed to pull himself together. Any red-blooded man would flirt with her, and he couldn't beat up every single one who did. She wasn't his and never could be. That had been settled long ago. Now, he needed to get his body aligned with his brain.

He added the ears of corn while he reflected on his jealous behavior, which was more protective now that he looked at it. Yes, he wanted to safeguard Maggie and meant what he said to Lance. She might not like Trent being overbearing, but she came to him for protection.

He rotated the corn, not wanting the ears to burn. The wind increased in power and howled through the trees. The smell of rain stained the air. The storm had gained speed as it moved across the mountain range. He loved this time of night when the setting sun left behind an array of brilliant colors streaking across the sky. The purple, orange, and red colors were framed by gray and black billowing clouds. In the distance, a flash of lightning added to the scene. His mind drifted off while he watched Mother Nature's show.

When he woke up in the hospital and was told Dalton hadn't survived, a part of Trent had died that day, too. He vowed that he'd stop at nothing to topple Falcon the day he was discharged. What Trent hadn't realized at the time was that the injuries he sustained would require so much rehab. When he learned he'd been removed from the case due to his compromised identity, he'd lost his head. That decision robbed him of avenging Dalton's death.

Trent rubbed at his shoulder, trying to ease the ache from the cold—a parting gift from Falcon. Trent's arm and leg always told him when inclement weather approached.

Falcon cost me everything. A flicker of movement caught Trent's eye, and he glanced upward to see Maggie approaching. *Well, almost everything.*

"It's getting cold." Her beautiful voice penetrated his sullen thoughts. "Want me to bring you a sweatshirt?"

"No, thanks. I've got the grill to keep me warm. Did you get everything put away?"

"I did. Having a few things to wear that aren't four sizes too big. So, tell me, Trent, do you think I overreacted by coming here?"

He wouldn't pretend he didn't understand the context of her question. He also wouldn't sugarcoat it. "No, and I've got a bad feeling, but coming here was smart. What do you know about Falcon?"

Her eyebrows scrunched together as she searched her brain. "I assume you're not talking about the bird, so I'd say nothing. Should I?"

"Did your brother talk about his job or assignments with you in any detail?" Trent opened the lid and rotated the ears of corn again.

"No, I've heard snippets of things over the years but didn't pay attention. He certainly didn't divulge any details. Why? Who or what is Falcon?"

Trent turned toward Maggie. His mind raced with how to summarize the case. "It's the last assignment we worked together. Falcon had been in play for several years. This organization supplied military grade weapons and drugs to the Middle Eastern and African warlords. The US government wanted this group dismantled because America's finest were being killed by their own weaponry peddled to the highest bidder. So many agents across multiple agencies and organizations invested their lives to infiltrate this group. Those deep cover assets endured the daily routine of watching these monsters act like gods and kings. Not to mention all the horrific acts they had to carry out to keep their covers intact."

Maggie's eyes widened. "What? I don't know what to say, that's horrible in so many ways."

Trent grabbed his tongs and flipped the steaks. The aroma of grilled meat made his mouth water. "It's a necessity to bring down these types of organizations. Your brother and I were responsible for following the money that would eventually tie suspects to weapons and drugs. The only way to decimate Falcon was to deplete their funds. Intel gathered suggested that Falcon's leader was an American, either from the military or a covert agency, but his identity remained unknown. All we have is his code name: Talon. The two biggest problems were that the leader of this organization never surfaced and following the trail of money had been almost impossible, but we're making progress. This cartel ran a tight ship and had countermeasures for every scenario."

Her mouth gaped, and her gaze darted back and forth. "What are you saying? That this group is who killed my brother? Do you think they were the ones to leave the knife? Oh, God."

"Slow down. At this point, all we know is what you've told me. Yes, whoever left that knife is tied to Dalton, which probably means it's tied to the FBI. Falcon makes the most sense but could be any of our past cases. It could also be something entirely different, although I would bet on the former." He had wanted to talk about this earlier today, but she had seemed so happy, and he hadn't wanted to darken her mood. "I have more questions for you, but how about we tackle them after dinner?"

A loud boom of thunder caused her to jump. "Holy smokes, that sounded close. Uh, sure. After dinner. Do you want me to prepare the salad?"

Trent nodded at her. "Everything's on the counter, and I have several bottles of dressing in the refrigerator. The steaks will be done in a few minutes."

Her hips swayed as she walked toward the house. He appreciated her candor and direct questions. Man, he couldn't believe she was here with him. They still clicked and melded together as if they hadn't spent time apart. The only difference was that her brother would never join them. She tried to mask the pain, but he had the secret decoder ring. Those green eyes told a story all on their own.

He would do anything to erase that pain. Even now, she still calls to him on so many levels. He'd never been so drawn to a woman, and letting her go wasn't easy.

"Where's your mixer?" she hollered from the screen door.

Now, what was she up to? "Cabinet, next to the refrigerator."

He wanted to ask why but figured she didn't supply a *because* for a reason. Excitement bubbled in his body. He liked the thought that she had a surprise for him.

A flash of lightning, followed by another boom of thunder, made him look toward the sky. Large raindrops pelted his face and body. Again, the sizzle of electric energy split the sky, followed by the deep, resounding rumble that hastened his actions. The storm was escalating, promising to deliver a wicked show.

He removed the steaks and corn from the grill, covered them with aluminum foil, and placed them on the platter. Holding the plate, he turned the barbeque off before dashing toward the house.

As if she read his mind, Maggie met him at the door and took the dish out of his hands. "You're drenched. Wait here. I'll get you a towel."

She moved with a sense of purpose, but he heard a suppressed giggle trail behind her as she went to find him a towel.

MAGGIE DAMN NEAR SWALLOWED her tongue after returning with a towel. Trent had stripped off his wet T-shirt to reveal a chiseled chest that was a ten on the drool index. Raised pectorals with tiny, hardened discs strained from the cold air. Tiny goosebumps dotted his flesh. His chest was sheer perfection, with a slight dusting of hair that traveled down from his navel to disappear into the waistband of his jeans.

She couldn't help herself. She lightly trailed her fingers up his stomach, over every ridge of hard muscle that contracted under her touch. He emitted a low groan that sent shivers down her body. The fresh, cool scent of rain and mountain air clung to his skin. She wiped away the excess moisture with the towel before giving it to him altogether.

A lopsided grin formed on his face. "If you don't close that mouth, you'll catch a fly."

She caught her bottom lip between her teeth and tilted her head upward to look him in the eyes. "Your body is a work of art, and my hand acted on its own accord."

A heated blush worked up her neck at her brazen comment. She looked away from him and started to retreat, but a warm hand gripped her arm to halt her movement. His touch sent jolts of electricity directly to her core. Her heart pounded against her ribs, and pinpricks of excitement tingled across her body. Anticipation rippled through her body while she waited to see what would happen next.

"Thank you," he drawled. "And it doesn't hurt to have a good-looking woman tell me she can't keep her hands off me."

Maggie chewed on her bottom lip. "I appreciate that, but I know you're not interested in me *that* way anymore, right?"

He emitted a growl from deep in his throat, her only warning before he snared her wrists and maneuvered her so her back slammed flat against the door. The press of his much larger frame against hers was deliciously erotic. Her chest heaved, not from fear but excitement. He stole her breath.

He moved one of her hands downward between their bodies until it rested on his jean-clad erection. "Does this feel like I lack interest? I've been in this state since you arrived. You, Margaret King, are one sexy, smart, and beautiful woman."

Desire flooded her system, making it difficult to think. She trembled, and her nipples hardened into tight peaks that rubbed against the satin of her bra. A hot rush of arousal pulsed through her body. Oh God, what had this man unleashed inside of her?

She slid her hand slowly up his length, hating the denim that separated them. He stared into her eyes, lust darkening his pupils, and even his breathing increased. Her tongue darted out to moisten her dry lips. She never wanted anything more in life than this moment right now.

"So much better than a dream," Maggie whispered, not intending to voice that sentiment.

He ground his erection against her belly. "Yes, I crave you. You tempt me in ways I've never experienced. Your body is a wonderland of possibilities because I know you can handle my need to love hard and with abandon. Do you understand me?"

His breath feathered against her lips right before he covered her mouth with his. The kiss wasn't soft or gentle; it was raw and untamed. It represented all their missed opportunities, and that telltale of what might have been.

Her body burst to life, every nerve-ending zinging with happiness. A flash of light crackled, followed by a boom that seemed to rattle the house. The lights flickered briefly before the room went dark. In the absence of the soft electrical humming of the refrigerator, the only sounds were their ragged breaths mixed with the rain pounding against the house.

Trent stepped back and cleared his throat. That moment faded into the darkness, along with his touch the second he retreated. "Storm's getting worse. I should get flashlights and candles. And some dry clothes."

Maggie blinked as he fled, and the room went still as the hottest and sexiest moment of her life evaporated right before her eyes. She wanted to cry and scream with frustration. She wanted that damn kiss and whatever it brought afterward. She needed Trent Jacobs like a flower required water.

Her body shivered from the absence of his body heat. A profound and unwelcome feeling of loss slammed into her chest—a feeling she despised. What had changed his mind? Did he have another woman? Of course, he did. He always had someone, except her when he had the chance.

Her mind whirled with how to handle the awkwardness of the situation. Her head waged a war with her heart, and it sucked. She wasn't prepared for this intense resurgence of attraction. Worse, she wasn't sure she could resist it. She sensed his reaction was honest, but she didn't understand why he shut down. Then, something Annika had said drifted in the back of Maggie's mind. *I think he's struggling with survivor's guilt. He'll come up with many excuses, so stand strong and push right back.*

A word she would not use to describe herself was coy. She preferred strategic games, like trying to sink your opponent's warships, a game she and Dalton played for hours when they were children. As a teacher, that description would get you eaten alive by her students. She had to be firm yet loving in her quest to develop all those precious minds. Maybe Trent needed that approach, too. Blame stopped growth and only eroded the truth over time.

Trent padded back into the kitchen a few minutes in dry clothes and with a handful of lighting options. She accepted a flashlight and silently headed to her room to put on a pair of sweatpants and channel her strength. It was time to remind herself why she had come there. She hadn't expected the flood of memories and emotions that had inundated her, which was naïve on her part. They had history together, and with Dalton, and nothing would ever change that, nor would she want that.

The smell of sulfur penetrated her nostrils when she returned. Several candles burned, and a small pile of spent matches sat on the table. The soft flicker of light danced off every surface in the kitchen. It made the setting for dinner romantic, though that wasn't the objective. The storm caused all sorts of things to flap and flutter in the strong winds.

"What would you like to drink?" he asked, putting the salad she had prepared on the table.

"Whatever you're having is fine with me."

He took two wine glasses from the cabinet and the bottle of wine from the counter. They ate in silence while the bug screens rattled against the windows in between the rolls of thunder. Flashes of light illuminated the scaffolding erected outside the windows, creating an ominous scene.

"My steak is cooked to perfection." She forked another bite into her mouth.

"I can't wait to see what you made for dessert." The smile he flashed revealed his joy as the candlelight flickered against his skin creating a soft glow. He truly was a handsome man.

"How do you know I made dessert?" She scrunched her forehead with feigned confusion.

He hunched his shoulders and cocked his head to the side. "I'm pretty good at investigative research. For starters, nothing we've eaten so far has needed a mixer, which leaves dessert or breakfast."

She sensed him relaxing a bit, the easy banter flowing between them. That made her feel better and took some of the awkwardness out of the evening.

"Hmm, is that what you think?" She raised her eyebrows at him. "You'll just have to wait and see, Inspector Jacobs."

His cellphone chirped, drawing his attention from her and to the screen. "Hi, Mom." He listened for a few minutes and smiled. "Yes, it's storming here. I'm home. I do love your lasagna, but I'll have to take a rain check. Dalton's sister is visiting, and I'm helping her out with a few things."

She loved how his love for his mom reflected on his face. He didn't seem to want to rush her off the phone but also didn't want to have a long conversation. A pang of longing hit her in the chest, knowing she'd never get a call like this to have dinner at her parents' house. When they died in her senior year of high school, the immediate loss and pain was horrible, but losing Dalton almost killed her.

"Yes, she's doing well. I think she'd love your lasagna. It might take a few weeks to sort everything out, but if your schedule is open, we'll come for dinner." He winked before mouthing, "Sorry."

He finished the call and put his phone back on the table. "It seems we have a standing invitation for dinner and she's happy you're visiting. I'll start a fire in the living room while you serve up your surprise.

This storm sounds like it's going to last a while." He placed their dishes in the sink and left the kitchen.

The ingredients for dessert sat in the refrigerator. As she made the final preparations, she thought back to all the family dinners she had as a child. They would laugh and share stories about their day. It didn't matter if it was over a pizza or a full-blown meal. All that mattered was they were together. She missed those precious moments the most.

The pain in her chest deepened, causing her to squeeze her eyes shut to stop the flow of tears. Now, even her dinners with Dalton were gone. Rolling her head back and forth, she sucked down a deep breath and held it for several seconds. Now wasn't the time, she needed to focus on this threat and what it meant. She entered the living room with her treat in tow and leaned against the wooden frame to enjoy the view.

Trent waded up newspaper, the muscles in his back flexing, before he picked through a stack of kindling to find smaller pieces for the base. Once he'd erected a pyramid-shaped pile, he struck a match. Smoke tinged the air. He pressed the flame to the paper, and the edges changed color from orange to brown and then black before the material crumbled to ash. Just like life, vibrant and colorful one minute and gone the next.

Trent sat staring at the flicker of light.

"Penny for your thoughts?" she asked.

He ran his hand through his hair and sighed. "Many, but I'll start here; I crossed the line earlier, and I'm sorry. It's just...having you here...it's... never mind."

"Finish that sentence, Trent." She entered the room and set the tray with the wine, strawberries, and bowl of whipped cream on the coffee table. "Please."

He stood and placed the screen in front of the fire before moving to the couch. The second his butt hit the cushion she knew he'd buried his thought. The fire started to crackle, filling the dreaded silence that had blanketed the room. She refilled their wine glasses with the bottle of red he had opened for dinner. The glow from the flames flickered across his face in a golden hue. He looked like a Greek god.

"Overwhelming. That's a good way to describe it. Let's sit on the floor while we talk." Trent moved the table forward, giving them more room between it and the sofa.

She plucked a berry from the pile, swiped it through the fluffy cream, and hummed with delight. The sweet juice combined with the velvety texture of the cream melted onto her tongue. It didn't escape her notice that he watched her every move. Plucking another strawberry, she dipped it into her white fluff enjoying another burst of flavors. The simple act of sitting in front of a fire to enjoy a stormy evening with him calmed her, but it also made her feel alive. A dangerous acknowledgment, but one she'd worry about tomorrow.

"Don't eat it all," he groused before plunking a berry through the concoction and popping it into his mouth. "Delicious. I like that you made this for me."

"You're welcome, but it's not that hard to make." She winked. "So, what did you want to discuss?"

"Did you happen to take a picture of the knife and note?"

"No. Honestly, the thought never crossed my mind. I should've, but I freaked out and left."

He popped another berry into his mouth and spoke around the bite. "You did the right thing. I just wanted to know. Can you describe the paper used or the knife?"

She moved her gaze to the flames and watched them dance. "I'm pretty sure it had a black handle. The blade wasn't too large. More like a steak knife, but wider and sharper looking. The note was scrawled on a sheet of paper from my memo pad."

"That's good. Do you have any details about the van besides the color, like make or model?"

"Yes, and I even have the license plate number. I had planned on giving you that last night after dinner, but I was so exhausted it slipped my mind. I'll get that for you. I never really saw the two men up close. They wore baseball caps and always seemed to be looking down."

"That's my girl. So, a sketch artist is out, but the rest of that information is useful. Does anyone know why you've left town?"

Maggie rubbed her forehead. "I didn't tell anyone I was leaving town. I emailed my boss stating that I needed to use some vacation days."

Concern washed over his face. "I'm contacting my friend from the Bureau, Noah Parker, to help us. I'd trust him with my life. I want him to pull traffic footage from around your apartment to look for white vans. In the meantime, I'll run those plates, but I'm sure they'll come back as stolen. Whoever left that note is tied to Dalton."

"I agree."

The fire crackled and hissed in tandem to the rolling thunder in the distance.

"Do you think he'll find the van in any of that footage?" She reached for another strawberry.

"I hope so."

A sudden clap of thunder rattled the windows and caused her to jump. "Sorry, all of this makes me jittery. I'm not fond of horror movies, yet it feels like I'm starring in one. None of this makes any sense to me. I'm virtually a nobody. I'm not social anymore. I stick to myself."

"I remember a bubbly, funny, and stubborn woman. Even the stories Dalton told me about you in high school matched that description. What do you mean by 'sticking' to yourself?"

"You know, stayed at home by myself. It annoyed me when everyone always asked me how I was doing or told me it would get easier. It made me want to scream. I was tired of perfecting the art of loss."

Trent nodded. "When did you decide to quit being a teacher? I thought you loved teaching."

She shrugged and sighed. "After Dalton died, I couldn't teach anymore. All those innocent third graders would look at me daily, full of life and happiness. I couldn't deceive them any longer. I didn't view the world through that same lens. Now, I'm a freight auditor. I can work from home. Plus, I can take on as much work as I want to help fill the downtime. I live a boring life."

"I don't like that you've isolated yourself. Trust me when I say this, living in the shadows is not your place. Just like giving up on people is not the answer. You're too bright and caring. Why would you do that to yourself?"

Her shoulders slumped. "Something deep inside changed when he died. I guess the world became unstable, and all the bad you two talked about became real for me. Trusting people seemed harder. Losing those I loved devastated me. I'm tired of that cycle. I miss him...and I miss my parents. My heart has been ripped from my chest too many times. Now it's irrevocably broken."

Her voice cracked, and hot tears ran down her cheeks. "I can't risk that type of loss again. To me, the solution was easy: no love, family, or friends equaled no more loss."

"I should have reached out and been there for you instead of leaving you to grieve alone." He slid her trembling body into his lap and cradled her in his arms. "I miss him too, but hiding won't stop the pain."

"No, but it prevents future pain. Watching your family dwindle to nothing as they're violently ripped from your life, rendering you the sole survivor, is brutal. Words like 'traumatic' and 'devastating' only scratched the surface. Therapy helped some after my parents' death, but it also drilled home the concept that everyone goes through the cycles of grief differently, and there isn't a right or wrong way to grieve. Doing what I need to do to survive isn't wrong, which is why I found a quiet corner and stayed there after Dalton."

It was on the tip of her tongue to ask him why he'd been so distant during the funeral, but the warmth of Trent's arms and the rush of her tears prevented her from asking. In an odd way, it felt like she'd finally been given the chance to purge her grief with someone who understood the profound impact of losing her brother. This moment could have only been shared with one person, and his arms were wrapped tightly around her. This night belonged to the memory of her brother. Tomorrow belonged to solving the puzzle of who had threatened her.

Four

O N FRIDAY MORNING, MAGGIE watched out her bedroom window as a crane lifted metal roofing sections from the ground to the crew on the roof. The concert of noise grated on her nerves. The high-pitched whine of metal scraping across itself, followed by the constant *pfft-pfft-pfft* of the nail gun and the stomping of worker's boots, played over and over. This was her entertainment while Trent took a call in his bedroom.

He'd worked from home the last few days while they spent a good chunk of time talking about old times. It had been ten months since they had spoken, but all that time melted away the moment they came together. Trent had already run the license plates from the van, which came back stolen. He'd updated Noah, who was still scouring surveillance footage in his spare time.

The mechanical sound of the crane. Scraping of metal. Stomping of feet. *Pfft-pfft-pfft* of the nails. Repeat.

Aargh, she craved peace and quiet. She admired everything Trent had achieved with his renovation but wished the roof upgrade was complete. The strange men wandering around made her anxious, not due to the workmen, but because she feared the owner of the knife would find her.

The last three days alone with Trent had been pleasant, but she was more than ready to head into the station with him today. He had a job to do, and her unannounced visit had taken him away from his duties.

Needing a break from the chaos, she exited the house and walked toward the edge of his property. The sun glinted off the creek as it ran along the meadow, the picture framed by a deep blue sky dotted with clouds. The view was both beautiful and tranquil. The afternoon breeze ruffled her hair, and the slight smell of earth and pine filled her nose. Turning her face toward the sun, she loved how the warmth radiated across her skin. Well, at least nothing had happened since she left Dallas. She'd feel horrible if she brought trouble to Mill Creek.

She tried not to dwell on the past, but it did provide a certain level of comfort. The downside was that it allowed a person to wallow in self-pity. That intense sense of loss made her leery of close relationships. Not that they enhanced her quality of life, but they provided the separation she needed to survive.

Basking in the sunshine's warmth, the chaos of the roofers faded into the background. She focused on the sounds of the babbling creek and aspen trees vibrating in the breeze. Two butterflies challenged each other in the distance, flittering above the water back and forth, then left to right, as they dueled before disappearing into the tall grass.

Did she and Trent look like those butterflies as they fought this attraction between them? The chemistry had always been there, but now it burned bright and white hot. She hated the nagging feeling that he could be ripped from her life, too. Death had a mind of its own. A reality she knew all too well.

She smiled, thinking about how sexy Trent had looked while dripping wet from the storm the other night. His deep blue eyes matched a smile that would melt the panties off any girl. Being with him had put her loneliness on the back burner and given her a reprieve from reality.

Leaning on him made a difference and offered a sense of security. He was familiar, so she trusted that bond, but she couldn't allow herself to blur the line any further with her heart.

To belong was a precious commodity, to feel the joy of being home, even if temporary, made her ache for a future she could never have. She intended to enjoy the benefits of having people around who cared. The thought warmed her insides, and the muscles of her mouth widened with her smile. Now, what did she do with all these intense feelings for Trent? She had to compartmentalize her feelings.

A deep, urgent voice penetrated the fog of her mind. "Maggie? Where are you?"

"By the creek," she answered. When she saw Trent's face, panic threatened to seize her throat. "Wh-what's wrong?"

"Don't just disappear," he answered, his tone sharp. "I need to know where you are at all times."

"Oh, sorry, I needed to clear my head."

"Things have escalated, so you're not leaving my side."

"What does that mean?"

Trent clutched her upper arms and lowered his voice. "Noah located the van, which still had the stolen plates. It showed up in a police report."

Maggie perked up at that news. "That's good news, right? Now we can find out what those men were doing."

His grip tightened on her arms. "Not exactly; they're still at large. The officer who found the abandoned van also found a maintenance uniform with three more stolen plates and what appeared to be cables and wiring left inside. My guess is that someone ripped out the surveillance equipment in a hurry. What's the name of your apartment complex?"

Her heart flatlined. "Sagebrush."

"That's a match. It means those assholes had access to your property. Maybe even your home unit. This reminds me of the night you arrived when you mentioned that you'd found your front door ajar before. What did you mean by that?"

She stood ramrod straight, her gaze unfocused while she accessed the recesses of her memory. "When I came home from the funeral, my door was open, and a maintenance man had been exiting. He muttered something about checking smoke detectors, I think. He told me if I had any questions to refer to the note from building management. I figured I'd missed it with everything going on. I was numb, Trent."

He dragged her against his body; warmth and security enveloped her. His hand lightly stroked her hair. "I'll have the maintenance logs checked. Noah also recovered footage of that van around your complex on multiple days and camera feeds in the area. That corroborates your story. I didn't doubt you, but facts are key. That means those men were watching you. Going forward, I would rather be overly cautious than take unnecessary risks."

Maggie dug deep to keep herself from falling apart. She needed to be his partner, not a woman on the verge of a breakdown. Trent had a job that needed him and a town that depended on him. Together, they would figure out who left that note and why.

She pulled from his embrace and steeled her spine. "Don't you have bad guys to apprehend?"

He used his index finger to tip her chin up. "Nope, my days are typically bad guy-free, but if you're up to it, I should probably head to the station."

"Well, Sheriff Jacobs, I noticed the wall of new filing cabinets. And since I'm not a sit-down and twiddle my thumbs type of girl, do you need a highly organized person to help set up those metal drawers?"

Trent figured having her with him was better than being separated. "I'd love your help, but you'd have to check with Aimee. That's her domain and her call."

"Done. I'll offer my assistance when we get there."

The afternoon passed quickly as she and Aimee mapped out a plan to tackle the file cabinets. Aimee practically cheered when she found out Maggie was willing to help. They shared quite a few laughs throughout the day, and they worked well together.

Aimee blew a rogue strand of hair out of her eyes. "Ugh, at this pace we're going to have to pull those old file boxes out of storage in a day or so to see what's lurking inside."

"Dust and more dust?" Maggie tossed over her shoulder, adding more files into the drawer labeled Closed Cases.

"As long as there aren't any gross or buggy things inside, I can handle going through each file."

"Lucky for you, I can audit with the best of them. My job as a freight auditor might come in handy when we dig through them. I can categorize and cross-reference like a pro."

They both giggled and continued plowing through the boxes.

"Wow, you two were productive. It's almost five. Since we skipped lunch, Maggie, I thought you might be ready for dinner." Trent said from behind the two women.

Maggie spun around. "Holy crap, it's five? Aimee, are you good if I leave for the day?"

Aimee wiped the side of her nose with the back of her hand. "Yes. I'm ready for a shower and to call it a day."

Trent held out his hand to Maggie. "How about pizza?"

She placed her hand in his. "Yum, you had me at ooey-gooey cheese. Gosh, I could eat an entire pie myself." She looked back about at Aimee. "Want to join us?"

Aimee dusted off the knees of her dress slacks. "No, thanks. I'm looking forward to a quiet evening with my new novel."

"Oh, what do you read? Romance? Suspense?"

"Actually, this one's a combination of both. It's a new author, so I'm ready for take-out and my book."

"Okay, but if you change your mind, you know where we'll be." Trent tugged her toward the exit. "You should have told me you were hungry," he said, raising an eyebrow.

"Oh, get over it. I was busy, and so were you. You're just being fussy because now *you* have to entertain me all by yourself."

He placed a hand on the small of her back, guiding her toward his truck. The warmth from his touch soaked into her skin. "So many ways to interpret that demand."

The ride home was in companionable silence, but the moment the gear shifted into park, Maggie popped out of the vehicle. Her focus before dinner was to clean up and change. She couldn't remember the last time she was giddy about something as simple as dinner. She'd be lying if it didn't make her feel good to dress up to remind Trent what he had walked away from when he broke things off. The trick was just to enjoy and not to build on those feelings. Her focus was to live in the moment; she could do this because emotional entanglements were a thing of the past. Those led to heartbreak, which was a no-no.

TRENT HELD OPEN THE door of the PB&S Cafe so Maggie could enter ahead of him, determined to keep his head screwed on tight and not cross the line with her again. He had practically swallowed his tongue when she walked out of his guest bedroom wearing an orange and white sundress. How anyone could look so adorable and hot simultaneously mystified him. The dress fit her perfectly, from the formfitting bodice that framed her full breasts to the skirt ending just above her knees that swayed with each step.

"This place is so cute," Maggie said.

He thought she'd like farmhouse-style decor with wooden tables and mix-n-match metal chairs. Every table had an antique milk bottle with assorted herbs or flowers. An enormous chalkboard menu hung over the counter, and as usual, a line of people was waiting to give Lauren their order. Her restaurant served a wide variety of food, from fancy pizza to sandwiches and salads, typically made from ingredients she sourced from local farms.

"Everything smells amazing. Do we order at the counter and then grab a seat?" Maggie asked while she surveyed the room.

The restaurant had people everywhere, either dining in or picking up orders to go. "Yup. What do you like on your pizza?"

She chewed on her index finger as she perused the big menu. "Surprise me," she said, then turned to find a table.

Oh, he could do that easily. He enjoyed making her smile. Hell, if he were being honest, he enjoyed having a companion that made him want things in life he didn't deserve. He had to calm down and get his brain back on track. The problem was that she revved him up faster than any other woman. He needed to focus on the fact that she came to him for protection.

He ordered their pizza and two salads, remembering that Annika always said the green shit was important.

Trent headed to the table Maggie had chosen and put his beer and her wine down. "Okay, we're all set. Hey, I'm sorry about the house. I didn't realize how loud a roof replacement could be. Not to mention the crew walking around."

"Well, it's not like you knew I was on the way."

He took a sip of his beer and placed his napkin in his lap. "True, but finished will be nice. Kane did a great job with the renovation."

Lauren approached their table with a salad in each hand. "Hey, Sheriff, here's your kale Caesar salads."

"Thanks. Lauren Granger is the owner of this gem. And this is my friend, Margaret King," he said, gesturing to Maggie.

"This one's a charmer." Lauren hooked her thumb in Trent's direction. "It's nice to meet you."

"Likewise. I love how you decorated your restaurant."

"Thanks, it's been fun to see this place evolve and grow over the last year. Enjoy your food," Lauren said with a smile before she turned toward the counter.

"Lauren's fairly new to town. She opened the place right after she arrived this past January."

"Wow. Based on the crowd, I think she's a hit."

They reminisced over dinner about funny stories and times they'd spent together. Having a connection to someone with a connected past and being able to share those memories was a cathartic release. He hadn't laughed or felt much warmth in his heart when he'd thought about his friend. Revenge and anger had taken over, muting all those memories. Now that he sat there with Maggie, she had helped him open a door he thought had been locked forever.

As they left the restaurant, Trent waved to Lauren and hollered, "Thanks. Delicious as always."

Maggie turned to him when they cleared the building. "That was one of the best pizzas I've ever eaten. This little town has amazing cuisine."

His smile widened as he rubbed his belly. "Mill Creek is a small-town foodies paradise."

"I'll have fun eating my way through all the different places and menu items. It's nice to see local eateries thriving instead of just chain restaurants. I might need to take daily hikes to keep my clothes from getting too tight."

Trent placed his palm on the small of her back as he guided her toward the city park. The thought of her staying there long-term to take those hikes had his heart thumping in a happy cadence. The crisp evening air held a subtle scent of fresh-cut wood. As they strolled toward the park, he pointed out several buildings and shared more pieces of the town's history.

"When I was eight, my grandfather took me trout fishing for the first time. We packed a lunch, caught some grasshoppers to use as bait, and spent the day lying in wait in the tall grass. That day, I caught a twelve-inch beauty that we had for dinner. Thrilled to the core."

"Don't you stand or sit to fish?"

"Not creek trout as they hide alongside the bank in alcoves. Shadows and sounds can spook them, so you have to stay low and quiet," he answered, wiping off the park bench so she could sit. He took a seat next to her and when his jean-clad leg brushed against hers, it caused a jolt of energy to surge through his system.

She folded her hands in her lap. "Your grandfather must have been so proud of you, especially if he were alive today to see you as sheriff."

"Don't give me that much credit. I'd still be an FBI agent today if my boss hadn't decided to remove me from the case," he countered, a deep sigh escaping his mouth.

She turned her hand over so she could lace their fingers together. "So, that's why you left the bureau?"

"Yes. Looking back, I let my anger have too big of a vote. But being stripped of the opportunity to avenge Dalton's death gutted me. To this day, I still object to my superior's rationale; cover or not, I still could have worked the case."

He looked away to stare at the buildings in the distance, needing a moment to quell the anger that instantly simmered low when he rehashed this topic. The seconds felt like minutes as he sat quietly. This wasn't a topic of conversation he liked to discuss, but he owed her the truth about why he resigned, even if he couldn't divulge the entire story. The weight he carried on his shoulders plummeted to his stomach, churning the pizza he had just consumed as his mind opened the door to his past.

Maggie squeezed his hand. "Sorry. I shouldn't have asked—"

"Don't apologize. I should have shared this with you before now. I should have died alongside Dalton—a part of me did. The injuries to my leg and shoulder were gruesome, requiring several surgeries to repair the damage. Rehab sucked. What got me through was I funneled my anger into getting stronger so I could put an end to Falcon. When that goal was ripped away, I lost my direction. That's when I heard about the special election for the Sheriff of Mill Creek County, and now the rest is history."

"I wanted to visit you while you were in the hospital, but I had so much to do with Dalton's funeral. I'm sorry I wasn't there for you."

"You had enough on your plate. Besides, I'm the one who should be apologizing. I haven't been there for you at all, starting with the day of his funeral." Trent inhaled sharply.

Why hadn't he reached out and offered her comfort? She'd been forced to grieve alone while she figured out how to move forward without his support. His fixation on his anger and pain consumed him while he punished himself. He had to fix the damage he caused, but the fear of failing her strangled his heart.

"I always wondered why you hadn't, but I never really thought about everything you were going through, too. We're a pair, aren't we?"

He'd meant everything he said to her, but what if he let her down when she needed him the most? Guilt gnawed at him because he knew he'd take that opportunity without blinking an eye if he ever got the chance to bring down Falcon. That alone was why Dalton didn't want his sister with anyone in their line of work. Her brother wanted her to come first and to be with a man who understood that importance. A man whose job brought him home safe and sound every night and put Maggie first. Not one who put his life on the line while trying to make the world a safer place.

Trent cupped Maggie's chin and tilted her head back until she looked him in the eyes. "I'll protect you until I take my last breath. Noah will, too, because you're Dalton's family."

Her eyes widened, followed by a sharp intake of breath. "No! I'm not worth anyone's life. I won't lose anyone else I care about. I can't..."

He released his grip. "Shh, I'm not planning on going anywhere for a long time." Her reaction to his declaration caused another rush of guilt to punch his system. She'd endured so many heartbreaking losses. To be that young and to have buried your entire family was a trauma he couldn't fathom. Eliminating this threat and keeping her safe was his main focus. Those were his one and only priorities.

"It's been a difficult time for both of us. Don't get me wrong, I could have used some help packing up all his trophies and books. Gosh, if anyone in high school knew that my jock brother was a closet bookworm, there would've been a riot. Anyway, I had Maggie Moo to help me through some of it."

"Who's Maggie Moo?"

Maggie looked at him as if he'd grown a third eye. "My stuffed Holstein cow that must have been in the bedroom when you brought me clothing the other night. Don't you remember how Dalton used to call me Maggie Moo? It was his nickname for me. He gave it to me during his last visit and told me that whenever I missed him or needed a hug, it would be like I was hugging him. That way, he was always with me. Of course, he also told me not to lose it. Commanding to the end, I guess."

Trent nodded and raised his eyebrow. "That's right, and it also answers the question of why a girl on the run brought a stuffed cow with her."

She blurted out a laugh. "Maggie Moo goes everywhere with me. It's my brother's doppelgänger."

Trent laughed. He was pretty sure Dalton would grimace at being compared to a cow. Maggie rested her head on his shoulder while they sat silently, watching the night sky transition from dusk to dark. The stars shone brightly, dotting the sky. He enjoyed tonight, even when the conversation turned toward uncomfortable topics.

Tomorrow, he'd check them into the Mill Creek Hotel. His house wasn't the best place to keep her safe. He also planned to cut back his hours to spend more time with her. At least he had a chance now to right a few of his wrongs by putting her first.

Tomorrow morning, he'd call Noah to share his suspicions about her being under surveillance. He'd also call in a favor to see if Oscar would be willing to enter her place to retrieve the knife and any possible fingerprints. Whoever entered her home had some unfinished business with Dalton.

T RENT WAS OUT OF bed before his alarm sounded. It didn't matter if it was the weekend or not. Usually, he'd head into the office on Saturdays to catch up on paperwork since he spent the weekdays out in the field, but today, he'd rather spend his time with Maggie. She needed to have some fun infused into her life, and he was more than happy to oblige. He had decided to take her hiking to see one of his favorite spots, followed by a picnic lunch. First, though, he wanted to get them settled in the hotel, then he'd call PB&S Cafe to order lunch.

As he showered, he made a mental list of things he needed—sunblock, a blanket, and other necessities. Afterward, he dressed in cargo pants, a black T-shirt, and boots. He rummaged around in his closet until he found his backpack and filled it with the supplies for their hike. He'd grab the ice cooler when they left since it was in the garage. In the kitchen, he went about making coffee.

When the burp and gurgling of water started to flow through the maker, he took out his cell phone and dialed the Mill Creek Hotel. He was making the reservation when he saw movement out of the corner of his eye.

"Good morning," he mouthed when Maggie entered the kitchen. "Okay, I understand. If possible, one room on the first floor, closest to the back corner."

"It's booked and ready when you arrive," the front desk clerk cheerily replied.

"Perfect. Thanks, Michelle."

After ending the call, he spun around to tell Maggie his plan and punched his solar plexus. Only moments ago, her face was rosy and shiny from her shower, but now it was white as a ghost. She would never be able to hide behind those beautiful orbs, which were so expressive and telling.

Even her hands shook as she fidgeted with her fingers. "What's wrong—"

"Y-You're sending me...away...n-n-now?" Maggie croaked.

His heart nosedived at the fear that had overtaken her features. Her eyes were wide with panic. "Come here," he demanded in a tone that brokered no argument as he held his arms out.

Without hesitation, she moved into his embrace, her skin cool to his touch. Her immediate instinct to trust him immensely pleased him. His need to protect her while shielding her from anything that upset her tightened his chest. He never wanted to see that look of panic radiating from her eyes again.

He wrapped her up in his arms and rested his chin on the top of her head. Crushing her body tight against his, needing the contact as much as she did. The scent of vanilla and oranges from her lotion filled his senses. "I'm making reservations for *us* at the Mill Creek Hotel until my roof is finished. I want you to be safe and comfortable. I tried to book two adjoining rooms, but the hotel is sold out for the summer season. One room is all I could get, so I'll see if they have a roll-away bed, or I can sleep on the floor."

She pushed out of his embrace enough to look him in the eye. "I'm sorry for jumping to that conclusion. I know you won't leave me. One room is fine, but I'll take the roll-away bed. They're made for smaller people."

He trailed the back of his fingers down her cheek. "I'm sorry for the confusion. You're precious to me. Now, go pack your bags. After we check in, I have a surprise for you."

He waited for Maggie to pull from his embrace, but instead, she squeezed him even harder. Their combined heat encased his body, and the growing bulge in his pants told him he should break off the contact. Something about this moment drove him to act on her impulse.

He sucked in a sharp breath. His hardened length dug into her stomach. "You're tempting the beast inside me," he growled.

She tilted her head backward and licked her lips. The pink tip of her tongue worked over her soft flesh. Ever so lightly, he brushed his lips over hers, then nipped along the seam of her lips. He slid his hands lower until they rested on the globes of her ass. His insides shook from the pinpricks of arousal that rushed through his body. All his senses were heightened. Her nipples hardened to tiny points that stabbed at his chest. All this, and they hadn't even taken off any clothing. *Damn it.* He was screwed. He wanted her with every fiber of his being.

When she opened her lips to moan, he chose that moment to devour her. His tongue met hers, tasting every corner of her mouth. She tasted like peppermint and sunshine. He pulled back, leaving them both gasping for air from this sensual assault. Her eyes darkened with arousal.

"I love that your lips are red and swollen from my kisses." Gripping her head, he angled it perfectly to claim her mouth again. He broke off the kiss at the sound of his cell ringing. The device displayed Noah's name.

"What's up?" Trent answered.

Noah spit out the update while office chatter filled in the background. "The DPD has updated its report. Two men were found not far from that van. Murdered, execution style."

"That's not good and can't be a coincidence." Trent watched Maggie pour a cup of coffee before sitting at the kitchen table. He paced back and forth while he spoke.

Noah added, as he typed, "Oscar agreed and will be at her home within the hour."

"Thanks, man. Let me update Maggie and we'll head to the station."

Trent turned around and raked his hand through his hair. He closed his eyes and blew a deep breath as he came and sat next to her. "An agent Noah and I know has agreed to enter your apartment to retrieve the knife and dust it for prints. I also want him to sweep for bugs since you've seen maintenance inside your place, and that uniform was found inside the van. There has also been an update from the Dallas police department that two men were found murdered, execution style, not that far from the abandoned van."

Her eyes went wide, and her mouth gaped. "Executed?"

He grabbed her shoulder and squeezed. "It has the markings of a professional hit. The men were killed with a shot to the head and two in the chest. According to the medical examiner, the time of death is somewhere between twenty-four to forty-eight hours ago."

She pulled her hand free and pressed it to her forehead. "Wh-what does that mean?"

"Time of death isn't a precise calculation. The best theory is that someone took care of loose ends, but we still don't know why or that this is related to you. Now, my goal is to retrieve that knife, dust for prints, and see if we can tie any of it to those two dead men. That will determine our next steps."

Maggie stood, but Trent snagged her hand to stop her departure. "About earlier—"

"Stop it, we're both adults, unless you mean you don't want to—" she pointed between them "—with me? Or do you have someone else? I wouldn't be surprised, you always did."

Trent cursed to himself. Everything had come out wrong. This should be simple. He wanted her, and she wanted him. So, why did his guilt and his sense of loyalty have to intervene? "No. This isn't what your brother wanted for you or me, either, for that fact. Our jobs are dangerous, and you deserve better. I can't stand the thought of you being put in harm's way because of my career. Besides, this isn't the time."

Her body recoiled, and she fisted her hands at her side. "Seriously? Is that your reasoning? Dalton didn't get to interfere with my life when he was alive. He certainly won't from the grave. He may have tried, but it's my life, and I'm the only one who makes the decisions. Death can change a person's priorities and outlook on life."

"You're not seeing the bigger picture. We need to get to the station." He hated how the brightness in her eyes dulled.

What could he say? *I want you, but I'm conflicted, and I feel like I'm taking advantage of you. Or that my guilt is screaming, I don't deserve you.* He ran his hand through his hair and sighed. His actions didn't match those sentiments. He had to get a grip on his emotions, even if his body had staked a claim to a woman he could never have. He wasn't worthy of her. He couldn't spend more time discussing this. Their plans had changed, and he had to get them to his office for the next installment of Maggie's shit show. He'd stop and check them into the Mill Creek Hotel on the way.

Five

PERSPIRATION CLUNG TO MAGGIE's body, her skin itchy and warm, even with the air conditioner running. Her nerves were on fire as dread filled her stomach. Silently, she sat in Trent's office, looking at the television mounted in the corner. Soon, it would broadcast the live feed of her apartment from the body camera attached to an FBI analyst. This was not how she expected to spend her Saturday. This was not something she expected to experience ever in her life. Instead, she'd rather be immersed in Trent's surprise, not focused on her worsening situation.

She still couldn't believe someone might have been in her home for nefarious reasons. She was a nobody, so why would someone waste their time? The thought of being spied on made her skin crawl. No, scratch that: it scared the shit out of her.

Trent sat behind his desk, his fingers moving rapidly as he accessed the software to log them into the live feed. A stupid thought crossed her mind—at least her bed was made. *Idiot, like that, mattered one iota.*

A trickle of sweat traveled down her spine, tickling her on its descent. "If those things are found, I don't know if I can handle knowing my house was bugged."

"Remember, information is power. If it is, we'll handle it." Trent's voice was soft but firm.

Maggie sat quietly, sipping the iced tea they'd stopped to get on the way. The cool liquid slid down her throat, leaving a soothing trail in its wake. Her mind raced with worst-case scenarios, hating the helpless feeling that hovered over her. It didn't help that she was still pissed at Trent for how he ended their last confrontation, but she had to set that aside for now.

"Okay, the feed is running." He snatched the remote and turned up the volume on the television. "Oscar, can you hear me? It's Trent, and I'm with Margaret King."

The snowy image sharpened and bounced up and down, right and left, making her a little dizzy before a man emerged on the screen. He looked to be about thirty years old, with a lanky build and short brown hair. He screamed science or computer geek to her. "I can hear you, Trent. It's good to see you, man."

The camera image swirled, blurring images right before her front door came into focus.

"Thanks for doing this on such short notice." Trent raised the volume button a few clicks.

"I'd do anything for you. Things just haven't been the same since you left. Okay, Margaret, do I have your permission to pick your lock and access your home?"

Her stomach dropped. She forced confidence into her reply so she sounded stable, not a woman on the verge of freaking out and screaming, uh, hell no. "Yes, but please, call me Maggie."

"Will do," Oscar replied, his hands using two metal instruments to breach her lock. After a second, the front door opened wide.

Trent had updated her on the ride over about Oscar's expertise with high-tech gadgetry. According to Trent, Oscar's lab was a righteous playground for all geeks worldwide. Now, he stood in her hallway. *Geez, what's the point of locks?* Oscar placed a black bag, like airline pilots carried, on her kitchen counter. He opened it and removed several gadgets and tools, placing each on the counter. Then, he donned a pair of latex gloves.

Oscar's voice echoed over the speaker, "Let's begin with the knife and note. Then, I'll start in the kitchen and work clockwise around your apartment to look for bugs, transmitters, and cameras. Unless you have a question, I will just sweep, clear, and secure each room."

"Understood," Trent replied.

Oscar photographed her office before he bagged and tagged the note and knife. "Our assailant thinks he's creative. There is nothing special about the knife, a typical folding lock knife. From my cursory glance, it looks like whoever broke into her apartment focused their efforts in this room."

They watched as he worked diligently from top to bottom, then left to right around the room. The next stop was the kitchen. Activity filled the line, and minutes passed like hours. A series of beeps and high pitch squawks made her jump. Determined to remain strong and not dissolve into a puddle of water, she forced herself to take several deep breaths. *Knowledge is power. Knowledge is power.* The problem with this understanding was that it left her exposed and on edge. A stranger had breached the one place where a person should feel safe.

The sound of the power drill came next.

"Did you see anything that's missing?" Trent asked in a low voice. "It looks like your desk and file cabinet were of interest. I noticed a file labeled Dalton on the floor."

She glared at him as if he'd grown a set of horns.

Maggie slid her gaze sideways toward Trent. "Seriously? I watched, but nothing came into focus. I didn't even see that file on the ground. What I can tell you is that there's nothing exciting about my files. That file with my brother's name on it is full of his funeral paperwork and death certificate—"

Maggie's eyes widened when she saw several small devices cupped in Oscar's hand as he held it toward the lens. "W-what are those things?"

"Not good news. They're electronic bugs." Trent's lips smashed into a straight line.

"You mean someone could listen to me?" Her skin prickled with a mixture of shock and panic.

Several long minutes later, Oscar's voice came across the line. "I have a camera in the office and bathroom, along with two more bugs."

Her hand flew to her chest. "Oh God, this is so bad."

Trent stood and moved around the desk. He pulled her against his chest and held her while her body trembled. In a low, deep voice, he spoke against her ear, "Serious, yes. But now we know more than we did yesterday."

Her assessment didn't seem that glowing. She didn't utter the word that sat on her lips. *Violated.* Stripped of her privacy and security. The solidarity of his actions reminded her that she wasn't facing this alone—the one fact that meant the most to her now. She trusted Trent with her life.

He ran his hand down the back of her head and cupped her neck. "Now, we take all the evidence we're gathering and find the connection that ties all of this back to Dalton."

Maggie's feet tingled while a chill washed over her body. In total, ten devices were found, four of which were cameras. Her cheeks heated with embarrassment until it morphed into anger. God, she hoped nude pictures of her weren't circulating around the internet.

She listened to Trent update Noah on his cellphone while Oscar placed each device into evidence bags. "Oscar is going to see if he can lift any prints. My newest theory is that the same person who broke into her home to install the surveillance equipment will match the prints lifted from one or both of our dead men."

Her head pounded, and acid churned in her stomach. She dashed toward the trash bin, barely reaching it, before she emptied her stomach of bile and iced tea. Her throat burned as hot tears burned her cheeks. It didn't take long for those to give way to sobs as she crushed the can to her chest. What the hell was she going to do?

A cool paper cloth pressed against her forehead, followed by a deep, soothing voice. "I've got you. Everything's going to be okay."

He gathered her hair in his hand while she dry heaved once more. His gentleness and presence calmed her, and she needed that right now. When she quieted, he moved the bin and lifted her so she sat in his lap, cradled against his chest.

"I'm sorry. I didn't mean to fall apart." Her voice sounded more like a croak.

"I'd be more worried if this didn't bother you. You're a strong woman, but you're human, Maggie. Don't apologize for that."

He made her head spin. One minute, he slammed the door on their attraction, and in the next, he made her feel precious. Forever wasn't in her plan because the constant worry that Trent could be killed would consume her. She'd been down that road and couldn't do it again. What she wanted was to experience what could have been. At least she'd know what she'd missed out on. *Damn you, Dalton!*

She looked over her shoulder at the blackened screen. "Where's Oscar?"

"He's gone and is taking the devices with him so he can check them for fingerprints. If we're lucky, Noah will run those through AFIS—Automated Fingerprint Identification System."

The pounding in her skull ramped up, which made thinking overrated at the moment. Instead, all she could do was nod at his statement. The questions she wanted to ask would have to wait; her energy reserves were drained. Never in a million years had she thought they'd find spy things in her home. Wow, had she underestimated the danger her brother faced daily.

Now, her residence gave her the willies. Whoever had infringed on her space made her want to use an obnoxious amount of bleach before she'd feel comfortable there again. Who knew what else they did while they were inside her home? Great, one more thing she'd have to deal with later.

"I should call my office and tell them I need to take another week of vacation."

Trent adjusted his hold of her. "Let's head to the hotel and relax. Later, I'll grab some takeout, and we can eat dinner in the room."

"How long will the fingerprint process take?"

He stood holding her until she slid down his body and her feet touched the floor. "Oscar's going to the lab tonight and hopes to have something he can send to Noah in a few hours."

Her thoughts drifted back to the day she found the knife. She'd barely started her day as she sat at her computer with a cup of coffee. She had a restless night and had risen early with plans to start another auditing assignment. That was a nice perk of her job. Once she made her quota for the month, any additional audits she completed were bonus pay. Her mind, not focused on the freight bills, drifted to her brother's last impromptu visit, which had always bothered her. That, in and of itself, worried her because he never did anything without over-planning every detail. Now that she thought about it, he'd been edgy and apprehensive.

That morning, she'd grabbed the USB drive Dalton had given her during his visit and inserted it into the slot on her laptop. She reviewed his legal documents again and another document with several names listed on it she'd glossed over before. Trent's name and two other agents who worked with the Bureau. The other name she didn't recognize, so she typed it into her search engine only to learn that the man had died. He must have been a friend of her brothers. The other file contained photos she wasn't ready to open.

"Trent, I just thought of something. I don't know if it means anything, but Dalton wasn't himself during his last visit. First, he just showed up, but something wound him pretty tight. I mean, I've been nagging him to get his legal paperwork in order since everyone in our family seems to die. He always resisted and told me he'd be around forever to pester me. My jaw practically hit the floor when he handed me a flash drive containing all that information."

"That's good. Do you remember anything else that seemed off? Did he share anything job-related?"

"I remember seeing the van in the parking lot the day we buried him. The only other thing that comes to mind is that he was extra bossy. He mentioned several times that I should let you handle his final arrangements, which pissed me off. I kept thinking I could take care of my own family. Oh, and to make sure I never lose Maggie Moo. Do you see what I mean? The man looked like Dalton, but he was acting crazy."

Trent nodded but didn't say anything further. She figured he was processing everything. On their way out, Maggie headed toward the restroom to rinse out her mouth and put herself back together. She was pretty sure she had dragon-barf breath and didn't want to kill Trent with it.

She stopped short of the bathroom door and turned to Trent. "Hey, earlier, you said you had a surprise for me. What was it?"

A devious smile split his lips. "I'll pick another day."

T RENT REFUSED TO BE shut out when it came to Maggie. He'd learned his lesson when she'd shown up on his doorstep. She didn't have to shoulder any of this alone, but he couldn't help her if she didn't tell him what was bothering her. Since they had returned to the hotel, she'd barely spoken two words. His phone lighted displaying a next text message. He pressed the message icon to read Noah's note.

Oscar got prints. I'm running them now against AFIS. I figured my system would be faster than yours.

Trent relayed Noah's text to Maggie and then spoke out loud as he typed his reply. "Good. *Pull the prints from the DPD police report. I know your mad hacker skills can handle that easily. See if they match.*"

That's not a challenge. I could do that in my sleep—

He put his phone down to see Maggie glaring at him. Dark smudges marred the delicate skin under her eyes. A look of defeat colored her face. "What's going on in that pretty head of yours?"

"I'm tired, frustrated, and worried. Not to mention, I practically threw up all over your office." Maggie exhaled, taking a seat on the bed.

He gave her a small grin. "You hit the can. I'd call that a win-win." He slid his hands into his pockets and leaned back against the dresser. "You don't have to keep everything bottled up inside. Talk."

She pinned him with a serious look that faded into defeat. "I don't know if you'd understand. It's like I'm standing on the outside of my life looking in. Nothing makes any sense, and I feel out of control."

He didn't like the dull gaze that stared back at him. He needed Maggie to relight that fire that burned so hot inside her. A mad Maggie beats a deflated Maggie any day of the week. "The unknown is the worst part, but we don't stop until we've uncovered the truth. Today was good. Let's hope AFIS can help us out."

She shot up and fisted her hands. "Good? That was far from freaking good—"

"That's not what I meant, and you know it. This is a significant find that's going to lead us to more answers and new avenues to investigate. Knowledge is—"

"Power. I've heard it before, but you'll have to excuse me because I don't feel empowered. And from where I'm standing, I've put my whole life on hold with my thumb up my ass until we find out who's behind these attacks."

His phone chirped again for the umpteenth time in so many minutes. This time, it showed a text from his deputy. *Boss, Clarke Dragoon has left two voicemails for you. In the last, he stated that he'd like to speak to you tomorrow morning.*

Trent replied back to his deputy that he'd head toward Mr. Dragoon's place tomorrow and shoved his phone into his back pocket. Mr. Dragoon had zero patience, and he wasn't ready to hear another disagreement between him and his neighbor, Irene.

Trent ran his hand through his hair. "Your life's unfolding in real time, and I'm afraid there isn't a pause button. The important part is that you're not alone in this because I'm not going anywhere. We have a puzzle to solve, and that's what we're going to do."

"I'd rather DVR it and see if I like the ending before committing more time to it," she muttered under her breath. "The other item we need to solve stems from our earlier conversation."

Trent crossed his arms over his chest. "We did, you just didn't like the messaging. Dalton wanted something better for you...stability and—"

"Stop quoting my brother," she snapped. "He doesn't get to voice his opinion. He's dead. Besides, the whole stable and home for dinner scenario didn't work so well for my parents, did it? That argument is nothing more than my brother trying to dictate the course of my life. It's past time we hashed this out because it's been between us for a while."

Trent held her gaze. "Dalton had a valid point. Our jobs were practically twenty-four-seven, and there was always the potential that danger could follow us home. What type of life would that give you?"

She marched forward until they were nose to nose. "You're both crazy and overbearing bastards. This is ridiculous. I get to pick who I want in my life. Risk and reward. Isn't that the stupid phrase you two tossed around all the time?"

Trent lowered his head so he could see her. "Uh, yeah, but that was in reference to work."

"Semantics. This is my life, Trent, and I'll choose my own destiny."

"You're just speaking crazy now, and it's pissing me off. All I meant is I shouldn't be taking advantage of you, considering everything that's happening. Besides, after this is over, you will head back to Dallas, right? What's the point?"

Maggie huffed out a frustrated grunt. "The point? I'm curious, did you even think to ask my brother if you were included in his mandate or are you just assuming? Well, at least I know why you dumped me. Honestly, I think my brother would be happy knowing you were the one in my life. He admired, trusted, and loved you. You may want to wrap your head around that fact. Or was it for another woman? You and Dalton always seemed to have plenty."

"Stop it. You don't know what you're talking about. And I didn't dump you, for fuck's sake, but my career didn't align to your desire to start a family. I care about you, Maggie. Walking away from you was the hardest damn thing I've ever had to do, but it was the right decision. That's my point."

"Don't you want to know what it would have been like between us? I can't help but be insanely attracted to you. Oh, never mind, this is coming out all wrong. You're a good man, Trent."

Her statement was like a knife to his gut. "Opening Pandora's box is never a good idea. I'm far from being a good man. And this thing between us is my fault. I do want you. I don't deserve you. There's a big difference between the two. For the record, I haven't been with another woman since the day Dalton was killed."

Her mouth opened and then snapped shut. She stood silently, her gaze lingering on him for at least a minute. "I'm taking a shower."

He hadn't meant to say that, but she could fire him up faster than anyone he knew. Wanting her wasn't the problem. His greatest fear was letting her down. That he'd fail Maggie just like he failed Dalton. The other, she'd hate him when she learned the truth about that fateful day.

Trent exhaled, rolling his neck to alleviate the tension that had taken over his body. He walked toward the window and stared at nothing in particular. His vision blurred as his mind travelled backward to when he pulled into the abandoned railroad warehouse that morning to meet Dalton.

Their debriefing at FBI headquarters in DC to update the team on Falcon's latest intelligence, had been pushed to the afternoon to accommodate Dalton's last minute travel plan to see his sister. Trent planned to grill him later because something had taken up residence in Dalton's ass making him deviate from his planned and organized self.

He arrived at the abandoned building's parking lot forty-five minutes late. The metal building resembled a warehouse. Most of the windows were either broken or missing, and the few remaining were coated with spray paint. The lot's pavement showed signs of age, marred with large cracks and weeds growing between the gaps. The lone car in the lot sat empty.

Where was Dalton?

Trent slid his gaze to the rearview mirror before casually taking in the view to his left and right. Everything appeared quiet and calm. The sun shined brightly on the cloudless day, giving him a clear view into the distance. His scalp prickled. The quiet and stillness bothered him—something was off.

He retrieved his SIG Sauer P226 from the glove box. When he exited the car, he tucked the pistol at the small of his back, just inside the waistband of his pants. The coo of pigeons grew louder the closer he moved toward the building. His gaze swiveled, noting everything as he approached the wall by the open doorway.

The sound of a single gunshot rang out. The flap and flutter of scared pigeons fleeing faded to the sound of a man groaning. Instincts and training took over as he reached for his gun. He systematically assessed the situation and his options. The moans intensified as someone floundered, scraping along the ground.

His heart thumped hard against his chest. He eased his head around the doorway, not wanting to give up his position or alert anyone to his presence. The sight of tortured flesh froze the blood in his veins. He snapped his head back against the wall.

Shit, it was Dalton. What the hell had happened?

And whose body lay next to him?

Trent's throat constricted, and his mouth went dry. God, this man had stood by his side and had his back countless times. He wasn't just his partner. He was one of his best friends, which was why the conjectures surrounding Dalton's motives still pissed him off.

"Trent...Trent? Are you ignoring me?" The press of Maggie's hand on his back caused him to flinch.

Needing to purge those images from his mind, he closed his eyes to wipe the slate clean. He gulped a breath before turning to face Maggie, whose skin glistened from her shower. She looked more relaxed, and he didn't have the heart to tell her the truth.

"Sorry, I was processing all the evidence we've collected so far and didn't hear you." He hated the falsehood the moment it slipped past his lips, but he wasn't permitted to divulge any details surrounding Dalton's death.

She had taken a seat on the bed, watching him. "So much has happened so quickly. It's overwhelming and makes me tired."

"No, that's from the adrenaline crash. Get some rest. I'll go down to the front desk and get a roll-away—"

"Seriously, those suck for comfort, and the last time I checked, we're both adults. We'll share the bed. If you snore, I'll elbow you. No, I have one better. If you snore, you can do laundry tomorrow. I'm running out of clothing."

Not going there...This is about sharing a bed for rest, nothing else.

"Appreciate it, and I'll do the same. Just be forewarned, I only have two loads—sheets, towels, and everything else."

She rolled her green orbs at him and then shook her head. He'd take it. At least she had a little play left in her after this crap-tastic day. Unfortunately, more would come. Right now, he'd take comfort in the fact that despite their issues, she had sought him out and had asked for his help.

"Maybe the worst is behind us?" Maggie asked, her eyes pleading with him.

He wanted to tell her anything but the truth, but he refused to lie to her. "Unfortunately, I think we've only scratched the surface, so we need to remain observant and careful."

Six

THE FOLLOWING MORNING, TRENT pulled into Clarke's driveway and killed the engine. This to-do item was one he wanted to cross off his list. The front door opened to reveal the hulking man with a bald head. He stood about six-feet-five-inches tall but had to weigh at least two hundred and fifty pounds of pure muscle. When you put the whole package together, Trent had to agree with Irene. Clarke did look like he belonged to a biker gang, but looks could be deceiving.

"It's about damn time. I figured the response would be quicker in a small community." Clarke groused, not leaving his front porch.

Trent rested his hands on his hips. "I'm sure you're familiar with nine-one-one, you know if there's an actual emergency. Lance told me you had something to discuss?"

"I have a problem," Clarke responded, his arms crossed over his chest.

Trent's hackles went up. "Okay, I'm listening. Do you want to take this inside?"

Clarke studied him for a minute, then separated his arms. Tucked in one hand were some papers he held out to Trent. "Porch works."

He approached Clarke to take the proffered pages and then flipped through the pictures. Anger bolted up Trent's spine, digging its claws into him. It took a great effort on his part not to rip him a new ass. "This is a picture of Irene standing at your door with a pie. This is called being neighborly."

Clarke made a clicking noise with this tongue while he shook his head. "Nope. That there is called subterfuge. That pie you see in this image," he pointed at the dessert, "gave her a reason to be on my porch. She's peering into my windows. I'd call it trespassing with intent."

Trent's patience meter flatlined. He had hoped this call wasn't about Clarke and Irene, two grown-assed adults who couldn't play nice. They would have to learn to coexist, or he might lock them up until they find common ground. He didn't get the sense that this man was a menace to society, just a pain in everyone's ass. It's a huge difference, but he could rub people the wrong way with his arrogance.

"I'm in no mood to play mediator today. Are you seriously claiming that Irene intentionally entered your land without consent? This is what you're wasting my time with this morning?" Trent asked.

Clarke ticked off every offense on his fingers. "First, she didn't have my permission. Second, she's already complained to you that I'm the one causing problems. Third, I've never trespassed on her land—"

"Stop it," Trent snapped. The muscle in his jaw clenched. "Your argument is weak, which I'm sure you already know. No trespassing signs are posted, and you don't own this property. That concern would need to come from the owner. Act like a grownup and get to know Irene. She's a good woman who loves this town and all of its residents. I have more important things that need my attention today. Goodbye, Mr. Dragoon."

Trent turned on his heel then strode to his truck. He'd planned to stop by his house after this meeting to grab a few things on his way back to the hotel with breakfast.

Clarke cleared his throat and stated in a blunt voice, "We haven't discussed *your* problem yet?"

Trent stopped mid-step and pivoted, ready to lay into Clarke, but his facial features had darkened which made him pause. The cocksure man that had irritated only moments before had vanished. "Let's hear it."

"Do you know anyone in the area who has two high dollar drones?" Clarke asked.

"No, why?"

"Well, whoever owns these babies is skilled. They flew them in a grid style search pattern around the vicinity of your house. It reeked of gathering intelligence on either someone or something. Nothing about it seemed normal which bothered me."

Trent's eyebrows narrowed, and his gut churned like he'd just been sucker-punched. "I don't require people to register drones, but I appreciate the information. If you notice anything else suspicious call me directly. I'll see if I can find out who might own them." He removed a business card from his wallet.

Clarke palmed the card and nodded. "Will do."

Trent turned back toward his vehicle. Irritation prickled at his neckline, but it had nothing to do with Clarke. The fact that someone had flown two drones close to Trent's home told him that whoever was after Maggie knew she was in Mill Creek. The stakes had just increased—tenfold.

M AGGIE STOOD IN FRONT of the window in their hotel room, watching the people on Main Street go about their daily routines. A reminder that life went on, even without those loved ones filling in the space around you. A restlessness simmered under the surface of her skin, threatening to engulf her body and mind. She didn't recognize her life anymore. That was a problem. Why did everything have to be so complicated?

Now, all she seemed to have were questions. Why did she think isolating herself from everything familiar would help her heal? Why had someone targeted her? It all didn't make any sense. What had become blatantly clear was that she had to push past her grief and reclaim her life again. Would it be easy? Hell no, but she had to try. Nothing would ever minimize the pain of losing someone she loved, but she had to start moving forward.

The pane of glass cooled her forehead when she rested against it. She remembered the day her parents stood in their driveway, waving at their children before they left for their cruise. Armed with luggage and an itinerary outlining everything they wanted to explore, they beamed happily. Instead, horror and tragedy struck.

She wondered if her parents had suffered or had a merciful death. Were they together or separated when the cruise ship sank? More questions she'd never have answers to, which meant she would always wonder and speculate. No closure.

The hard truth was that no one had forever with the people they loved. She had to hold tight to the here and now because tomorrows were limited. Had the time come for her to fight for the chance to create new memories? To see where things could go with Trent?

A shiver ran down her spine at being vulnerable, but at the same time, butterflies danced in her belly with the possibilities. The mechanical slide of the door lock engaged, pulling Maggie from her thoughts. She turned in time to see Trent walking through the door carrying breakfast.

"Let me help you." She rushed over and took the bag from his grasp so he could place the tray holding their drinks onto the table. The aroma of buttermilk, bacon, and coffee filled the air. "Oh, man, this smells heavenly."

"Here's your coffee and iced tea." He winked at her before digging into the sack. "Bacon or sausage?"

"Surprise me," she said, eagerly grabbing the wrapped sandwich he offered. She took a large bite of buttery biscuit, fluffy egg, gooey cheese, and crisp bacon. As the flavors melded on her tongue, she groaned with delight.

She spoke around a mouth full of food, "Yum, this is awesome."

"I couldn't have you passing out on me while you do my laundry. I mean, you did build a log cabin last night."

She punched him in the arm. "Whatever, my nose was plugged."

"Uh-huh."

After they polished off their sandwiches, he picked up the basket containing their laundry and motioned for her to lead the way. Thankfully, it seemed to be a slow Sunday morning, so they jumped on the open washers and dryers.

The hotel's small laundry had a nice layout and even a few chairs to sit and wait in. The smell of fresh linen and lavender-scented detergent floated in the air. When one load finished, Maggie and Trent folded the clothes while the second went through the drying cycle.

As they worked side by side, Maggie thought about what she'd told Trent last night. He needed to know how he made her feel. It didn't change her outlook on marriage and children, but one never knew what tomorrow would bring. Time with the people she loved mattered. He was all she had left. The trick was to keep her heart wrapped tightly so it didn't expand.

Trent's cell phone buzzed in his pocket. "Hey, Aimee, what's up? I'm putting you on speaker. Why are you in the office today?"

"Okay. A few things...I came into work to wrap up a few reports I didn't finish last week since we worked on the filing cabinets. The most important thing is the budget, which has to be finalized and submitted for the coming year. All I need is your signature. Second, Mr. Dragoon called super early this morning and wants to meet with you. He's even threatening to come down here and wait."

Trent rolled his eyes. "I've already met with him so you don't have to worry about that. Let me wrap up what I'm doing, and we'll be there in twenty minutes."

"Oh, that's great to hear. Thank you, and I'm sorry to bother you. You practically live here, so I'm glad you took a day for yourself. Well, until I interrupted it." Aimee sounded relieved.

He suppressed a laugh. "Don't worry about it. See you in a few."

Maggie placed her hand on his arm the moment the call ended. "Is Aimee all right?"

"Yes, I have a new resident, Clarke Dragoon, who is hellbent on getting on everyone's naughty list." He grabbed the stack of clean clothes and loaded them into the basket. "To make a long story short, he's only been in town since June, but he already has one of my lifelong resident's panties in a twist. She's convinced he's up to villainous activities because he's up at odd hours and always in his yard walking around, looking at everything. She's even accused him of knowing the exact weed and rock counts. As for Aimee, I think he's interested in her if you know what I mean."

"Oh, got it. Just take his recess away. That always worked to settle the boys down in my class."

Trent chuckled. "With that man, we should jump straight to the principal's office for a good paddling."

She scrunched her eyes together. "Uh, that type of discipline isn't allowed anymore. Geez, Trent, corporal punishment is wrong."

"Come on, I've got to get to the office. Let's get this last load folded."

T HIRTY MINUTES LATER, MAGGIE found herself glued to the window inside the sheriff's station with her heart lodged in her throat. She couldn't believe what she saw.

"Aimee, come quick," she cried out. "There's a dog loose, and it's headed toward Main Street."

Aimee ran to the window and peered out. "Oh, crap. I'll get Trent so he can stop the traffic and rescue the dog."

"What's happening?" Trent's deep voice asked as he stepped outside of his office.

"Trent, hurry. A dog's running free," Maggie rattled off while running toward the front door.

"Stop," Trent barked at her, but apparently, Aimee thought he was speaking to her. Now he had two women standing still, looking at him like he'd lost his damn mind. "Aimee, get Lance on the radio to head toward Main Street to see if we can intercept the dog. Maggie, stay with Aimee."

"No, I can help. I've wrangled third graders. One dog is nothing. Let's go," Maggie pleaded, then smiled when she saw that Trent had accepted that he'd lost this battle because he was already moving toward his truck.

The dog had made it to Main Street and seemed panicked with all the commotion. People had gathered to watch the scene play out. Trent turned on his lights, but not the siren because he didn't want to spook the animal anymore. He parked his truck and strode with confidence onto the scene. He commanded the bystanders to form a semi-circle around the dog to cut off the open side of the street. He held a pole with a loop at the end in his hand. The poor dog would need love and comfort once safely contained.

He'd slipped the snare over the pooch's head and secured him in no time. Deed done, he dropped to one knee and praised the animal in low tones with his free hand extended.

"Good boy. That's right. No one's going to hurt you," he told the dog repeatedly.

The dog was cautious but curious as he approached Trent's hand to sniff it. The fuzz ball quickly assessed and decided that Trent was solidly in the friend category. His rear end wiggled side to side with every tail wag. Trent continued to praise the dog as he scratched him behind the ears. When Trent stood, the dog leaned against his leg, nuzzling against his new friend. This adorable canine looked like a mixed breed of golden retriever and poodle.

"Hey, sweetie," Maggie said to the dog as she squatted beside Trent. "What are you doing here? Where's your family?"

Trent flashed her a smile. "This guy is making new friends today. If you feel comfortable holding him, I have a leash in my vehicle, and I'll go get it."

She nodded. "Do you have any water? I think this guy is thirsty, considering his tongue is hanging out of his mouth."

Trent hollered over his shoulder. "I'll see what I can find."

"What a good boy you're being," she cooed into big, innocent, brown eyes. "You don't have a tag on this collar, but you have this pouch."

The dog started to bark and wiggle when Trent approached a few minutes later with a blue nylon lead and a water bottle. "Let's get him into my vehicle, and then we'll take him to Micah Parker."

"Is that a vet?" she asked while she poured water into Trent's cupped hands.

"Yes, he's the town's veterinarian and owns the clinic. I hope this boy has a microchip to help us locate his family." He wiped his hands on his pants and then opened the passenger door for Maggie.

"Check the pouch on his collar, too. He's too cute to be lost," she said over her shoulder.

Trent loaded the dog into the seat behind the driver. He tugged upward on the Velcro flap and retrieved a flash drive.

He frowned. "This is odd, but maybe it contains information about the family." He tucked the drive into his pocket and slipped behind the wheel but didn't fasten his seat belt.

She would raze him for not buckling up when he backed into a parking spot in front of the Knotty Pinetree.

"Hang tight. I'll be right back." He slipped out of the vehicle and into the diner.

She scrunched her brows together and shrugged. It seemed like a strange time to get lunch. The sound of panting made her turn around to talk to the cute boy in the back. He was a beautiful, well-mannered dog.

Hopefully, they would be able to reunite him with his owners.

About ten minutes later, Trent reappeared with two drinks and a bag. He handed her the drinks and placed the bag between them.

"What's that?" Maggie asked, pointing to the bag.

"I figured Fido might be hungry."

Her heart melted at the kind gesture. When they reached the clinic, Trent ushered everyone inside, keeping the dog at his side. As soon as the door closed, their furry friend sniffed the air, whined, and promptly turned to leave through the same door he just entered.

"Hi, Sheriff," Micah said from behind the counter. When he approached, the dog hid behind Trent's legs.

"Whoa, fella, he won't hurt you," Trent said in a low voice. He patted his leg, and the dog came forward and sat on his foot. His head angled upward, waiting for his next command.

"This is my friend, Maggie King, and this feller is the one I recovered on Main Street. I'm hoping he has a chip."

Micah shook her hand. "Pleasure to meet you." Then he walked closer to the dog and squatted to his level. "Hey, fuzzy bear, everything is going to be okay."

The warmth in the veterinarian's eyes and the way he interacted with their rescue told her all she needed to know. This man loved animals, and it showed, judging by how the dog's tail wagged. Micah was easy on the eyes and had a sweet disposition. His wavy brown hair dusted his shoulders, and chestnut eyes sparkled as he spoke. Even his crooked nose, obviously from some type of injury, gave him a rugged look.

The office smelled of a mixture of food, medicine, and cleaning chemicals. No wonder their little friend had turned tail to leave right after they'd entered the clinic.

However, she really liked the beautiful mural on the top half of the wall behind the front counter. Someone had painted all types and breeds of animals sitting with their back to the customers on a grassy knoll covered with flowers and trees as they watched the sunrise. It was a peaceful setting everyone could enjoy.

"I picked this up at the diner for him." Trent handed Noah the bag of food. "This guy doesn't have a tag, but he had a USB inside a pouch. Ever heard of that before?"

Micah squinted and held out his hand. "Can't say that I have, but the technology exists, so maybe someone thought this was better than a tag."

When Trent deposited it into his palm, Micah went to the computer behind him and inserted the drive. "I hope it doesn't have a virus on it," he said.

When the video file appeared on the screen, Micah clicked the Apology icon and waited for it to play. "It's a video...uh, Trent, you need to see this. It has nothing to do with the dog."

Trent moved behind the counter, and his stance immediately became rigid, as his jaw clenched. She moved toward the computer and froze when she saw what was on the screen. Two men were kneeling and pleading with someone standing before them, *"I'm sorry. Please don't do this, man."*

The sound of three gunshots rang out, followed by a pause, then three more. Both men in the video dropped to the ground. She sucked in a sharp breath and covered her mouth. *Oh my God.*

"I'm sorry about this, Micah. Will you run your checks and take this guy to your shelter? I'll have Aimee reach out to you," Trent instructed, extracting the drive.

Micah nodded and accepted the lead. "I'll take care of him. It seems you have your hands full."

The warmth from Trent's palm barely registered as he placed his hand on her back. He steered her out of the clinic and hugged her tight.

"What was that?" she mumbled against his chest.

"I'm pretty sure those were the two men DPD found executed. I need to call Noah. Are you okay?"

No, she wasn't okay. She was far from being okay. Instead, she nodded and turned away from him to compose herself. Now was not the time to freak out. Trent stood on the sidewalk's edge with his phone at his ear. A prickle began at her scalp and traveled down her spine, leaving a cold trail in its wake. Now, he was talking about drones. What the hell was going on?

The moment he ended the call, she asked him about the drones.

"My meeting earlier with Clarke was about two drones he saw flying over my property. We should get back to the office and send this file to Noah. It needs to be shared with the authorities but under the auspices of the FBI."

"Oh my God, they've found me, right?"

"Yes, it's a good guess to say they know you're here. The question is what they intend to do with this knowledge and why are they targeting you?"

Seven

L ATER THAT NIGHT, TRENT paced their hotel room while Maggie took a shower. His mind raced with so many thoughts that his brain might explode. There was no doubt in his mind that Falcon was behind everything that had happened to Maggie, but why? Why was she important to them? He couldn't fucking believe that he was involved with this cartel again, giving him a second chance to avenge his partner. The time had come to involve the FBI because they had enough proof to corroborate their theory.

Early during dinner, the disquiet rolled off Maggie while she fidgeted throughout their meal. The bathroom door cracked open, and a puff of steam billowed from the opening. The familiar scent of orange and vanilla hit the air, along with the clean smell of soap. He'd pulled the shades closed and placed two bottles of water on the small table in the room.

This was not really the type of conversation that brought forth good dreams, but delaying it wasn't an option. He needed her to understand the entire picture and what involving the FBI would mean.

She emerged wearing one of his T-shirts, looking sexy as hell. He liked how she looked in his shirt and how the material would carry her scent afterward. Her hair was slicked back, and her skin glistened a rosy hue from the hot water. She looked so innocent and soft.

When she padded over and took his hand, it shocked him. Especially when she tugged him toward the bed. The blood in his head surged south, causing his member to stiffen. "Maggie, wait—"

She released his hand and turned back to him, placing her index finger over her lush lips. "Wait a moment." When he complied, she peeled back the covers on the bed. As if reading his mind, she instructed, "Sit in the center of the bed, cross-legged. Dalton created this forum to discuss important stuff when we were kids. It's called the circle of secrets."

"Not even remotely close to where I thought this was going," Trent said in a husky voice. He folded his legs and grimaced. "And clearly, your brother didn't do this when he was older."

A tear trailed down her cheek. Her voice wobbled when she answered, "Actually, he did the last time I saw him."

She wiped the tear away and held out her hands to the side of her legs, palms up. When Trent mimicked her actions, she grabbed his wrists, encouraging him to do the same. When he gripped hers, closing the circle, she continued her explanation,

"This is the circle of secrets; whatever is shared is sacred. Anything can be discussed, but everything said must remain between us. No lectures or bossiness inside this circle, just a place to listen and vent. Suggestions and ideas can be discussed, but the other can't overtake the situation. Then, once the circle is dissolved, lips are sealed."

Trent scrunched his eyes together and pursed his lips. "Wait, let me get this straight. Your big brother, 'Mr. Overprotective of my little sister,' never intervened on his own...like never?"

A small smirk zipped across her face. "I've had my suspicions, but I've never known him to break my trust. So, do you agree to these conditions, and will you uphold the code?"

She sat quietly and studied him. This had Dalton's creativity written all over it and doubled as a great way to get his sister to confide in him. Trent would also bet his life savings that Dalton had discreetly taken care of anything that ruffled his sister's feathers.

"Yes, I agree," Trent declared.

"Well then, Mr. Jacobs, I'm pleased to announce that you are now an official member of the circle," she said in a regal voice, as if to showcase the magnitude of his moment.

The huge smile that covered her face slid downward along with her shoulders. Her gaze dropped to the center of the circle. He sensed she was gathering her strength for whatever came next.

After several seconds, she inhaled and let it all out in what seemed like a long, run-on sentence that she'd never be able to finish if she stopped.

"I believe in my heart that Dalton wouldn't be mad about the two of us. In fact, I know he'd be happy because he loved you like a brother. I'm not sorry I came here, but I'm worried I brought trouble to Mill Creek. I don't want to put others at risk. I-I'm scared too, Trent, that whoever is after me might hurt you. I just found you again; I-I can't lose you."

He let that statement hang in the air between them for a minute. When she finally raised her gaze to meet his, he saw the flash of doubt and vulnerability in those green eyes. He didn't like that one bit. In fact, it made him want to beat his chest and remove every single thing or person who had caused her anguish. It took a Herculean effort on his part not to break their circle and tug her into his arms.

"None of this is your fault. If something should happen, that isn't on you either." Pride swelled in his chest at her bravery in speaking her mind and not holding back. "You've always impressed me. You're handling an extremely difficult situation with strength and fortitude.

Not once have you curled up in a ball and given up. You're a fighter. All I can promise is that I'll do whatever it takes to keep you safe and try not to get myself injured in the process. Thank you for trusting me enough to share your burdens."

Relief washed over her face, and a small smile tugged at the corners of her mouth. "Really? I don't feel that impressive."

"Trust me, you're one of a kind," he growled. "It's also why I know Dalton would kick my ass if he could read any of my thoughts regarding his baby sister."

She opened her mouth to reply, but Trent cut her off with a squeeze to her wrists and shook his head. "It's my turn now. You need to hear the latest. We've been able to link both sets of fingerprints from our two dead men to the van and the bugs we pulled from your place. Noah even took it a step further and has linked the brand and type of bugs we found to other cases Dalton has worked on."

Maggie's grip tightened. "Holy crap. Okay, what do we do next?"

"Facial recognition software is being used to identify the dead men and any potential connections to other cases. As sheriff of Mill Creek County, I have no case-related reason to obtain those photos from DPD, so Noah's doing this for me under the radar. At this point, it's time to take all of this to the FBI. I've asked Noah to update his boss on what we've learned and our assumptions. We should hear back from him in a day or so as to what's next."

Her smile widened. "Wow, that's awesome." Then, instantly, morphed into a horrified frown. "Oh, my God, this is really bad."

"It's not good, but knowing who's after you beats not knowing a damn thing. I haven't met his boss, Special Agent in Charge Tim Guzman; he came into the picture after I resigned. The next few days will be interesting, and if Guzman agrees with our assessment, the FBI will lead the investigation."

"You think my brother's last case is behind all of this?" she asked in a small voice.

"A prudent approach is to verify the evidence against Falcon, but every fiber of my being says that they're involved."

Why would they care about me? I'm nobody to them." She stared at him, but her gaze was unfocused.

It pissed him off that she was involved. Revenge? That didn't make sense, but something had put her in their sights. He knew the FBI had never found anything Dalton might have secured, so why now?

"The easiest connection is you're Dalton's sister, but their focus on you makes no sense. That's what we have to figure out."

"I don't want to talk about this anymore tonight. We can focus on all this tomorrow. Instead, I would rather spend the time forgetting all this ugliness exists. Make me forget, Trent." She reached across the space and cupped his face. "Don't think about all the reasons you shouldn't, let's just enjoy the simplicity of each other and the connection we share."

Trent closed his eyes. When he opened them, he shifted to straighten his legs and pulled her onto his lap. She wiggled in his lap, grinding herself against him with each movement.

"If you don't stop moving, I will lose my control."

Her throaty moan intensified his desire. "Good, I want to forget."

"This doesn't solve anything, yet I find myself unable to resist you. God help me, but I don't want to resist your temptation any longer. Tomorrow, I'll face the consequences of my actions, but tonight, I'm going to live my fantasy."

His mind short-circuited, and the only thing left that mattered was getting inside this vibrant woman who made him want to believe that they had a future. Emotions he no longer denied swelled deep inside him. He loved her spirit and compassion and knew she'd keep him on his toes. If she needed him to erase all the bad, for just a few precious moments, he do it because he'd do anything for her.

"Trent, I need you, please don't push me away." Her plea tore at the last thread of his resolve. Sliding her off his body, he laid her down on the bed and hovered over her.

Crushing his mouth to hers, he took what he wanted. She tasted like hope and mint toothpaste. Her mewl of delight reverberated on his tongue, lighting a fire in its wake all the way down his body. She was so damn tantalizing.

He lifted his head so his lips barely hovered over hers. "Stop me now if you don't want this to go any further."

His heart beat wildly at the prospect of what came next. No other woman had made him feel this way.

"Yes, don't you dare stop," she replied breathlessly.

When she walked away, he'd be crushed, but he'd let her go because it would be for the best.

The stands of her damp hair were cold against his palm as he twisted a handful to maneuver her head to his liking. When he found the perfect angle, he slammed his mouth against hers, devouring her like she was his last meal. He demanded, and she obliged. He couldn't remember being happier. The moans and whimpers that escaped her throat drove him higher.

Breaking off the kiss, he rested his forehead against hers. He nudged his hardened length against her stomach. "This is because of you. I've wanted you since you arrived. No, scratch that, I've wanted you since I met you."

"Mmm, you should see what you've done to me," she shot back in a low, sexy murmur.

That was the plan, but a sense of urgency drove his movements, making him clumsy. This was not a moment he wanted to rush.

Instead, he forced a deep breath into his system. He trailed his hand down her body, between the valley of her breasts and then lower.

When he reached the hem of the T-shirt, he slowly inched it up her delectable body, exposing milky, soft skin, inch by inch, until she laid naked. Only a strip of white lace adorned her body, covering her sex. "God, you're beautiful."

Trent trailed his fingertips over her flesh, leaving a trail of goose-bumps as he continued his exploration, taking his time to touch and caress every inch of her skin. He buried his face in her neck and inhaled her scent. He crushed her breasts to his chest. He loved the feel of her erect nipples as they rubbed against his body.

He palmed her soft globes, then shifted to torment her nipples. Each pull from his fingers had her back arching off the mattress. Soft moans escaped her lips, which made him increase the pressure on each pinch and twist of her tight buds. Her eyes had darkened with arousal. The sheer knowledge that she wanted him this badly thrilled him.

"Your breasts are so responsive to my touch," he murmured, his determination to drive her higher evident with every brush of his fingers.

Trent dipped his head to lick and nibble along Maggie's jawline before sucking on her earlobe. Indecision overwhelmed every fiber in his body. He wanted to take this slow and ensure everything was perfect, but he didn't know if he'd be able to last. He hadn't been with another woman since he put sex above duty. However, one time with Maggie would never be enough to satisfy him.

Decision made, he rocked back on his heels, straddling her. He hooked his thumbs in the waistband of her panties, tugging them down her shapely legs. He tossed the slip of fabric over his shoulder.

The sight of her laid out in front of him with her blonde hair fanned out around her head made him groan with appreciation. Green eyes shone bright as her gaze followed his every move. Her inky black lashes fluttered against her pale, soft skin. The heavy scent of her arousal went straight to his dick making him harder than a rock.

"You're mine, Margaret King." He grabbed her ankles and pulled her toward him until her bottom lay flush with the edge of the bed. Her legs fell open to make space for him to kneel between them. Her lush body had curves that were meant to drive a man wild. "I'm not going to last this first time, but I promise I'll make it up to you all night long."

She sat up on her elbows and cocked one eyebrow. "What if I'm a one-time type of gal?"

There was no way, if he had any say, because he'd never be satisfied with once. He'd wanted this moment for far too long. He nipped along her inner thighs while his hand parted those soft lips that glistened with her arousal. "Not possible, baby. I have no doubt you'll be as addicted to me as I am to you. When I'm done with you, you'll never need another man."

He licked along her core, lapping and sucking until he found her bundle of nerves, then worked that delicate bud alternating between sucking and racking his teeth over the sensitive tissue. He slid a finger inside her tight channel, her body gripping his digit.

A flush washed over her body while she whimpered his name. No one had ever looked as beautiful or sounded better to him, which drove his libido to the edge. He'd be damned if he came inside his pants like a randy teenager. Instead, he needed to focus on branding her with the fervent pleasure that only he could provide. To create a need so intense that she'd never be able to leave him.

He pressed a second finger into her slippery heat. Rotating his hand until he hit the exact spot that drove her wild. Her eyes widened, and a moan tore from her throat. Ramping up the pressure and rhythm, he rubbed his thumb against her clitoris, and her inner muscles tightened. Satisfaction washed over her face as she writhed under his ministrations.

"Oh, Trent, why didn't we do this sooner?" she murmured.

He couldn't live life backward, so he swallowed down his reply. Leaning forward, he swiped a puckered nipple with his tongue and then the other. His teeth scraped over the tight bud before he sucked it into his mouth, before repeating the same process on the other.

"I've always liked my dessert first," he said in a deep, husky voice.

He claimed her lips, plundering her mouth while his digits mimicked the same motions. Her hips undulated until she clamped down and exploded. This image would stay with him forever. Her hair was a sexy mess, and her lush lips were swollen from his kisses. She tempted him in ways no other woman ever had.

She licked her lips and emitted a breathless moan of contentment like a kitten who had enjoyed its bowl of milk. His chest puffed out in an arrogant display, knowing he'd given her that look of utter satisfaction. He stood and peeled off his clothes.

When she pulled herself up onto her elbows and ogled him, he groaned. "You're good for my ego. You keep eating me alive with those beautiful eyes. We'll never get any rest."

Maggie rolled her eyes. "Sleep can be overrated at times."

MAGGIE SMILED BUT COULDN'T stop raking her gaze over Trent. She'd waited too damn long for this moment. His body was a work of art. He had muscles everywhere, and she couldn't wait to lick each one. His washboard stomach flowed into the tight muscles of his torso. In the center of his groin, his impressive erection jutted upward from a neatly trimmed patch of hair. Good God, he was huge. Her stomach fluttered with anticipation. The crinkle of a wrapper caught her attention just before he rolled on a condom.

"You ready, baby?" He knelt on the bed and moved over her until he blanketed her body completely. His erection rubbed through her slick flesh. Her body hummed with excitement and, with it, a fresh coat of moisture. She had never wanted anything as desperately as she wanted Trent to be inside of her.

"Always. Now get moving, I can't wait any longer," she demanded, her body simmering with desire.

His eyes dilated and darkened at her passionate plea. "Yes, ma'am."

His cock prodded at her folds, and with a flex of his hips, he surged deep, impaling her in one big thrust. He plunged his hands into her hair and kissed her hard.

A fullness she'd never felt before overtook her senses as nerve endings surged to life. She enjoyed the pinpricks of toe-curling pleasure as her body accommodated his size.

A breathy plea tore from her lips, "Please, Trent, please, fuck me. Hard. I want to forget everything but this amazing moment. I've never felt like this."

Then, in a command gruffer than he intended, he said, "Hold on to me, baby."

The pace was hard and fast as he shuttled in and out of her body, rubbing his cock over her clitoris with every movement. Her senses overloaded with pleasure as he pushed them toward the brink.

She clamped down on him, liking the fullness but needing more. "Make me yours."

"With pleasure, but don't think I'll be easy on you. I plan to enjoy this moment and each one to its fullest."

The bed squeaked from the frantic pace as he hammered in and out of her body. Her mind went haywire from the rush of sensations. Trent repeated the motion over and over, a delicious cadence that delivered right to her core. Her body contracted around him, trying to hold him deep. He'd pull almost all the way out, then thrust back in, making her interior muscles clench.

Heat licked across her skin, and jolts of pleasure zapped throughout her body. His masculine scent wrapped around her. He surged back in, his strokes constant and measured, driving her body toward orgasm.

Long. Deep. Hard. Repeat.

His strokes were constant, the friction between their bodies igniting a fire that threatened to consume her mind, body, and soul.

Her toes curled so tight she worried her feet would cramp.

Long. Deep. Hard. Repeat.

"I'm so close." She mewled and wrapped her legs as tight as she could around his body, wanting him closer.

Her body tightened as the final rush of electric energy pulsed right at her core. She raked her nails down his back as she climaxed. His frenzied pace slowed until he thrust once more. He roared his release as he emptied himself inside the condom. Tears pricked the corner of her eyes, not from pain but from the realization that they'd become one.

Their eyes locked for a few seconds as ragged breaths filled the room. She worked to slow her breathing while basking in the afterglow of the best sex she'd ever had...would ever have. Her entire body hummed, and she didn't want to lose this connection to him.

He kissed her forehead. "I don't know if I'll ever get enough of you." He rolled to the side and withdrew from her body then moved to take care of the condom. "Give me a minute to recover, and then we'll tackle round two."

"I like how you think, Trent." Maggie couldn't help the smile that spread across her face and warmed her heart. Trent would never know the effect his words had. They reached deep inside and called to a part of her she hadn't known existed. Maybe it was time to learn from her past and live in the moment.

She'd enjoy this magical night. It never hurt to add to the collection of amazing memories stored in her heart.

Fear squeezed her heart because she'd have to survive this threat.

Eight

TRENT WIPED THE SLEEPY grit from his eyes. How long had it been since he slept this soundly? He glanced down to look at Maggie. Never in his life had he felt this type of connection or peace with another woman. They complemented each other, and she made him yearn for things like love and family. That thought scared the crap out of him.

There were a million things on his to-do list this Monday, but his priorities had shifted with her curled tight against his body. The hard length of his erection rested against the warm flesh of her belly. He resisted the strong urge to roll her over and take her again. He'd kept her up into the early morning hours, and she needed to rest.

A rattle against the nightstand drew his attention toward his cell phone. He maneuvered himself so he didn't disturb his sleeping beauty and snatched it, grimacing when he extended his shoulder further than he should have.

He tapped the message icon to see Noah's update. *Guzman wants to meet in person—he is interested in theory and evidence. He's even authorized me to bring in more analysts to widen our search parameters. We'll meet in Boise tomorrow at 2 p.m. at the Aspen Inn and Suites.*

Trent's eyes widened, happy with the urgency, then told Noah they'd be there.

He nudged Maggie. "Wake up, baby. I have news from Noah. We're meeting with Tim Guzman tomorrow afternoon in Boise."

"That FBI guy?" a drowsy Maggie grumbled.

"Yes," he said. Not exactly the news he wanted to share first thing in the morning after an incredible night together. A sudden glimpse into the future slammed into him, making him want to bask in this sight every morning for the rest of his life.

He rolled so he sat on his haunches, straddling her. Her hair, rumpled from sex, combined with her sleep-softened face made her look adorable. Warmth radiated from her body, heating his thighs. Selfishly, he was determined to savor whatever time he had with Maggie. He'd store all these memories to relive later when darkness threatened to consume him. She only knew part of his guilt, and the part she didn't know haunted him.

He leaned forward on his elbows, careful not to crush her. "He's the one who replaced my boss leading the Falcon investigation. Now, let's get back to the really important information. Like how you're the sexiest thing I've ever seen in the morning."

"Keep talking, I'm listening," she replied in a raspy voice. Her words were sultry and low.

He pressed his lips against hers while his erection nudged the softness of her belly through the sheet. He nipped at her full lips before retreating so he could smile down at her. "Good morning, sunshine."

Her eyes opened, and when she stretched her arms, the sheet lowered exposing her breasts. "Well, hello there, yourself. I'm glad this is real and not a dream."

He rocked forward and laved and nipped each nipple before moving back to her lips, giving her a long, passionate kiss.

She turned her head to the side. "I could get used to this style of alarm clock. Have I mentioned that I love your nakedness? It makes me so happy." Her sing-song voice warmed his insides as her arms wrapped around his chest and squeezed.

"Touché." In one swift motion, he ripped the sheet from between their bodies until they lay skin to skin.

Her big green eyes darkened with her arousal. "Is this the snooze feature?"

He thrust his hips forward, leaving no doubt of what comes next. "No, it's called the 'I can't keep my hands off of you' feature."

She absently raked her fingernails across his shoulder blades. Not only did the sensation feel great, it sent jolts of pleasure straight to his cock. She undulated against his cock, making him hot and hard enough to drill through a layer of igneous rock.

"Good, because I can't upend your life forever," she muttered, cupping his face with her hands, "but I like how we're spending our time together."

"You can and will, if that's how long it takes to end this threat," his voice was thick with emotion and strong with conviction. "Your safety is of paramount importance to me."

Trent bent and claimed her mouth in a heated kiss to punctuate his point. She slid her hands down his back, tugging him even closer. He poured all his unspoken words and emotions into that kiss. All he wanted to do was focus on Maggie, no more talking about threats or her leaving. Determined to enjoy her bounty while he could because once he told her the truth, she'd hate him.

He withdrew from her mouth and trailed kisses and tiny nips along her jawline and neck. He worked his way across her collar bones. Arrogant male pride filled his chest as she spread her legs wider to make room for him

Working his way down her body, he teased and sucked every inch of her buttery skin. Her nipples were so responsive to his touch as they beaded into stiff points. Fueled by her little cries of pleasure as she whimpered and moaned beneath him, he slid his left hand downward, testing her readiness and stopping to torment her bundle of nerves.

"You're hot and bothered this morning," he said, his confidence oozing from every pore.

"Gee, wonder why?" she teased. "But less talk, more do."

"Such a demanding lover, but I'll do my best. You know, practice makes perfect." He winked before palming her thighs.

His phone rang out when he lowered his head for another taste of her pouty lips. "Don't move one inch. I need to see if this is important since I'm running a tad late this morning." He snatched his phone for the second time and grimaced. "Hey, Aimee, what's up?"

"Sorry to bother you if you're taking today off, but it's not on the calendar. We have problems. This new phone system is temperamental. I don't have the authorization code required by support to troubleshoot. All calls ring three times, then go to voicemail. When we try to access the messages, we get told we're not authorized."

Shit. Trent ran a hand through his hair. "That's because I haven't given it to you. Sorry, Aimee. I'll remedy that as soon as I get there. Give me thirty minutes."

He ended his call and muttered his frustration. He slid out of bed and tugged Maggie up and into his arms, walking toward the bathroom. "Phones are down at the station. We've got to get there as soon as possible. I'm sorry, but I promise I'll make it up to you if you allow me to."

Her whole face radiated happiness as she flashed him a toothy smile. "Deal. I'm greedy, so I'll take you however I can. Maybe tonight we can even indulge ourselves in the shower, that's a fantasy of mine."

Oh man, hearing that she had visualized them getting busy in a shower about blew his mind. A guttural whisper left his lips, "Hot damn! That makes two of us. We'll throw that into the rotation just to spice it up."

He ushered her into the shower before he took his razor, toothbrush, and paste from his toiletry case. He'd get this out of the way and switch places with her when she finished.

TWENTY-FIVE MINUTES LATER, TRENT climbed the station's steps, with Maggie following closely behind. He was impressed with her speed and willingness to hustle. He held the door for her to enter, loving the whiff of vanilla and orange as she approached him. As soon as he cleared the threshold, Aimee pounced.

"Good morning. You two were fast. The phones are still having issues, and now the internet is down. Lance is rebooting the system to see if that will fix it. Fingers crossed. There must be a full moon tonight."

"Great, do you have any good news?" he quipped, then winked at Aimee.

"Oh, I forgot, I most certainly do."

Trent wasn't sure he liked the devilish smile his assistant flashed him. "Okay."

"You have a visitor. Clarke Dragoon arrived about ten minutes ago to see you. It's a full house of fun today, that's for sure."

Trent walked toward his office and nodded at Clarke. "Mr. Dragoon, Margaret King," Trent introduced the two, then directed Clarke to follow him into his office.

He heard the man's booming voice behind him. "Thanks for making my day great, Aimee."

"Don't blame me for that, Mr. Dragoon," Aimee admonished.

"Mr. Dragoon, my office, now," Trent commanded, sitting behind his desk.

Clarke sauntered inside and took a seat opposite him. Yup, this big pain in his ass had a thing for his assistant.

"Why do you seem to frustrate all the women in this town?" Trent tossed out as he reclined in his chair.

Clarke plastered a lopsided grin on his face, feigning surprise. "It's truly a curse and a blessing. All of this comes with my charm and good looks."

"Down, boy. Maybe we should get you neutered. Leave my assistant alone unless she tells you differently. Have you offered an olive branch to Irene?"

Clarke didn't acknowledge a word he said, but Trent didn't expect him to either. Instead, the man reached behind his back, and leaned to the side to pull out some papers that were folded lengthwise from his back pocket. "I'm here because of these photos. After your visit yesterday, I went back to review my surveillance footage. This activity didn't trigger my alarms because it was outside my established perimeter, but my cameras captured the images."

Well, that answered the question of why Clarke walked around his property all the time. Trent took the proffered photos and studied them.

"The photo quality is poor, but they're dressed like hunters." He used his index finger and thumb to rub his eyes. "The only hunting I'm aware of, at this point in the year, is limited permit black bear."

Clarke stood and fished a flash drive from his front pocket. "That should be easy enough to verify. What interested me more is the hand signals they used...definitely military. Take a look at their movements—they're efficient and uniform. This group could easily be linked to those drones." Clarke flipped the small device to Trent then exited his office. "Later."

Trent caught the drive and nodded. "Appreciate the information."

The man could be intense, but what he just shared interested Trent. It also made him wonder why Clarke had top-of-the-line surveillance equipment. Trent pulled his keyboard closer and typed in his username and password into his computer. Each time he entered Clarke Dragoon into one of the databases Trent had access to, everything returned normal. *Squeaky clean.*

Maybe Irene had a point. A man who did that much reconnaissance in his own damn yard might need a more thorough background check. Trent knew the perfect man for the job, who had access to almost everything under the sun.

He sent Noah a text message: "*Clarke Dragoon, I want everything down to his underwear size. What I've searched comes back too clean." He just delivered another package of information that probably relates to those drones. I'll share it tomorrow.* Noah sent Trent a thumbs-up icon. Trent spent the rest of the morning updating files and working on the phone system. He loved technology but hated the learning curve.

When he exited his office, Maggie, Aimee, and Lance carried cardboard file boxes out of the storage room toward the bank of file cabinets.

"You two already emptied all those other boxes?" Trent asked, watching Aimee drop her boxes on the floor before returning to her desk chair.

She took a long sip of her water. "Maggie's a taskmaster, but having an extra set of hands is awesome. We should be done with all of this by the end of the week."

Maggie sat in the open chair by Aimee's desk. "Yeah, poor Lance. We persuaded him to be our muscle, because he can carry two times the boxes."

Lance flexed his arms. "What can I say, the ladies just like to see guns."

Trent shook his head, feigning disgust. "No, you got played, man. If you were married, that's called a honey-do list."

Feminine laughter filled the office.

"Want me to start working on those files, or can I do something else to help?" Maggie asked.

"How about going to lunch with me, instead? I need some fresh air and a change of scenery," Aimee suggested.

"Trent, do you want to head to lunch with us?" Maggie asked tentatively, unsure how much of her situation was common knowledge.

Trent paused and glanced at Maggie. He didn't want to stop her from hanging out with Aimee, but he'd feel better with Lance accompanying them. "As long as Lance can tag along. You don't have to sit together, but I'd feel better about everything happening. Lance, I'll fill you in later, but keep an eye open for strangers."

"Are you sure?" Maggie's tone betrayed her shock at his response.

"I'm sure I trust Lance to keep you safe. Will you bring me back something to eat?"

"Of course."

Trent watched the three of them head toward the front of the building and out the door. Obviously, Aimee wanted to spend some time with Maggie, and he wanted them to have a chance to talk and laugh. The two had hit it off, and he liked seeing them both happy.

When they returned, he'd give Lance a cursory understanding of what was happening and what to be watching for. Trent would wait to inform him about the FBI and Falcon at a later date.

Trent hadn't been in his office for more than forty minutes when a voice hollered, "Hello?"

"Be right there," Trent called out from his office.

A delivery man held a big bouquet of the oddest mixture of flowers Trent had ever seen. A dozen pink and red carnations, two long stem red roses, and black flowers? Who the hell had sent that ugly arrangement and to whom?

He pointed to the black flowers. "What are those?"

"Black Calla Lilly," the delivery man supplied. "These are for Margaret King. Is she here?"

Trent's world tilted, and daggers of trepidation stabbed along his spine. After pumping the delivery man for information—who knew nothing—his next demand was to speak to the shop owner. After several long minutes, he learned the meaning of each flower and that the order had been placed online. The owner provided her contact information, which he jotted down, in case he had further questions.

Once the man left, Trent donned a pair of latex gloves and opened the card. It simply read, in computer-generated font, *I love a good game of cat and mouse. Until next time.* The message and the symbolic meaning behind each flower now made the entire situation personal. Carnations signify grief, love, and loyalty, and pink signifies gratitude and motherly fondness. Red carnations represent love and affection, two red roses for love and romance, and black calla lilies for mystery.

What the hell did this mean? Nothing good, that much he knew.

T HE CHIMES JINGLED ABOVE the door to the Knotty Pinetree as Maggie opened the door. The scents of freshly baked bread, sweets, and bacon had her mouthwatering. Man, did she love bacon. It could be a food group all on its own. She'd worked up quite an appetite from all their bedroom activities. Holy cow, a simple touch from Trent ignited her blood, making her body pulse with need.

The restaurant was packed, but she spied a booth in the back that had just opened up. Lance nodded at them then headed toward an empty seat at the counter.

Maggie slid into the booth and smiled at Aimee. "I'm so glad you suggested this. It's nice to have a little girl time."

Aimee lifted her head from the menu. The flecks of green in her irises sparkled with amusement. She was small in stature with killer curves and gorgeous thick tresses of auburn hair. "Is everything okay with you? I mean, it's none of my business, but you know what Trent referenced back at the station?" Her face reflected concern.

"Sort of. Someone left an unpleasant surprise in my apartment which is why I came here to see Trent. It's tied to our past, so he's helping me with figuring out this whole mess."

Aimee frowned. "That sucks, and for what it's worth, I under-stand, in my own way. If you need anything, I'm only a phone call away."

Maggie smiled at her kind offer, but she also wanted to ask her some questions about what she'd experienced. Something in Mag-gie's gut told her to let it go for now. "Thanks, I really appreciate your offer. Hey, have you heard any updates on our furry friend?"

Aimee closed her menu. "I do, and it's excellent news. The dog and family were reunited this morning. The family even donated to Micah's shelter and practice to show appreciation. The strange part, the Wilson family reported that a man had taken their dog and drove off in a truck. Witnesses also reported that the same make and model of pickup truck stopped and dropped the dog off close to Main Street. Who would do that?"

Sally approached the table and said, "Hello, ladies. What can I bring you to drink?"

"Iced tea," Maggie answered.

"Ditto, and what's the special today?" Aimee winked at Sally with a big smile plastered across her face.

"Only my homemade fried chicken with potato salad, coleslaw, and a flaky biscuit."

Aimee bounced in her seat and clapped her hands. "That's right, Sally's fried chicken is to die for. Just hearing her talk about it makes my mouth water. It's the absolute best. I'll take two orders, one for lunch and the other to go."

Maggie shrugged. "With an endorsement like that, I'd be a fool not to order the special. I'll also need one to go for Trent."

Sally fanned herself with her order booklet. "I never grow tired of hearing such praise."

Aimee and Maggie laughed while Sally removed the pencil from behind her ear and wrote down their orders. "I should be humble, but facts are facts. Okay, two specials and two to go. You ladies, holler if you need anything else. Oh, and if you're sharing gossip, speak really damn loud."

They both nodded at Sally before she turned toward the kitchen.

"How long have you lived in Mill Creek?" Maggie asked as she unrolled her silverware and placed her napkin in her lap.

Aimee lowered her eyes. "Not long. I came about the same time as Trent rolled into town. Enough about me. So, do you like it here? Remind me again—you lived in Dallas, right?"

"I do. The pace is certainly slower, but the people are so friendly. I like the cozy atmosphere, and the food is crazy good. The only things I truly miss from home are my weekly fixes—barbecue and Tex-Mex. It's a rite of passage for any proper Texan."

Aimee giggled. "I thought you'd say big hair and the excessive use of the Texas state flag."

Maggie widened her eyes with mock horror. "That's not something we joke about, and you haven't seen my underwear."

Aimee laughed so hard she wiped tears from her eyes. Sally appeared at the table to refill their iced teas and drop off a bowl of packaged wet naps. "Ladies, you're having too much fun. Did I miss anything good?"

"Only that Maggie prefers panties with anything Texas emblazoned on them," Aimee supplied in a haughty tone.

Sally turned to Maggie and winked. "You, my dear, are full of surprises."

Maggie looked up when she heard the bells jingling for about the fifth time. Now, every seat in the diner had been filled, and the lunch rush appeared in full swing. Not a moment later, a powerful man with a bald head acted like the moon cast a shadow over their table.

"This must be my lucky day. You're still looking beautiful, Aimee." His voice rumbled from deep in his chest.

Aimee's neck and cheeks flushed with a pink tint. "Are you following me, Mr. Dragoon? Are there no other single women around here for you to pester?"

His stance widened as he propped large hands on his hips. A mischievous smile curled his lips. "I'd call it flirting, and I only have eyes for you. It's Clarke, by the way. Besides, it's fried chicken day. Who the hell would miss that?"

Maggie didn't know what to think about what was unfolding before her eyes. The attraction between Clarke and Aimee hung thick between them, but she seemed committed to ignoring it.

"You big ape, leave these women in peace." A voice full of righteous indignation taunted from somewhere behind the giant man.

Goading a man of his size didn't seem like a sane thing to do, but who was Maggie to judge? A moment later, a slip of a woman elbowed her way to the front of the table.

"Hi, Irene," Aimee replied. "Have you met Sheriff Jacob's friend, Maggie?"

Clarke stepped to the side, giving the feisty woman more space. She had long, white hair pulled back into a French braid. Beauty and grace came to mind, but her no-nonsense style fit her perfectly. She wore periwinkle blue linen pants and a white short-sleeved top. Not one wrinkle existed anywhere on her outfit. This woman had gumption and fire in her soul, and Maggie liked her instantly.

"Oh, you're the one everyone is talking about. Scoot over, dear."

She barely had a chance to react before Irene practically sat in her lap. Maggie's mind raced with ideas about what people might be saying. The last thing she wanted to do was place Trent at the center of the town gossip.

Once settled, Irene folded her hands on the table. "Mr. Dragoon, be a gentleman and go bother another table, or better yet, I have some weeds in my yard you can count."

Maggie would give Clarke credit. He took his dismissal from Irene in stride.

"Ladies, Irene, enjoy your lunch," Clarke said before winking at Aimee. He turned toward the counter and picked up a to-go that waited for him.

"I didn't realize the two of you haven't met." Aimee grabbed her glass, using the straw to stomp down ice.

"We haven't, but how fortuitous for me." Irene patted Maggie's arm. "You're the sister of his friend—the one killed in the line of duty?"

Maggie's heart dropped out of her chest at the unexpected question regarding her brother's death. She sucked in a sharp breath, trying to suppress the rush of tears escaping her eyelids. "Yes." Her voice wobbled.

Irene wrapped her slender fingers over Maggie's hand and squeezed. "I'm sorry for your loss, but I'm glad you and Trent have each other to lean on. I know that whole situation ripped his heart out. I've lived here long and consider most of these residents a part of my family. I've also known the Jacobs family forever. Come here, dear, I didn't mean to upset you."

Irene hugged Maggie tightly. Maggie took a minute to regain her composure. Although Irene's words were genuine and heart-felt, she was just stating facts. She dabbed her eyes on the napkin.

"Then, I bet you have some great stories about Trent?" Maggie asked, hoping to learn some tidbits about Trent's childhood that he hadn't censored.

Irene's smile made her eyes sparkle with merriment. "There are many gems like when he placed his dog's tooth under his pillow because he reasoned with his grandparents that the Tooth Fairy wouldn't know the difference. So, when he woke up and checked in the morning, he had a dog treat under his pillow instead of a quarter."

An instant later, she had managed to transition Maggie's pain into a treasured moment full of laughter. "You come and visit me anytime, and we'll reminisce. How long will you be staying?" Irene asked, patting her hand.

Maggie nudged the other woman, enjoying the camaraderie. "I'd love to, but I'm not sure. We're playing it by ear."

"Good. I'll look forward to it. There's no need to rush. Anything that's worthwhile will always build stronger and stronger over time," Irene stated.

Sally approached with plates stacked all over her arms. "Lunch is served. I'll swing back in a minute to refill your teas."

When all the plates were delivered, and Sally had retreated, Irene stood. "Enjoy your lunch. I have to get back to the library. Oh, before I forget, Mrs. Carter, a teacher at the elementary school, has resigned due to her husband's job transfer. If you know anyone who teaches and might be interested, send them to the school."

Maggie and Aimee nodded and waved goodbye to Irene. Maggie thought about what Irene had said about the school. She wouldn't mind going back to teaching because she missed it. Moving to Mill Creek didn't bother her either, and if she got this job, it would give her a way to support herself. This could be the change she needed, even if she and Trent didn't work out. Hopefully, they would still be friends. The table fell into a companionable silence while they ate.

"Oh man, I'm stuffed. This fried chicken is delicious," Maggie replied. She wiped her hands on the napkin and leaned against the back of the seat. "I can't believe we didn't talk at all."

"I know. It's a tribute to how amazing this chicken is, and it demands your undivided attention. This was fun. I think our next outing should be drinks at Two-Stepping. They have live music on Friday and Saturday nights. I've only been a few times, but I'd love to go again.

Going by yourself is kind of awkward. You game?" Aimee asked with a smile on her face.

"You're on, but you might be busy. It seems Clarke has a crush on you and may ask you out on a date."

Aimee's eyes flashed bright for a second before she schooled her reaction. "No, no, no, I'm sure he has a type, and I'm far from that person. Dating isn't a priority for me. It only leads to problems."

Maggie wanted to respond but had to agree with her, although for different reasons. She filed that tidbit away to approach another day. Aimee had a story, but first, Maggie needed to earn Aimee's trust so she'd open up. *If she would even be here to develop a friendship.* Suddenly, the thought of not being there depressed her.

Trent had mentioned that his assistant wasn't overly social and preferred to keep her life private. Without overthinking it, Maggie decided they both needed a night out. "Let's make it happen. I could use more girl time."

Happiness radiated off Aimee. "Done," she agreed, flicking her wrist to check the time. "We need to head back. I enjoyed today, and for what it's worth, your visit has been good for Trent. I hope you do stay for a while."

Maggie narrowed her eyes at her statement. "Why is that?"

"I don't mean to be intrusive, but he smiles more. He also isn't working around the clock, seven days a week. We all thought he was a robot or something before you arrived."

Maggie laughed at his assistant's repugnant expression. "Nope, he's just stubborn and very dedicated."

After paying her bill, she turned to see Trent heading toward her, his demeanor serious. The blood drained from her face while her stomach somersaulted, making her wish she hadn't overeaten at lunch. The tension emanated from his body and circled him like an aura.

Even his face was drawn tight. His long strides had him face-to-face in no time.

"What's wrong?" she asked and swallowed hard.

"Not here. We'll talk at the hotel." His tone was clipped and measured.

She followed Aimee and Lance out of the restaurant with Trent's hand on the small of her back.

Once everyone stood outside, he turned to Lance and Aimee. "I will be working online for the rest of the afternoon. Then, I'll be out of the office for the next two, but I'll check in periodically. Lance, you're in charge. I've already sent an email to the team. You can reach me on my cellphone."

"Sure thing, boss. Is there anything else I can do?" Lance asked.

Aimee's eyes went wide. "Will you be back in time for the annual fundraiser, or should we postpone it?"

"No, I'll be back. I wouldn't miss that one. You've all done so much work." Trent reassured her while his gaze scanned the area.

Aimee hugged Maggie. "Thanks for lunch, and let's do our bar night soon."

Maggie rested her head against Trent's chest and hugged him tight. The steady beat of his heart settled her nerves, along with the subtle scent of sandalwood, his shaving cream. His presence calmed her, knowing he would stand by her side for all the good, bad, and ugly moments. She longed for that connection, to share in something greater than herself.

Overwhelmed by emotion and the moment, she lifted her head and whispered against his ear, "Dalton and I were the lucky ones to have you in our lives."

The muscles in his back clenched. Why did those words make him uncomfortable? She was about to ask him when he abruptly pulled away. "We need to get back to the hotel. There's been a new development I need to share with you, and I have some work to finish before we leave for Boise in the morning."

Nine

MAGGIE OPENED HER EYES to see the early rays of light filtering in through the curtains. Tiny flakes of fibers and dust floated in the air without a care in the world. She rolled and eyed the slight indentation of where Trent had slept. She swept her hand over the spot. No warmth. The light in the bathroom leaked out from underneath the door.

Stretching her body, she smiled as her muscles ached and protested, a reminder of how they spent their night. More than a physical release, she had needed the closeness of his touch to reinforce all the good in the world. She felt safest in his arms, a luxury she couldn't afford.

She couldn't believe how this whole situation kept unfolding. Hell, she couldn't believe her brother, and Trent had dealt with all this chaos day in and out. Drones—seriously? The flower delivery weirded her out. Flowers were personal, and the message insinuated she toyed with people. How did that fit into the puzzle? A knife and a flower delivery were polar opposites that made her wonder if they were even related.

The bathroom door opened. "Good morning."

She tossed the covers back and headed toward the shower. She needed to get a move on it so she'd be ready for their meeting with the FBI. "Same to you. I'll be ready in about thirty minutes.

T HE WEEKDAY TRAFFIC MADE the commute from Mill Creek to Boise effortless. They hadn't conversed on the ride, but she was okay with that. It seemed Trent was using that time to mull over whatever had him occupied. He pulled into the Aspen Inn and Suites right on time.

"Wow, this hotel is right on the river." Maggie's head swiveled as she took in the scenery. She loved all the greenery and the tree-lined river that flowed around the property. A family of ducks waddled about in a grassy area. On any other day, she would love to take a stroll along the path. She took her messenger bag out of the truck and put the strap over her head so it sat across her body.

"Yes," he said, retrieving two additional bags from the backseat. He motioned for her to lead the way toward the elevators. Once inside the small car, he pressed the button for the hotel's top floor.

"Umm, don't we need to check in?"

"Done."

She blew out a short breath, trying to move a wayward strand of hair off her face. "I'll neuter you if you don't start using complete sentences. Right here, in the damn elevator."

He cocked an eyebrow and sent her a pointed look. "I checked in using the hotel's mobile app. The key is on my phone."

"I guess I don't get a key?" she grumbled.

He flashed her a smug smile. "One key is perfectly fine since you won't be out of my sight."

She didn't like the brooding Trent, especially when tension practically trickled from every one of his pores. When the elevator doors slid open, he thrust his hand backward to stop her. He glanced to the right and left before he exited and nodded in her direction. Once they were inside the suite, he checked each room before finally stowing their bags on luggage racks. She stood observing him and felt her head pounding. His pent-up tension had transferred to her. Even her skin itched with nervous energy.

"I'll send Noah a text to let him know that we've arrived."

"Okay, I need to use the bathroom," she announced. Her bladder was ready to release the large iced tea she had consumed during the hour-long drive from Mill Creek.

A short minute later, he stood outside her door to update her. "ETA 5 minutes."

Damn. She was torn between wanting more time and getting the meeting over with. Her stomach rolled with angst. When she exited the bathroom, she noticed the size of their suite. They had a bedroom, sitting area, and even a small dining table so at least they had room to move around. Not knowing where to stand, she decided next to Trent would be best. She fidgeted with her hands, nervous energy consuming her. "I'll feel better when this meeting is over."

A loud knock echoed through the room.

"That makes two of us," Trent replied. He turned to her and cupped the nape of her neck. "No matter what, we're in this together–to the end. Promise me, Maggie."

She sensed there was more to his statement, but there wasn't time to probe. "I promise, Trent, I trust you."

He strode to the door and opened it wide. "Special Agent in Charge (SAC) Guzman, Noah, thanks for coming. This is Margaret King," he introduced as they entered the small sitting room with a sofa and two armchairs.

Guzman walked directly to Maggie and accepted her outstretched hand. "It's nice to meet you, but not under these circumstances." He released her hand then took a seat on the sofa.

"Hi, Maggie," Noah greeted her, then placed a big file box on the coffee table. When he finished, he took the other seat at the end of the couch. He was an attractive man. His wavy, light brown hair dusted his collar, which made him look mischievous and approachable. His body didn't scream computer nerd, and his shirt clung tight against his muscular chest while his pants cupped him in all the right places.

Maggie sat across from the two men, leaving one for Trent. She straightened her spine and clamped her lips together, ready to listen and, God help her, not throw up. Confidence oozed from the SAC, but for a man in his early fifties, she assumed there wasn't much he hadn't seen over his career. He stood close to six feet tall. His presence filled the room, yet he wasn't overbearing.

"Where do you want to start?" Trent inquired.

Guzman leaned forward to rest his elbows on his knees. "It goes without saying that what's discussed here stays in this room." When both Trent and Maggie acknowledged, he continued, "As a courtesy, I've alerted the Salt Lake City field office that I'm in town." he said the last part directly to Trent.

"Good, that keeps everyone happy," he acknowledged.

"Trent, thanks for your report; I appreciate the detail and insight. So, here's what we have: an abandoned van, two men executed, fingerprints from the victims, those prints connected to the van, apartment, knife, and surveillance equipment. Traffic cameras placing the van at your apartment complex on several dates, drones surveilling Trent's property, which we assume is linked to locating Maggie, and a floral delivery. You may not know that I've contacted the DPD to let them know the FBI is taking over their case, and all related files are being transferred. The video of the executions has also been authenticated and confirmed."

Trent cleared his throat. "I've also issued a BOLO for the vehicle eyewitnesses, and my traffic camera footage confirmed a silver pickup truck with a white toolbox that dropped off the dog. I'm sure it will be reported as stolen if it's found, but we'll process it for evidence."

Noah interjected, "That would be nice for once. In another new development, I tied several surveillance devices to other cases Dalton had worked. Falcon, however, matched every single one."

Trent held up a flash drive. "I want to subpoena the maintenance records at Maggie's complex to see if the man she saw exiting her home the day we buried Dalton was legit. Also, one of my residents, who's in possession of high-tech surveillance equipment, captured these images. The piece that's interesting is the hand signals used. Their movements are uniform and precise, very military. The images are grainy, but I'm sure wonder-boy here can enhance the resolution to see if we can identify any of them."

Noah ran his fingertips across the pads of his thumbs. "My skills are legendary," he agreed, catching the flash drive Trent tossed to him.

Guzman scribbled on a notepad. "Agreed on the subpoena. That makes the drone scenario more interesting and would tie to Falcon's use of mercenary soldiers." His gaze moved between Trent and Maggie. "I've thought long and hard about how much to divulge. It seems your greatest champion, Trent, is Noah, and he's earned my trust. I did my due diligence and researched you prior to our meeting. I'm impressed with what I read, and your exemplary service record speaks for itself, even with the allegations of improprieties brought against you that were eventually dismissed. For what it's worth, I disagree with your superior's decision to remove you from the case. My assessment is that we lost a good agent the day you retired—Mill Creek gained a great sheriff."

Trent nodded and replied in a tight voice, "I appreciate hearing that."

Maggie whipped her gaze to Trent. What the hell did that mean? She wasn't aware of any of this. Her mind snapped back to a prior conversation with Trent. *I'm far from a good man, Maggie. I don't deserve you.*

Guzman turned his attention back to Maggie. "I don't know much about you, but we can help each other. I met your brother while training at Quantico, and he impressed me. I was sorry to learn his career ended so disastrously."

She sucked in a sharp breath to quell the sudden rush of emotions that flooded her system. The way he said that bothered her, but she couldn't put a finger on it.

He held her gaze for a few seconds before he directed the conversation back to the point of the meeting. "It's time for a different approach, and the current circumstances make you both a part of this. Understand there will be lines that can't be crossed, but we'll discuss those when they arise. I'm in charge, and how we proceed is my call; unless we're in Mill Creek, then we'll liaise with you, Trent. That said, you'll both have a voice at the table when we review our plan and formalize the next steps. All of this is covered in a non-disclosure agreement you must sign, Maggie."

Trent rubbed his shoulder. "I agree with the case, but anything related to Maggie's safety is run through me and must be approved. Those are my stipulations."

"Is run through us," she blurted, not wanting to be left out. "I don't want to put Trent in unnecessary danger either. After all, this is my problem."

Guzman sat forward and frowned. "Perhaps a discussion for you two later. I'm not being obtuse, but Trent can handle himself, and our jobs have their inherent dangers. I've heard your concerns, Trent, and I will do my best to abide by those conditions, but again, anything case-related is my call. Noah, please grab the NDA for Maggie if she agrees."

A scream lodged in her throat at Guzman's reply, but she got it. Noah's long fingers reached into the file box to retrieve a folder and pen. A moment later, he handed her the file. She flipped the folder open and read over the document before she scrawled her name on the line and handed it back to him.

"I'm trusting you," Trent said.

Guzman unbuttoned the cuffs on his dress shirt and rolled each sleeve to his elbow. "You have my word. Now, Maggie, I understand your brother visited you before his death. Did he mention anything that seemed odd or maybe gave you something to hold on to for him?"

"Not in the way that you mean. He never discussed his cases with me."

Trent ran his hand through his hair. "I've asked her the same questions; she doesn't have or know anything. The timing of his visit has always bothered me because it was last minute. Dalton planned everything, right down to when he'd take a shit."

What Trent said was right. Her brother took organization and control to another level, but that unexpected memory threatened to open the floodgates of her tears. A lump formed in her throat. She needed a diversion to get control of her emotions, so she looked past the SAC and started counting back from one hundred. Crying in front of these men would serve no purpose, and Dalton needed her to be strong right now.

Eighty, seventy-nine, seventy-eight. "It was a relatively normal visit, with the exception of him being spontaneous. He gave me a copy of his legal planning documents: power of attorney for financial and health-care and his will. We had promised each other to get that paperwork completed, and I'd been nagging him about it. We learned at a young age that having it in place is best because life is unpredictable. He also mentioned being out of touch for a while, but not to worry. I would say that looking back, he seemed apprehensive."

Guzman interjected, "Maybe nervous? Has he ever mentioned being out of touch before?"

"No, apprehensive is the better description, and yes, sometimes his assignments took him away, and we couldn't speak as often as we'd like."

Noah cleared his throat. "Dalton kept most things close to his chest. The one topic he spoke openly about was you. He loved you very much."

Seventy, sixty-nine, sixty-eight. Maggie's distant gaze re-focused on Noah. "Thanks for sharing that with me."

Trent looked at Noah. "What did you uncover on Clarke Dragoon?"

Noah glanced at SAC Guzman, then answered, "You're right, he's clean."

"All you need to know," Guzman offered, "is that Clarke is not your enemy. I'm not at liberty to reveal details, but Noah's digging caused a ripple effect and several phone calls. If you catch my meaning."

Trent cocked his eyebrow. "Okay, that's good to know since he has impressive surveillance equipment on his property. My guess is we might have captured footage of Falcon's mercenary soldiers. Obviously, they weren't expecting that on a random property in Mill Creek."

Noah's smile went wide. "Using any of those photos to identify them would be a huge win. The video of the execution could be that same group, but the videographer and executioners remain off-screen."

Guzman looked at Maggie. "Something put you on their radar. Our theory had been that Dalton uncovered information that could put Falcon at risk, but we've never retrieved anything to substantiate that hypothesis. That could be why Falcon was monitoring you. To know if your brother had given you anything to hold or act on, if something happened to him. The flowers are puzzling because that's more personal, but the note suggesting you're playing games doesn't make sense. Infatuation? Revenge? Information? Trophy? All of these are possible motives."

Her intake of breath turned three male heads in her direction. "I'm getting the distinct impression there's much more to the story. Like, what allegations were you two talking about a moment ago? Why did the FBI mandate a closed casket—a decision that robbed me of being able to face my brother one final time to say goodbye—naively, I thought it was FBI protocol."

Trent knelt in front of her and placed his hands over hers. "Don't do this to yourself. Dalton gave his life for a greater cause. He wouldn't want you torturing yourself."

Her understanding of Dalton's death made her stomach sour. "I was never told how he died, only that it was in the line of duty. No, I deserve the goddamned truth." Maggie pulled her hands free of Trent's grasp and glared at Guzman. "I want to know what happened."

He raised a perfectly man-scaped brow. "Knowing exactly what happened to a loved one is not information the family is always privy to. Let me ask you, does having the graphic details matter that much when the end result will be the same?"

Trent turned around and snapped at Guzman, "No! What the fuck are you thinking?"

"Yes," she pleaded. "First, my parents, and now my brother. I can't explain why it's important, but I'd like to have closure for once in my life. Even if that truth is horrible. Call it my price for helping you."

Time seemed to crawl while everyone stared at the SAC. He rubbed his forehead with both hands as if he were trying to stop a headache. How could he deal with life's unsavory people day in and day out and remain sane?

Guzman's jaw clenched. He seemed to be processing her request. She sat quietly, waiting to see what he'd decide to do. "Jacobs, this isn't your decision. It's mine. The closed casket was due to the severity of the torture your brother suffered—ligature marks, missing digits, cuts, and contusions—most of the damage couldn't have been concealed by the mortician. That day—"

"Enough! This should come from me because I was the one there." Trent's voice was distant and strangled.

Guzman glanced at Trent briefly, then turned his focus back to Maggie. "Are you sure you want to know more? Because once it's heard, you can't undo it?"

"Yes," she whispered, tears streaming down her face.

"Maggie needs to understand what Falcon is capable of since she's a part of this case now. Go ahead, Trent," Guzman directed. "But tell her everything."

T RENT CLOSED HIS EYES and sucked in a sharp breath. Reliving that horrible day was not what he wanted to do or exposing the demons that had haunted him for the last fucking ten months.

"As Guzman stated, when I arrived at the warehouse, Dalton was already inside and had been tortured and shot. I called for medical assistance and backup before entering the building. I sprinted through the doorway toward him when another round fired, missing us both. This time, I was able to confirm the location of the shooter, who sat high and to the left in the rafters. The unknown was how many more shooters were present."

Trent stood and walked toward the window, needing space because the walls seemed to be closing in on him. "The third bullet hit Dalton, the bloom of crimson from his abdomen staining his white shirt. The shooter was toying with us. I knew if I didn't act quickly, your brother would bleed out. I continued moving forward and slid to Dalton's side. I had to get him back toward the wall and away from the shooter's line of sight. I had my weapon in my right hand aimed at the rafters and grabbed Dalton's arm with my left.

"The flash of a muzzle caught my eye as another shot pierced my right shoulder. My weapon clattered to the ground. The next two discharges were in rapid succession and punctured my left leg just below the hip. We were sitting ducks for that sniper.

"I barked at Dalton, 'What the fuck is going on here, Dalton? This is a clusterfuck.' His face was tight with pain, and Dalton spent energy he didn't have to push my body to the side and covered me with his own."

Trent squeezed his eyes closed and pinched the bridge of his nose to hold off the headache threatening to unleash holy hell. Living this nightmare in real time had been difficult, but having to tell Maggie devasted him more. Tension thick like molasses filled his body, seemingly holding him upright as his mind snapped back to that dank warehouse and the last moments he'd shared with Dalton.

'Listen...' The air whooshed from his lungs. 'Last week...' Dalton tried again, struggling to put words together. "Code for Falcon's accounting records."

The coppery smell of blood and mold filled Trent's nose. His limbs were heavy and sluggish. "And you're only telling me this now?"

Dalton was pale, and his voice weak. "I didn't know if credible..."

Trent shoved at Dalton, trying to get him off him so he could apply pressure to staunch the flow of blood from his stomach. He could barely move. What the hell was wrong with him? "Get off me, Dalton, so I can help you."

"Too late for me," he rasped out. "Did you call for backup? We're all alone here."

"Yes, so you need to hang on and fight," Trent demanded, as a shiver worked down his spine.

Dalton sucked in a shallow breath. His body shuddered. Fluid gurgled up after each word he spoke. "Sunday night...informant...He called, begging me to take him into protective custody. Met here—"

"Save your strength. You can tell me this later," I bit out, trying to apply pressure even though he still laid on top of me. "I get the gist, ambushed and shit show."

A ripple of pain cascaded over his body. His eyelids were dropping. Where was the damn ambulance? Watching the life drain out of Dalton was akin to having hunks of flesh ripped from his body.

Suddenly, Dalton's eyes opened. Sweat beaded his forehead, and his color had moved from white to a grayish hue.

"The identities...syndicate's top players. I wanted everything." He coughed out the words.

Trent's vision blurred, but he had to ask. Using his good arm, he grasped his face. "Where's the intel?"

Dalton's eyes drifted closed right before his head dropped onto his injured shoulder. Searing pain coursed through him. Trent couldn't feel his leg anymore, and that both scared and relieved him because that only left the pain in his shoulder. In the distance, the blessed sound of sirens wailed.

Slurred words whispered in Trent's ear, "Promise me...you'll look after Maggie...keep her safe. You're the only one...don't trust...Moo-"

Finally, Trent heard the damn sirens. The edges of vision darkened, and the shadows grew with each passing second. His body trembled as the putrid smell of blood and death swirled around him.

"Trent...Trent, do we need to take a break?" Guzman asked, his voice disrupting him from his thoughts.

"No...sorry." Trent inhaled deeply before continuing, "In the distance, I had heard heavy footsteps running across the rafters and down a metal staircase. I figured it was the shooter moving to finish us off. After several tense moments, nothing happened. Dalton had mentioned something about data that had the syndicate's top players and their identities. Unfortunately, everything went dark."

Trent shifted away from the window and returned to his seat next to Maggie. Her gaze followed him, but her face masked any emotions she might be feeling. A ball of foreboding twisted in his stomach like a fist to his ribcage over what came next.

"When I regained consciousness in the hospital, the first visitors were not my parents; it was my boss and Agent Ben Knight who informed me that Dalton had died and that evidence had been found implicating him as a rogue agent. The evi–"

"What? Are you serious? That's the most ridiculous thing I've ever heard," Maggie declared, her face red with indignation. She fisted her hand and pressed it against her mouth.

Trent continued, "The evidence against Dalton: his service weapon had killed the man they found with him, and a printed numbered account with ten million dollars was also linked to him. The money had been wired the previous day. The circumstantial evidence doesn't look good when you add that into the picture: his unplanned trip to visit you and his comment about being out of touch for a period of time made it appear that he might be planning to run. It also never helped that the supposed intel Dalton had found never surfaced."

Her fingers turned white from the intense hold she had on that chair. "So, you're telling me my brother is dirty? He loved what he did. He gave his life for this stupid job. I-I can't even believe what I'm hearing. Why didn't you stand up for him, Trent? You were there. You were his partner."

Trent swallowed, trying to ease the tightness in his throat. He never wanted her to hear these lies about her brother. He had no words to comfort her. The events of that damn day and everything that followed haunted him. "I'm explaining to you what was found at the scene. I arrived about forty-five minutes after Dalton. There was also a handwritten note scribbled on a sheet of paper with my name and an account number, although no money had ever been transferred into that account."

"What does that mean?" she snapped.

Guzman jumped in and answered that question for Trent, "In the hospital, Trent had to provide a statement about what he'd witnessed while on the scene and was interviewed by both men. That's when he learned he was also under investigation for collusion and bribery. Ultimately, his SAC at that time removed Trent from the case because his identity had been compromised, and he was placed on desk duty pending the outcome of the internal investigation. Eventually, Trent was cleared, but his supervisor upheld his decision by removing him from the Falcon case. Soon after, he resigned, which brings us to the current."

The tension in the room thickened like old honey in a container. Finally, Noah stood and turned toward the window, his hands on his waist. Maggie sat silently, looking toward an empty part of the room. Trent remained in his chair, restrained by invisible ropes while waiting for the walls to collapse around him.

Guzman reached for the box on the table and slid it toward him. "Noah and I have a meeting with the team tonight. We'll resume in the morning to discuss the next steps of engagement and see if we can turn up the heat on Falcon."

Noah glanced at Trent as he followed Guzman out of the suite. The moment the heavy door clunked shut, his time was up. Trent had to face Maggie and handle the fallout, which seemed far worse now than when it had happened in real time.

She turned in her seat so she could face him. Her face was mottled red, with unshed tears in her eyes. "Heartbroken and devastated only begin to describe what I'm feeling. I don't even know where to start with what I've heard today. Since you were his partner, why weren't you with him? You should have had his back by being there."

He stood and strode to the big window of their suite. He needed to flex his muscles. The Boise skyline twinkled to life with the setting sun. In the distance, he focused on a flashing red light atop a tower. "You're right, I should have been there and had his back. Your brother had flown back earlier than expected from visiting you. When he called me that morning to meet, I was with a woman. He'd told me he had news to share, but instead of getting ready to leave, I indulged in another round of sex. That's why I was late."

Maggie's audible gasp equated to a knife slicing through his heart. He forced himself to turn around to see the distress on her face. "The list of *ifs* overwhelms me. If I had acted differently, Dalton wouldn't have been tortured or killed, and I'd know what he found or who did this to him. No, I don't believe Dalton is dirty, but the opportunity to avenge his death and clear his name was taken from me."

Her mouth opened and closed, then spun and headed toward the bedroom. Exhaustion had long ago drained the last of his energy. Now, she knew everything. And if she never wanted to speak to him again, he'd honor that. But not until she was safe and this threat against her was eliminated. He owed Dalton and Maggie nothing less. Trent would spend the rest of the night pouring over the files that Guzman had left on Falcon to bring him up to speed on the latest developments.

Ten

DESPERATION TORE AT MAGGIE. She couldn't take it anymore. What she needed to do was close her eyes and forget what she heard. Afraid her rubbery legs wouldn't hold her, she hastened toward the bedroom. Her nose prickled from unshed tears while her heart lodged firmly in her throat.

Sinking onto the edge of the bed, she didn't know if she wanted to scream or barf. Warm tears trickled down her cheeks. What the hell had her brother been thinking? She hated the truth. She dove onto her stomach, planted her face in the pillows, then yelled until her throat burned.

White-hot rage and pain flowed through her system. She punched the bed, desperate to release her pent-up anger. Over and over, she pummeled the bed until her arms hurt.

Dammit, Dalton, I'm mad at you for dying—for being reckless. What have you been thinking? Even worse, what the hell was the FBI thinking?

She rolled from the bed and fumbled in her bag until she found Maggie Moo. She hugged the stuffed Holstein cow to her chest, the closest thing she'd ever get now to a hug from her brother. When a loved one died, the damage it left in its wake irrevocably changed those left behind. She still had to learn how to pick up those pieces, pivot, and move forward.

But when she mixed in the parts of Dalton's death, she didn't know that information had been overwhelming and crushed her. Bile churned in her stomach like hot lava. How dare the FBI think her brother was dirty. He would never betray his country or try to profit from illicit activities. He didn't blur the lines of justice; he upheld them. Guzman had been right. A person can't forget the gritty details once you've heard them. Was it fair to be angry and disillusioned at her brother? At Trent? Confusion and heartache clouded her mind.

Curling up on the bed, she held onto the soft stuffed animal and thought about everything they had done together while growing up until her tears dried up. Had it really been just over a year ago, Dalton and Trent had planned a quick weekend visit to Dallas?

She'd surprised them with VIP passes for a day of fun at the local area amusement park. They were both adrenaline junkies—roller coasters and laughter had been a perfect idea. The last part of her surprise, since they both loved Christmas and had missed many due to their jobs, she deemed it Christmas in July, complete with presents and her mother's holiday dinner.

Her breath hitched when she realized that was the last time they were all together. She laid on the bed for the remainder of the night, her mind working overtime until she drifted to sleep.

The next morning, she awoke to Trent rapping on the bedroom door, announcing that they had a little over an hour to get ready before Guzman and Noah arrived to finish their meeting. She had been thankful that he'd ordered room service for breakfast since she had missed dinner. Thankful that the morning was a bit rushed, not leaving any time to talk, she hid behind her breakfast. She knew it would come, but she didn't have the energy now and hadn't finished processing her thoughts.

Maggie and Trent had just finished breakfast when they arrived. He had ordered extra coffee and Danish and motioned for Noah and Guzman to serve themselves. Today, they chose to work at the dining table as Noah unloaded another box with maps, files, and pictures.

"Good morning," Guzman said. "We have quite a bit to get through, so let's get moving. Noah and I are due back in DC tonight."

Noah thrust the photos toward Trent. "The video images suck, and the team can't enhance them more than this."

Trent studied the images. "Clarke mentioned they were just outside his camera's range."

"That pisses me off," Guzman declared. "I'd love to ID those bastards. How sweet would it have been to catch those assholes off guard?"

Trent handed the photos to Maggie. "The part of this that puzzles me is that Talon seems to have expanded his MO to that of a personal nature with Maggie. What triggered this drastic change? What's his end game?"

"I've created a visual reference of Falcon's activities over this past year." Noah pulled out a long, folded sheet of paper. Sticky notes had been affixed to include her incidents. "Nothing on this timeline denotes their activities as out of the ordinary, except for Maggie. The addition of her is where our paradigm shifts."

Guzman pointed to the chart and drew a circle around a time period with his finger. "This is when Dalton was killed and buried. I think we can safely assume that any activity here is related to the suspected data breach." Then, he circled another area on the paper. "Maggie, can you think of anything that was out of the normal around this timeframe? Something you stumbled on, received, or found, or maybe someone paid you a visit? Anything?"

She scrunched her brows together while she thought about his question. "Other than the apartment fire next door and the break-in, no additional things stick out in my mind. As I said before, Dalton didn't talk about his cases with me."

Guzman leaned back in his chair. "The timing on all this is interesting. This group is known for being cautious, organized, and strategic. Yet, all these latest incidents have been at breakneck speed. Last night, we received credible intel that a large shipment of weapons is moving within the week to South Sudan. We're trying to narrow the window with our deep cover assets. All the various agencies are working together to develop strategies to intercept and deal a blow to the network."

"If we're successful, that would certainly gain Talon's attention and may cause him to retaliate," Noah added.

Trent rubbed his shoulder, then massaged his forehead. "It goes without saying that I'll protect Maggie, but we should have at least one additional agent assigned to her protection. Having another set of eyes looking for potential threats wouldn't hurt."

"I agree. In fact, I've already sent an undercover asset to Mill Creek," Guzman announced. "At this point, my priority has to be South Sudan.

Guzman interlaced his fingers, his elbows resting on the armrest. "Since you're taking the lead with Maggie's security, my agent will provide backup for you. That way, we will always have eyes on her. I've assigned an agent, Peter Lindholm, from the Boise office, who is checking into the Mill Creek Hotel today. His job, besides security, is to poke around and see what he can learn. His room will be directly across from yours, and he has already seen pictures of you both."

Noah tossed a folder across the table toward Maggie and Trent. "Inside is his contact information and photo," he said, then tucked other items into his box.

Trent added the agent's contact information to his phone and studied the picture. "Maggie, memorize this photo so you'll be able to recognize him." When she finished, he handed everything back to Noah.

Trent turned to Maggie. "Do you have any questions?"

She shook her head. "No, I'm good."

Everyone stood to shake hands and voice their goodbyes, and right before Guzman walked through the threshold, he announced over his shoulder, "Noah will keep you informed regarding progress with Sudan. If anything happens on your end, report it to Noah. We'll talk soon."

Noah waited until it was just the three of them in the room. He looked directly at Maggie. "I can't imagine what yesterday felt like for you, but I wanted you to know that I never believed the allegations against Dalton. We just haven't uncovered the truth to clear his name. I thought you should know where I stood on the matter."

"Thanks, Noah, that means a lot to me," she replied.

Trent nodded at Noah. "Good luck, man. We're going to head back to Mill Creek."

SINCE THEY HAD RETURNED to town a few days ago, Maggie and Trent had barely spoken, except to exchange pleasantries or to remind her that he had to be her constant shadow. She'd battled with herself over wanting to return to how things were between them. The problem was that it wouldn't make her happy either—knowing the truth surrounding her brother's death mattered. Trent hadn't bulldozed her into talking, which she appreciated. Instead, he'd given her the room she needed and told her he'd be available when she was ready. *Ready? Ready for what?*

This whole situation left her distraught and strung tight from the emotional toll. Even his demeanor had shifted to quiet and intense, and he was basically on high alert at all times. The strain from the situation weighed on them both.

She'd spent her days at the station with him while he worked or rode with him when he had to leave to go on calls. The only thing that helped to pass the time was helping the team prepare for the annual sheriff's fundraiser. She loved the idea of the sheriff's office doing an event for the betterment of the community. This year's proceeds were going to Micah Parker's AMC Animal Wellness Clinic for the new animal shelter he was building.

Tonight was the night at Two Stepping, who partnered with the sheriff's department—twenty dollars per adult for a beer or soda, cheeseburger and fries, and live music. Her job at the moment was to tear off different colored raffle tickets for each item and place it inside an envelope to hand out after each person paid. Irene had even volunteered her services to watch the town's children who weren't old enough to stay home alone at the library.

Maggie's cellphone chirped, jolting her from her thoughts. "Hello?"

"Hey, it's Aimee. Do you want to join me at Two Stepping? I thought we could indulge in an early snack before the festivities begin at five o' clock. Lance and I just finished setting up so we have some time. This should be a great night all around, plus, I've been told that Friday nights usually bring good bands."

Maggie checked her watch. "That sounds perfect. I'll bring the envelopes with me so we won't have to go back to the station. I'll let Trent know, and see you in a few minutes."

"Hang on, Lance told me to tell you he'll meet at the station and walk over with you."

"Okay, I'll be ready."

A surge of happiness she had missed the last several days swirled in Maggie's body. The routine and camaraderie within this office made her smile. She quickly finished the last few envelopes and shoved them into the box before heading toward Trent's office who seemed to be on a call.

He motioned for her to enter. "I'm on mute. What's up?"

"I'm going to meet Aimee at the bar, and Lance is on his way over to help me carry everything."

"Thanks, Maggie. I'll text the agent so he knows. I'll be over after this call."

She smiled and turned to leave, his voice stopping her momentarily as he continued, "Hey, I know everything is far from okay, and despite it all, you've been a huge help. I appreciate you, Maggie, and what you've done to help everyone."

Deciding not to look back because, at that moment, she thought she might just crumble, she hurried to the ladies' room to touch up her makeup and check her hair. This would probably be the last time she'd get this chance once the fundraiser started.

When she reached the door at Two Stepping, she opened the door wide to give Lance extra space since he insisted on carrying both boxes. She inhaled the scents of wood and stale beer as she moved inside the doorway, stopping to let her eyes adjust to the darkened interior. The bouncer checked her identification and gestured Lance through. Once she could see, she looked around until she saw Aimee waving from a booth off to the side of the stage.

He dropped the box of envelopes onto a portable table just past the bouncer to collect the admission for tonight's event. An easel holding a poster explained how the proceeds would be distributed and who they would benefit. The bar's motif leaned toward cowboy chic, from the checkered tablecloths with fresh flowers in mason jars on every table to the hand-painted mountain and prairie murals on the walls. She loved the wooden fence that framed the dance floor and stage.

"Hi, Aimee," Maggie said as she sat in the booth across from her. "The place looks fantastic." She picked up the four-by-six note card that provided even more details about how the Mill Creek Animal Wellness Center would use the money and even how to donate more for anyone interested.

"Thanks, I just hope the night is a success. This town is really cool with how they support their own. Sometimes the small-town vibe can be a little intrusive, but for the most part, the people here are very cool, and I've come to enjoy it."

Maggie placed the card off to the side. "Yeah, it's different, but what I like is the feeling that you're home—you know, like you belong. Big cities can swallow you whole, and no one will know."

One thing she had been mulling over just crystallized in her mind, and the decision didn't worry her. "I'm going to need your assistance. I want to apply for the open teaching position. Things might not be perfect now, but for some wild reason, moving here feels right if I get the position."

Aimee's eyes went wide. "That's amazing news because I like hanging out with you. Whatever help you need, let me know."

"It's always good when you have a friend to welcome you," Maggie replied. It felt beyond good to make a plan for the future.

They studied the menu. Maggie's stomach rumbled, reminding her that she'd skipped breakfast. She wiggled her eyebrows at Aimee in a playful manner. "I'm in the mood for fried, greasy, yumminess. Let's split the mozzarella sticks and potato skins. You game?"

Aimee grinned. "I like how you think, but we must add the brisket sliders and cream cheese stuffed jalapeños."

"Done! I knew I liked you for a reason," Maggie said, some of her tension fading over friendship and fried food.

"Are you okay? You look so tired since you returned from Boise." Aimee asked, her gaze intent and steady.

Maggie picked at a perfectly fine fingernail while emotions she would rather remain hidden tickled her throat. "I don't know. How lame is that answer? I mean, I'm living and breathing, but I don't know if I'll ever be okay again. I don't even know if I'm making sense."

Aimee reached across the table to hold her hand. "I do understand, and that makes us soul sisters. I'm here for you if you ever want to talk. My best advice is just take it one day at a time."

Maggie squeezed her hand lightly before releasing it. "Thanks for inviting me for an early bite. You don't know how badly I needed this."

The waitress delivered two iced teas Aimee had already ordered. She relayed their food order while Maggie sat politely, tucking away her thoughts and reactions. Once her mask was firmly in place, she lifted her gaze and smiled at the server right before she left the table.

The wait staff uniforms were really cute. She liked the denim bottoms matched with a white short-sleeved button-up shirt, a red bandana tied at the neck, and cowboy boots. They were a perfect balance of country and sexy. She loved the vibe of this bar.

"Oh look, the band has arrived." Maggie pointed as the group's guitarist opened his case to remove his instrument and begin tuning it.

Aimee leaned forward so she could be heard over the chords he played. "I love music, so being able to be here and enjoy the night is so cool."

The drummer and sound check man moved through their sequences, adding to the noise level. Another server arrived with plates stacked on her arms to drop off their order. The aroma and sight of each item made Maggie's stomach cheer. She selected a few pieces and placed each on her dish. Her moans of satisfaction made them both laugh while they nibbled and talked throughout their meal.

A tall, sexy man at the bar caught her attention. His jeans were molded to his long muscular legs perfectly, and his pants cupped his butt like a second skin, just begging for her to grab it. She might be upset at Trent, but he looked too good. It hadn't shocked her that she felt his presence. He'd changed out of his uniform and wore a T-shirt with the Mill Creek sheriff's emblem. That damn man caused her system to go topsy-turvy. She craved him and wanted to smack him at the same time. How was she going to handle everything that happened?

When he turned and found her in the room, he gave her a casual nod. She'd be a liar if she said his attentiveness bothered her. The moment she arrived on his doorstep, he'd made it clear she was important to him and that he'd protect her. She watched Trent and Lance talk for a few minutes before focusing on her food. They had about ten minutes before heading to their tasks for the evening. She and Aimee were working the table collecting admission while Trent and the other deputies ran food and other condiments to help support the waitstaff.

Two hours later, the doors had closed, and the bar was full of residents and visitors. The band was playing, and those not eating were dancing.

"I'd say this was a success," Maggie said, handing Aimee the contents of her till so she could tabulate the total dollar amount.

"This is awesome. We made eighteen-hundred-fifty dollars," Aimee announced enthusiastically. "I have to go give this to Trent. He's going to thank everyone for coming and announce the grand total in a few minutes."

"Wait, you have one more person to collect from for tonight," Maggie replied, eying the man walking up to them and extending her arm to stop Aimee.

"Hello, Mr. Dragoon," Aimee greeted in a bubbly manner. "It'll be twenty dollars."

"It's Clarke, and here you go, keep the change," Clarke corrected, handing her a hundred-dollar bill. "I'm beginning to think your insistence on calling me by my last name is your version of flirting."

"I'll give you that you're persistent, Mr. Dragoon, but I'm in too good of a mood to argue with you tonight. Thank you for the extra donation. Have fun tonight." Aimee updated her tabulation and paused to look back at Maggie.

"Go," she shooed. "I'll clean this up and be over in a few minutes."

"Here, let me help you." Clarke handed her the big box to fill. After she finished filling the box, he turned the table upside down to fold the legs into itself. Once it was flat on the floor, he picked it up and leaned it against the wall.

"Thanks. Will you put this box in front of it?"

She wouldn't have thought such a hulking man would be so agile. Why, she hadn't a clue, but his deft movements told a different story. He was certainly comfortable in his own skin. Arrogant, yes, but behind that façade, she sensed he had a good heart. He came across like the ultimate bad boy with all his tattoos and bald head. His look screamed crazy, biker, gang member, but she sensed that was more of a characterization. He also seemed to have it bad for her friend.

Just as she and Clarke finished, the lights brightened in the bar area, and the room went quiet. Trent had taken center stage, standing behind the microphone the singer had just vacated. He scanned the crowd, calling out names in greetings or funny one-liners. When he got to Micah, he uttered the phrase, 'Who let the dog out.' The crowd erupted into whoops or laughter. He motioned for Micah to approach the stage.

When Micah stood next to Trent, he continued, "The residents of Mill Creek are a special group. Why, you ask? We protect our own. We welcome newcomers. We give back to the community in which we live and work. Thanks to a last-minute anonymous donor, we raised twenty-four hundred dollars for the Animal Wellness Clinic's pet shelter tonight." Trent paused, his gaze found Maggie's and held it for a few seconds before stepping aside for Micah.

He approached the microphone like it could bite him. "Speeches aren't my thing, but I want to thank everyone for your generosity. More importantly, the animals thank you. I can't believe I've been here for two years. Time has flown, but in the best possible way. I must echo what Trent said—I'm so fortunate I found this town to call my home."

Applause and hollers came from the crowd. Trent turned and nodded to the band, who appropriately started playing an upbeat rock song that had everyone heading toward the dance floor.

Maggie stood back and watched the energized crowd, mostly of neighbors and friends. The warmth and spirit of this group humbled her. All these people worked together to support a common goal and each other. Trent's point hit her squarely in her chest. *We protect our own.* Ignoring the issue between them wouldn't make it go away or change the outcome. No, the time had come for them to talk. Even worse, her body craved him and his exquisite touch, which made her want to use him, if only for the moment. To give them both an outlet. She wasn't sure if they'd come out of it whole in the end.

Eleven

T RENT LATCHED THE SECURITY lock on their hotel door, and when he turned, Maggie sat on the edge of the bed. Guarded green eyes studied him. His skin tightened from her scrutiny and what would come next. A myriad of thoughts and emotions flooded his system. He deserved her anguish and would take whatever she unleashed at him. She hadn't moved a muscle, so he remained glued to the spot where he stood by the door.

She sucked in a deep breath. "I can't imagine how difficult it had been for you to tell me everything that happened to my brother. I'm grateful it was you instead of anyone else. I can't describe what it means to have closure and stop the horrible scenarios that ran through my head. I didn't like what I heard, but I finally know."

Lowering her head, she sighed before continuing, "Look, I'm struggling to find the right words. I don't want to fight because what's done is done. What I want to do is be open and honest with each other. I do have a question for you. Did my brother indicate that he thought he was in trouble or that something was wrong that morning?"

Trent clenched his jaw to the point he thought he might break a molar. "No, I never expected to walk into that clusterfuck, but that also doesn't absolve me of my actions."

"No, I suppose it doesn't. Do you think my brother was dirty?"

"What? No! I think he was set up, and I'd bet my life on it. His moral compass was sound. He held himself and everyone around him to high standards."

Maggie nodded, her gaze roaming around the ceiling for a few seconds. He figured she was processing whatever thoughts or questions churned in her brain before she spoke, "I don't blame you for my brother's poor decision-making. That was on him. He didn't tell you what was happening, and he never should have entered that building without backup."

Trent started to talk, but she stopped him. "Don't make excuses for him; you know I'm right. Guilt has a way of gnawing away at facts and twisting that knowledge to rewrite its own story."

Trent slapped at his chest, every word he said dripping with heartbreak. "If I had been there, the outcome might have been different. That's a fact."

She stood, her face red with anger. "You're not God, Trent, you don't control destiny. Could you have stopped a portion of what happened? Maybe, but you could have also been killed."

Her hand flew to her mouth, and she spun around, hiding her face. It gutted him not to reach out and try to comfort her. His stomach twisted into a painful knot. "I never meant to hurt you. I'm so sorry, Maggie. This is all my fault."

Her shoulders shook, and her voice wobbled. "I know, but you did. Reluctantly, I understand that you couldn't tell me about my brother. What I don't understand is why you kept what happened to you from me. It feels an awful lot like a lie. You shut me out, then you cut me off."

"I don't know. It took me a while to regain my memories from that day. I had so many emotions running through me, and depending on the day and my mental state, I had different reasons and excuses," he answered, his voice strained with emotion. Her accusation was akin to having his heart ripped from his chest. "All were selfish and cowardly because the truth is, I didn't want to face you. I couldn't even tell you that I'd work tirelessly to avenge his death and find out the truth because I'd been removed from the case."

The room fell silent, the only sound of soft sniffles. He'd moved behind her but didn't touch her. When Maggie turned back around, she pinned him with a gaze so broken and desperate it almost brought him to his knees. Her eyes were red-rimmed and shiny from another layer of unshed tears.

"At some point, you'll have to decide if you'll forgive yourself. Just like I'll have to decide if I can forgive you. What bothers me is that you kept something that was important from me once. Would you do it again? Right now, that puts us at another impasse. What I want, Trent, is to feel something other than pain."

Her movements were lightning-fast, catching him by surprise. She'd launched herself into his arms, shoving him back onto the bed with her momentum. After they bounced together on the mattress, she straddled his waist. She shoved his T-shirt up his body, and he helped her get it over his head. Next, the rapid fire of a snap being dislodged and the hiss from his zipper filled the silent room.

Leaning forward, she kissed his lips before sweeping down his neck and across his collarbone. When she pressed a kiss to the puckered scar on his right shoulder, he trembled.

Her fevered paced and actions had a warning bell blaring in his head. He cupped her face so she'd look at him. "Maggie—"

"Don't talk, remove my shirt. I need to forget, make me forget, Trent."

He wrenched the hem of her shirt free so he could slide his hand against her warm flesh. Eventually, he moved higher until he gripped her shoulders and tugged her down so he could kiss her. She nipped his lip with her teeth. He took control of the kiss, needing this connection. Unsatisfied with the amount of her nakedness, he jerked her shirt off her body. The next garment to go was her bra.

Using his hands, he tortured her nipples. He pinched and twisted the tight bud between his fingers. Her whimpers of delight fueled his lust. The need to reconnect with Maggie drove his actions. He had hated the distance between them—one he caused. His muscles bunched, and his cock surged to life. He rolled them both over to hover over her and sat back on his heels.

A beautiful offering laid out before him. Her eyes were half-hooded, and her face flushed with arousal. This image would stay with him forever. He slammed his mouth down on hers again and devoured her. Their tongues dueled and connected just as he would with her body. He craved more, ending their kiss, loving how her lips were swollen in response.

He backed off the bed to remove his shoes, pants, and boxers. The bed dipped when he crawled over her body. His mouth found hers again as he trailed one hand down her supple flesh until his finger pressed inside her. Satisfied she was ready; he settled his weight on top of her.

"Please, just fuck me," she demanded.

That plea was akin to a needle scratching across a vinyl record. No, this was all wrong. She would never be just a fuck to him. He'd given his heart to Maggie, even though he hadn't said the words. She mattered to him. He refused to go any further.

"I'm sorry, you mean more to me than physical release. When I make love to you, it's because I want all of you. The good, the bad, and the ugly. If you can't give me that, I understand, but I won't use your body." He rolled off the bed and padded into the bathroom.

He needed a cold shower and some time to regain his composure. It was time to shift his focus and change his strategy. Giving up on Maggie wasn't an option. He'd fight for her and what they had together. As the water pelted his skin, an idea formed in his head. He'd revisit the surprise he had planned to do earlier. Spending the day together, hiking in the fresh air, would benefit them both. He'd text the agent in the morning, giving him their itinerary for the day.

S ATURDAY MORNING CAME MUCH too early after a long night of tossing and turning. Maggie hadn't slept well after Trent's refusal to have sex with her. He'd put his feelings on the table, and his words touched her deeply because he'd spent his life enjoying casual sex. He'd made her feel special and she panicked. Fingers danced across the skin of her arm.

"Wake up, Maggie."

"It's early. Don't you ever sleep in?" she replied in a groggy voice.

"I had an idea. I thought I'd revisit the surprise I planned for you earlier. What do you say? Shower. Food. Surprise."

She sat up and finger-combed the hair out of her face. "Ooh, the possibilities, and I do love surprises. Okay, I'm game, and I think we could use a change of scenery."

She rolled out of bed and had her toothbrush in hand with a large dollop of toothpaste covering the bristles. "You jump in the shower first since you're faster, then I'll follow."

She was excited about the possibilities of where Trent would take her. She was more than happy to spend the day doing something fun, and a change of pace was exactly what they needed.

The day had been perfect, full of sunshine, creeks, fresh mountain breezes, and one very handsome man. She couldn't help it; she'd been attracted to him forever. Whether she wanted to admit it or not, they had history, and because of that, she could never fully cut him out. Denying her last night irritated her because she wanted a release, but she respected him for doing it. Doubt nibbled away on her conviction like mice eating cheese in a trap.

As promised, they stopped to grab sandwiches from PB&S Café before he drove them to a scenic lookout behind Main Street. Once they parked, it was a short hike to the most breathtaking spot. Lush meadows and a babbling creek blended into thick groves of pine trees and aspens that ran up the hill. Nestled in the middle was a well-maintained wooden multi-story house-like structure with a big wheel that churned water as it rotated. *Mill Creek.*

She had been stunned to learn that this mill produced compressed air to support local area mines in the early nineteen-hundreds. Now she understood where the name came from for both the county and town. She thought this place was picture-perfect during the fall when the foliage changed colors to vibrant yellow, red, and orange hues.

It would have been nicer if they didn't have an agent lurking in the woods behind them, watching their backs. Trent had made sure Parker had their itinerary before they left the hotel. One thing she knew for sure was that Trent took her protection seriously. On the way back to the hotel, they were both hot and sweaty from their adventure. He stopped to get iced tea and an afternoon snack to go. Maggie felt lighter than she had in the last several days. She'd missed the simple pleasures they shared.

The front desk clerk waved and cheerily greeted them as they strode through the lobby. "Hi, Sheriff. I have an envelope that arrived for you today."

Trent turned toward the desk and took the proffered letter. "Thanks."

"Just sign here to acknowledge receipt," the employee said, holding out a pen.

Trent signed his name and nodded at the clerk. "Appreciate it."

He held Maggie's hand, and they walked in silence toward their room. Once inside, she put her drink on the small table and flopped onto the bed. The cool bedspread felt heavenly against her back, and when she stretched, she practically purred. The air conditioner kicked on, blowing a cool breeze into the room that wrapped around her sun-soaked skin. Her muscles were sore, and her eyelids fought gravity.

"Let's take a nap." She patted the space next to her. "Someone, who shall remain nameless, had a restless night."

When she didn't get an answer, she cracked open an eye to see what had his attention. Trent's posture was stiff as he stood in the center of the room, staring at the contents of that envelope with a grave expression on his face. Chills slithered down her spine, not from the room's temperature but the rapid shift in his demeanor. His mood had transformed from easygoing to grim in a matter of seconds.

An unsettled feeling pitted in her stomach as she rose from the bed. "What is it? What's wrong?" she asked from behind him, wrapping her arms around his waist.

He turned and showed her the typed note.

I love the flirting phase of attraction. Or is it the thrill of winning the trophy? Someday soon, you'll be my wife. Please don't fret, no one but me will ever see this photo. I protect what's mine; I hope you liked my flowers.

Her hand flew to her mouth as she sucked in an uneven breath. "Do I even want to see the photo?"

"Photos," Trent clarified, then showed her the first one. A photocopy of a photo that showed her backside as she stepped from the shower and written across the top, *my Maggie.* The second was of Dalton and a man taken inside what she assumed was a warehouse.

"Oh God, Trent, that's creepy and much worse than the flowers. I'm naked." Her stomach plummeted, and the room spun out of control. She rushed to the bed and sat down. Her body trembled from dread and fear. "What the hell? I'm not marrying him. What does that mean? Does he really think I'd even consider something so vile? Is that a picture from the day Dalton died?"

Air rushed around her as Trent knelt in front of her. He rubbed soft circles on her back. "Deep breaths, baby. In through the nose, out through the mouth," he said softly, supporting her through her meltdown.

His presence made her feel safe. God, he was right, this was a lot worse than she had even understood. It was one thing to know she had an enemy. It was entirely another when she was caught naked and in the crosshairs of that person's threat.

He cupped her cheeks and tilted her head upward until he could see her eyes. "We'll get through this together. I need to send those pictures to Guzman and Noah. Now, we know the personal aspect and Talon's expectations.

"I'm so naïve. Just today, I thought that maybe he'd lost interest in me."

Trent pulled her into his chest and held her tight. She wasn't sure how long they sat that way, but she needed to feel him surrounding her. To help her chase away the sickening thoughts that jerk had put in her head.

"That sick fuck needs to die a slow and painful death," she grumbled. "Who's that man with my brother?"

"I agree with you on that one. That's from the day Dalton died. That was the dead man lying next to him when I arrived. I don't recall his name. I'll ask Noah when I send all of this to him."

She absently nodded. Why would a man linked to destruction and death around the globe be obsessed with her? She just hoped she could help the FBI nail that bastard. What he deserved was to be rotting in a small concrete cell for the rest of his life. The other reason was she didn't want to spend the rest of her life looking over her shoulder.

Her mood fizzled as dread settled in her stomach. They chose to eat dinner in their room again. Afterward, they tried to watch an in-room movie to take her mind off the giant elephant that sat on her chest, but that didn't work. Finally, she'd lost track of the time as she drifted off to sleep. A few hours later, she awoke to the muffled sound of a male voice.

She immediately turned toward Trent, but he wasn't next to her. The sheets were tossed back, and his space was cold under her fingers. She heard his voice again, realizing it had come from the bathroom. Her heart rate increased. Why had he gone into the bathroom? What now could have happened? The revolving door of fear was getting old.

She peeled back the covers, got out of bed, and padded toward the bathroom. Her hand hovered mid-knock when she overhead something that pissed her off.

"I don't care what it takes. I want a safe house, and I'll get her there. Get that authorization now," Trent whispered in a low tone that still had an edge.

"Trent?" she announced instead.

"I'll be out in a second."

She stood outside the door, purposely eavesdropping on the rest of his conversation. Anger pulsed through her body. That had to be Noah on the other end. Damn him, he knew better. He'd promised her that they be a team, and that he wouldn't try to sideline her participation. She concluded that she'd finish this for her brother, and if she were lucky, they find the evidence needed to clear his name.

"I've got to run. Maggie's awake. Good luck taking down those assholes."

She swiveled and then returned to the bed. The second he exited she pounced, hoping he'd tell her the truth. "Who were you talking to?"

She flicked on the bedside lamp so she could see his face.

His features were reserved. "Noah. Everything's okay. I didn't want to wake you so I took the call in the bathroom. We discussed the photos."

Her shoulders slumped, and she expelled a long sigh. "It hasn't stopped you before when I'm sleeping," she said, her tone pleading with him to come clean.

"I know, but you'd just fallen asleep after tossing and turning for a while. He also mentioned that the timeline had been moved up on the Sudan shipment."

"Nothing about a safe house?" she shot back, her anger bubbling over.

"Yeah, that's something I want in the event it's needed. A personal GPS tracker was issued for you to wear as a precaution. What's wrong?"

"Nothing." Her shoulders relaxed.

"Are you sure, because it doesn't feel like nothing?"

She expelled a frustrated growl. "I'm sorry, I thought you were trying to keep the safe house from me. All this has me on edge, and I totally overreacted."

He sat on the bed. "Come here." When she did, he hugged her tight. "This is stressful, and I understand why you'd jump to that conclusion."

"Thanks. So, when do we meet again to discuss this horror show that's now my life?"

"In Boise, as soon as they wrap up Sudan. If they succeed, Talon will most certainly be pissed."

"Well, I hate all of this. It scares me, but I've decided I want to help the FBI in any way I can because just maybe we can stop Falcon, which is what my brother died for. I didn't ask for this, but I'm not backing down since that Talon guy has involved me. I just don't want you or anyone else getting hurt or worse in the process."

"Risk is a part of life. Every second of every day, it all comes down to our decisions. Talon has a large organization of bad men willing to do his bidding. There is always someone desperate to move up and do his dirty work. I'll do my best to make solid decisions, but I expect the same from you."

"Deal, but I still worry."

"Oh, I almost forgot, Noah confirmed the man in that photo is the suspected informant, Barton Schamko. But the FBI has never been able to validate it."

Maggie jumped out of his grasp and stood. "Wait, that name sounds familiar. Why does that name sound familiar?" she asked herself while she paced. "That's it. That's the name I searched the morning before the break-in. Remember, I told you I hadn't recognized it. Well, he's dead. I figured it was a friend of Dalton's he wanted me to contact. When I saw his obituary, I let it go. Damn it, Trent, I missed this."

"You mean it was tucked within the legal stuff Dalton gave you during his last visit?" he asked. Grasping her hand, he tugged her back to the bed.

"Yes, his name and two agents were listed on a miscellaneous page."

She assumed Trent's silence meant he was processing what she just said.

"Holy hell, Dalton had obtained some data. Can I see that file?" he replied.

Tears burned her eyes. "Oh God, I've had this information the whole time. I didn't think that name meant anything more than a person my brother knew who had died. It just makes me sick."

"Why would you? Your brother didn't exactly explain his intentions to you or his job," he answered. Trent moved to the small table and pulled a chair out for Maggie. "Grab your laptop and show me."

The electronic bong of her laptop sounded. Her fingers swept over the keyboard when it finished booting. Then she inserted the drive. After a long minute, she clicked the icon and rotated her laptop toward Trent. A folder labeled photos and five Word documents were inside. The first four were typical legal documents: Trust, Will, and Power of Attorney. The next was a document labeled miscellaneous, which she opened, and inside, she showed him the notes on how Dalton envisioned his memorial and funeral. At the bottom of that page, it listed out three names—Trent Jacobs with the notation—*take everything to him, he'll help you with the planning*, Ben Knight, and Bart Schamko.

"I would guess that at the time he wrote this document, he didn't know that man would be dead. Have you gone through all these?"

Maggie sucked in a sharp breath. "Everything but the photos. I wasn't ready to look at old memories. Open it. Let's see what's in there."

Trent wrapped his arm around her and tugged her against his body. His warmth penetrated her chilled skin. When he clicked on the file, a bunch of photos appeared across the screen. In the thumbnails, she could see various pictures of her parents when they were younger, wedding photos, and childhood pictures of her and Dalton. With each picture, her heart warmed. Her brother had taken all the photo albums, printed photos, and digitized them so they would always be protected.

Hot streaks of water streamed down her cheeks. What an amazing surprise, and she couldn't even fathom how long it had taken him. Hundreds of images filled the screen. *God, I love you, you were the best brother.*

"Hey." Trent squeezed her side. "I've got this, if it's too much? I didn't mean to upset you."

"No, no, these are good tears. My brother did this for me. These are all the old prints he converted for safekeeping."

Trent kept scrolling until a series of photos toward the bottom caused him to slow down. He sat upright and clicked on an image until it filled the screen. Each image had a handwritten note across the bottom in Dalton's handwriting stating that Bart would provide the identity.

Maggie's eyes widened. "I've had this information the whole time?"

"It seems so, but we don't have everything. We have faces, which is a start. Are you sure he didn't give you anything else?"

"I'm super positive, but maybe it's embedded inside the other files?"

Trent agreed and moved her laptop closer. Together they poured over every file and picture, but didn't find anything else.

"I'll let them know what we've found, but since they are tied up with the Sudan operation, we'll bring all of this to our next meeting which should be soon.

When she stood, he jerked her toward him and kissed her briefly. The solid beat of his heart thudded against her own. Two hearts beat as one, in tune with each, creating a masterpiece. Could she forgive him and mean it? She wanted to survive, and the only thing that stood in her way to achieving that goal was Falcon.

Twelve

THE NEXT DAY, TRENT headed into the station for a team meeting. Maggie stayed behind to finish her book. She longed for a day that a change in schedule like that didn't immediately necessitate a text to an FBI agent. The babysitter aspect annoyed her, but she understood the big picture and appreciated his support. This whole nightmare couldn't end soon enough. Trent would swing back and pick her up afterward so they could head to Micah's to deliver the check from the fundraiser.

Her cellphone screen caught her gaze as it flashed the battery less than ten percent message. *Crap.* She'd forgotten to charge it last night. Popping out of her chair, she laid her phone on the small table then plugged the charger into the outlet behind it.

Ten minutes later, a loud knock on the door jolted Maggie's attention from her novel. She wasn't expecting anyone.

A man's voice hollered through the door. "Maintenance. I need to change the filter in the A/C unit."

She cringed. A prickle of doubt washed over her body. *Wouldn't the hotel inform their guests of scheduled service?* Then, she thought about her apartment. Since when had she started to doubt everyone's sincerity or intentions, but something in the back of her mind told her to reject his offer.

"Now's not a good time. You'll have to come back later."

"It'll only take a minute. If I don't get this floor done today, my boss will be pissed. I was supposed to have this finished last week. I don't want to lose my job," the man's voice pleaded from the hallway.

She hated her paranoia. She shoved Maggie Moo and her e-reader into her backpack, then she moved toward the window. Why did she do that? She didn't know, but she stayed right there. Her heart thumped hard against her throat. Each second seemed to take a minute to pass. She looked through the glass and saw only landscape and people walking in the distance.

A decision was made, and she slid the window open and popped out the screen. "Sorry, I just got out of the shower. I'll call the front desk to let them know when you can return."

When the man didn't reply, she let out the breath she'd been holding. A giddy laughter escaped her throat. Great, now she'd have to explain why she removed the screen. Embarrassed by her actions, she shook her head and gripped the edge of the window to close it. So, all this talk of bad men had her acting instead of just calling the front desk to verify.

Just as the window inched forward, a loud thud hit the door. Her head snapped to the right as the door splintered, sending pieces of wood into the room. Oh, crap, she wasn't crazy. She squelched a scream then shoved the window open. Her pace quickened as she scrambled up and over the windowsill.

When her feet hit the ground, the roar from the man who entered her room had her feet moving even faster. Two gunshots rang out behind her, followed by one more. She didn't need any more encouragement. Her breath sawed in and out of her chest. Her mind whirled as she tried to figure out how to get to Trent. She ran as fast as her feet would move her toward Main Street. Only a man on a motorcycle approached. She jumped off the curb into his path, flailing her arms to get him to slow down.

"What the hell? Are you trying to kill yourself?" the big man spat at her.

"Nope, just the opposite," she shot back. She fisted a handful of his shirt and swung her leg up to sit astride his bike behind him. "Go, fast—very, very, fast."

She said a silent prayer when he roared the engine and tore off down the street. Her arms couldn't fit around his waist, so she grabbed the material of his shirt and held it on for dear life.

"Where are we headed?" he asked in a loud enough voice she could hear him over the engine.

The bike vibrated underneath her body, and her brain slowed to a crawl.

"I-I don't care. Just away from here." She had trouble focusing and only knew she had to call Trent and warn him.

The man didn't say another word. He expertly navigated his motorcycle through the various streets toward a house on the same road as Trent's home. She felt marginally better that her random savior at least drove safely and seemed to have a protective streak.

After he pulled into the driveway and parked his bike, he removed his helmet. She dismounted on wobbly legs while her entire body trembled. In a flash, he extended his arm, stopping her from falling unceremoniously to the ground. Her eyes started to water from not wearing protection. Her confidence stopped because she was pretty sure the waterworks were moments away. She didn't want to cry in front of this good Samaritan, and she worried that if the waterworks fell, they wouldn't end.

"He might have seen me jump on your motorcycle." Her voice trembled as she looked upward to see his face. "Oh my God, Clarke,

I'm so happy to see you. Do you have a garage?" She feared her heart would pop out of her chest from beating so fast. When she took a step toward the house, she stumbled and almost hit the ground, but strong arms stopped her.

He flipped her up into his arms and carried her inside his house. Once in the laundry room, he bent and pulled a trap door open, all without even putting her down. Then, he descended a flight of stairs into a room resembling a fallout shelter.

Or the secret room where he plans to kill me, but she didn't get that vibe from Clarke. She rather liked the massive man.

Once her feet hit the ground, she followed his index finger which pointed at a cot behind her. "Stay here while I pull my bike into the garage. When I return, we'll talk."

She scanned the room, her head on a swivel. She sat on the cot and placed her backpack next to her. Geez, this place looked like the bat cave with the volume of gadgets and computers. Against the back wall where she sat were two locked, chain-link, fenced-in areas. One was empty, and the other held guns and other items. Then, on her left, four large monitors hung two by two, and computer equipment, a printer, and various electronic devices sat on the desk. Across the room were shelves with food and medical supplies. Who was this man, and why was he preparing for the apocalypse?

Heavy footsteps pounded down the stairs, dragging her from her musings. Nervous energy zipped through her body and settled in her stomach. He moved to a refrigerator she had missed and withdrew a bottle of water. "Drink, then tell me why you broke rules number one and two." Clarke stood with his legs spread and his arms crossed against his wide chest.

Why did she always get stuck with the bossy men? She took a sip of the water, and the cool liquid soothed her parched throat.

"I'm not familiar with rules one and two." She held the water bottle.

"Rule one, stranger-danger. Rule two, you don't jump in front of moving vehicles. That's a good way to become roadkill."

She couldn't help herself. She laughed. Who the hell was this man? "Uh, those rules don't count when you're in danger. And you're not a stranger."

He raised his eyebrow. "You didn't know who I was until you stood in my driveway. Now, spill."

She lowered her gaze, hesitant with how much to divulge. A tremor racked her body,and her damn eyes filled with tears again. She scanned the room and weighed her options.

"Maggie, I won't hurt you. I brought you to this room because it's the safest spot in Mill Creek. I'm also trusting you to keep your knowledge of this place between us. What has you scared to death? I can't help you if I don't know."

She sat silent, unsure what to say or what to do. This whole fucking situation had her second guessing everything. She didn't want to betray the FBI, and she didn't really know if she could trust him with that type of information. Her mouth popped open then she snapped it shut.

Clarke assessed her patiently before addressing her in a calm voice. "Earlier, you were concerned that you might have been followed. Who's following you?"

"It's kind of a long story…"

He smiled and pressed several keys on a keyboard. "Let me show you something."

Several images of his property came into view. Something deep down reassured her, and she remembered what Guzman had said. "I need to call Trent." She reached into her bag to pull out her cellphone.

Where the hell was it? Damn it, she'd left it charging in the room. "I need to call Trent to let him know I'm okay and what's happened. I left my phone in the room."

"First, tell me what's going on. I can't protect you if I'm in the dark. Then, if you give me Trent's number, I'll send him a coded text."

"A man posing as maintenance broke into my hotel room. I escaped out the window, and when I heard gunshots, I ran toward the street. I think all of this is tied to some problems I had at home, which is why I came to see Trent. He and my brother were partners in the FBI."

Clarke smiled. "You're doing great. Where's home?"

"Dallas, Texas." The water bottle crinkled as she moved it toward her mouth for another drink.

The pounding in her chest had moved to her head. Blindly, she shoved her hand back inside her bag to find her ibuprofen. Maggie Moo kept getting in her way, so she removed the stuffed animal, which gave her enough room to locate her bottle of pills. Tapping two out, she popped them into her mouth, and washed them down with the last of her water.

"How do you think they tracked you here?" He opened a plastic crate and removed two paddles. "This is a metal detector, and this one is a counter surveillance sweep. I'd like to scan you and those belongings."

Her mouth gaped open. "Oh, okay, but should you have those things?"

His face broke into a smile that made him look ten years younger. He motioned for her to stand with her hands outstretched at her side. He moved each wand over and around her body, one at a time. "An enthusiast is the easiest answer. Committed to safety is another. You're clean, but I need to scan your backpack. Dump out the contents, and afterward, I'll send off that text to Trent."

A mechanical chirp split the air, and lights danced on the wand. Clarke ran the wand over her wallet and nothing, but when he picked up Maggie Moo, his devices came to life in light and sound. He up-ended the cow to examine the bottom, and his gaze locked with hers.

"Where did you get this stuffed animal?" he asked, scanning the fluffy body. "This seam has been altered and re-stitched. If you press hard on this spot, you can feel something inside." He handed her the cow then walked toward his desk. When he returned, he held a pocketknife.

"It was a gift from my brother. Please be careful."

Clarke worked the tip of his knife into the seam, paying close attention to each stitch to avoid damage. He might come across like a bull, but underneath that façade was a caring and respectful man. One willing to protect another person without knowing all the facts and potentially putting his own safety at risk. The next time she saw Aimee, she planned to tell her that, in her opinion, Clarke was a keeper and one Maggie considered a friend.

"Got it, but it's not a tracker. It's a flash drive." He held the small device up into the light to analyze it. Then, he grabbed his wand and confirmed that was the source.

Maggie plopped back down on the cot, stunned and speechless. What the hell had Dalton hidden in her stuffed animal? She thought back to his last visit. He'd given her Maggie Moo and another flash drive that contained paperwork and photos. He'd never told her he placed a drive in the toy.

Then her memory snapped back to when Dalton had given her the cow and USB drive. *If anything happens to me, take both of these to Trent. Let him handle the final arrangements.* He'd reminded her ad nauseam that she should always keep the cow close, and if *anything* ever happened to him, take it all to Trent. That he'd protect her. At the time, all that did was piss her off. In reality, Dalton was trying to tell her his secret without revealing it. *Oh my God, is this more of the missing information?*

"Maggie," Clarke barked. "Where did you go, are you okay? I've texted Trent. Hold on, sweetheart."

If Trent had been with her earlier, it would have been him who had to deal with that bad guy when the bullets started to fly. If anyone were hurt or killed, that could have easily been him, too.

She swallowed the panic that bubbled up inside her. She can't handle any more trauma. Tremors wracked her body.

Clarke's face hardened, his gaze intense. "Hey, don't pass out on me. Come on, I can tell you're a brave one. Keep talking. Do you know what's on this drive?"

She squeezed her eyes closed, forcing a deep breath into her system, then exhaled slowly. Her mind raced with how to handle this discovery. She wanted to tell Clarke, but she figured Trent should be there when they found out what was on that device. If this is what she thinks it might be, then Dalton trusted her to get it to the right people. Lives depended on it. She had what Talon had been looking for all along.

T RENT HAD FINISHED HIS team meeting earlier and had just signed out of the payroll system. When the emergency call blasted through the office, his heart stopped. *Shots fired at the Mill Creek Hotel, suspect armed and at large, one victim, GSW, paramedics dispatched.*

He stumbled and thought immediately of Maggie? He prayed to God Parker Lindholm, the FBI agent assigned to watch her, had been able to protect her. Trent wasn't sure what he'd do if she were killed on his watch.

Turning to Aimee, he snapped, "Is the victim male or female?"

She shook her head, a look of concern etched on her face. "I-I don't know."

He left the question hanging in the air between them as he ran from the building to jump into his truck. He slammed the gearshift into drive then peeled out into the street. Sirens blared behind him as every first responder headed toward the scene of the shooting.

Once he arrived, he parked his truck and dashed inside, heading straight for their room. When he entered the hallway, he knew that the attack was aimed at Maggie. Two employees stood in the hallway blocking the area a few doors ahead of his room. A mixture of sulfur and charcoal lingered in the air. A hard lump formed in his throat, and tightness constricted his chest.

He nodded at the workers as he passed, then steadied himself for what came next.

"Sheriff...Oh, God, this man. H-he died," Doug Pebbles, the owner of the hotel, stated in a distraught voice, tears staining his cheeks. "I-I tried to save him, but I couldn't. Help me. This guy kept repeating that Margaret King escaped."

Trent turned away and squeezed his eyes closed, needing to force a steady stream of oxygen into his lungs to regain his composure. Another agent had given his life. When Trent opened his eyes, his heart went out to Doug, who sat on the ground next to the lifeless body, clutching a bloody towel. Working to save someone's life, only to have them die, changed a person forever, something he knew firsthand.

He grabbed a bath towel from the bathroom and draped it across Lindholm's body. Then, he squatted next to Doug and said, "You tried; that's what matters."

"All I can think about is that I'm glad my wife and daughter were visiting her parents. And here, this poor man lost his life. How terrible is that?" Doug's voice cracked on the last word.

"What matters, Doug, is when it counted the most, you were here, trying to save him. It's human nature to protect the ones you love." Trent looked up when his deputy entered the room.

Lance smiled at Doug, then addressed his boss. "You taking lead on this one?"

Trent shook his head. "No, you've got this. I have to find Maggie. What have you learned?"

Lance held up his hand so he could listen to the chatter on his radio. After issuing a command, he turned back to Trent. "Sorry. The perimeter is secure. We also have several witnesses who are giving statements and descriptions of the man and woman who exited through this window." He pointed to the open window in their room. "I've already issued a BOLO on the suspect."

Trent pointed toward the hallway then guided them away from everyone. "The victim is an FBI agent. I need to call Special Agent in Charge Guzman to update him on what's happened and to see how he wants to handle this scene. In the meantime, keep the scene secure and keep me posted on anything you find. Be vigilant. I trust you implicitly to get the job done. I've got to focus on Maggie."

Trent's phone chirped with an incoming text. "Hold on a second, this could be Maggie." He looked at his screen and scowled. *Your package has been delivered safe and sound. You can retrieve it at the annex next to the library.*

What the fuck did that mean? It made zero sense, because he wasn't expecting any packages, and the library didn't have an annex. His face screwed up in thought as he reviewed the message. Holy shit! He *did* know who sent the encrypted message and what it meant, and he might just have to hug that bastard.

"Hey, Sheriff," another deputy announced as he approached Lance and Trent. "Two witnesses have reported that a woman fled the hotel and hitched a ride on a motorcycle."

Trent couldn't stop the smile that covered his face. His mood improved for the first time since the damn emergency call. "I've got to go."

On his way to Clarke's home, Trent dialed Guzman directly to update him on the latest, including what they found in Dalton's legal paperwork—the informant's name and the photos. More importantly, he told him what happened to Agent Lindholm and Maggie. Trent figured Guzman would want one of his agents working this scene.

When he pulled into Clarke's driveway, nerves formed in Trent's stomach. He couldn't think about anything else right now until he had Maggie in his arms. To verify for himself that she was unharmed.

Clarke stood inside the front doorway. "It took you long enough. I thought my clue might have proven too difficult."

Ah, yes, there was the man who irritated the shit out of him, but at this moment, he might just kiss the jerk. "I owe you a debt. How's she doing?"

Clarke jutted his chin for Trent to follow him inside. Once they both crossed the threshold, he bolted the front door. He studied Trent for a minute before answering, "Feisty, and she has guts, but she's in shock. We found something that's pushed her over the edge. Oh, and if she were mine, I'd also chew her ass for jumping on a motorcycle with a stranger."

"You're not exactly a stranger," Trent replied. "Where is she now?"

"I was when she hopped on the back of my motorcycle," he chided and motioned for him to follow.

Trent followed Clarke down a hallway toward the laundry room. Off to the side, a trap door lay open. Clarke pointed downward, then turned to head back to the kitchen. Trent appreciated that he was giving them some time alone.

When his foot hit the last step, and he had a chance to take in the small room, it helped to know that Guzman vouched for Clarke, and he stood on the right side of the battle lines. Holy hell, this room looked like a command center.

"Trent, you're here," Maggie said, her voice distant and gruff, right before she launched into his arms.

He pressed his nose into her hair and inhaled her scent of vanilla and oranges. Cradling her soft, warm body against his harder frame. He couldn't stop himself. He kissed her forehead, taking a few minutes to hold this precious woman who was safe and unharmed in his arms.

"Tell me what happened," he demanded in a soft voice.

She stepped back and fiddled with her fingers. "A man who claimed he worked for the hotel wanted to change a filter or something inside my room. When I refused, he kicked down my door and shot at me while I climbed out the window. Once I was clear, I ran toward the street. Luckily, I jumped on the back of Clarke's motorcycle, which brought me here. Is everyone all right?"

It took him a few seconds to respond because he hated telling her the truth, but he had no other choice. "Yes, Agent Lindholm was killed."

Her intake of breath had him reaching for her. "None of this is your fault. As harsh as it sounds, you were his job, and he performed it with honor and valor."

As she leaned against his body, the woman inside seemed a thousand miles away. Clarke descended the stairs and stood behind them.

"Well, his family may not feel that way. They won't get to hug that man again," she said in a flat voice. "Clarke, will you explain how your toys uncovered the flash drive?"

Trent reluctantly released Maggie and turned to face Clarke. "Another one?"

The big man explained his gadgets and how they found the hidden drive. When he finished with the rundown on his spy equipment, she turned to Trent and added, "I haven't looked at it yet. I wanted to wait until you arrived."

Clarke said, "I can leave you two alone to review the contents if that's better."

Trent pierced Clarke with a dire look while Guzman's assessment of him swirled in his head. His decision was made, and he nodded at the man. "No, stay. If this is evidence, we need to be careful with it. Can you open it for us?"

After a few seconds, Clarke pounded away on his keyboard, and the contents loaded. Trent didn't have time to analyze the details, but he'd seen enough to validate its legitimacy. "Can you copy it?"

"Sure, how many?"

"Just one, and I'll need you to store this for me. If something happens, we're counting on you to get this to Special Agent in Charge Guzman of the FBI directly—hand to hand. I'll send Noah this update tonight, but when I spoke to Guzman earlier about the situation with Agent Lindholm, he informed me that they're flying back from the Sudan mission tonight and would be in Boise tomorrow to meet in person.

"Understood, I'll guard it with my life," Clarke acknowledged. He made a copy, then moved it to a wall safe and placed it inside.

He returned to his workstation and flipped one of the monitors to a local channel. "It seems your dead man is already breaking news."

"Nothing gets past the reporters, does it?" Trent groused as he picked up Maggie's bag. "Thanks for everything, but we need to leave for Boise. Guzman has already made arrangements and has additional agents in route to meet us."

He stood and glanced at Clarke, giving him a quick nod of the head. "Again, thanks. And don't worry, what we saw down here tonight in your bat cave is a need-to-know basis."

"What room?" She smiled.

Trent offered her his hand, and when she took his, hers was ice cold. He motioned for her to lead as she climbed the stairs. Once he had her loaded into the passenger's side, he rounded the front of his truck and slid behind the wheel. When the engine roared to life, he blasted the heat to help her combat the shock overtaking her body.

Big, green, sad eyes stared at him. "I'm scared, Trent. So much could have been lost today."

"We're going to a new hotel with full security. One of the female agents on site has been tasked with purchasing a few essentials for you. After we arrive, you can check out what she purchased. If you need anything else, just create a list, and it'll be supplied."

Maggie stared out the window. "Is it safe to check in using our real names?"

"Nope, another agent has already checked us in under assumed names. We'll pick up those key cards in the supermarket's parking lot around the corner."

She didn't utter another word. She'd withdrawn, which he understood, but it also worried him because she'd been through so much. When he reached the market, he pulled into the lot and parked alongside the described vehicle. He met the agent outside and took the proffered keys and bags. After Trent placed them in the back of the truck, he turned back around and saw a face he hadn't seen since Dalton's funeral, not that they'd spoken that day. Ben Knight, one of the agents he worked with back in the day, was also tasked with investigating him.

Trent extended his hand to the man. "Ben, what are you doing here? I haven't seen you since…"

Ben accepted it in greeting. "I know, it's been too long. Can you believe we're getting another chance at Falcon? Guzman is sending me to take over the investigation in Mill Creek."

"That's great. I'll call my deputy, Lance Charles, to let him know you're coming."

"Appreciate it. Hey, and I'm sorry, man. I was just doing my job. I wanted to say this to you earlier but never got the chance. Also, I wish I had gotten to know you and Dalton sooner. His call shocked me. Losing him sucked."

Trent sucked in a deep breath and ran his hand through his hair. "I think we all have regrets from that day. Seeing you was good, but I need to get to the hotel."

When he jumped back inside the truck, tears stained Maggie's cheeks.

Slamming the truck into drive, he pulled straight out of the parking lot. The distance seemed to be growing by the second between them. Giving up on them wasn't an option, not when she made him realize they were better together. He would fight for their love, and every damn tomorrow he could get.

Thirteen

T RENT CLOSED AND LOCKED the door. The room looked like every other, except for the color scheme and prints on the walls. He put their plastic bags on the bed and turned to face Maggie.

"Go take a shower and get some rest," he said. "Tomorrow will be another long day. Maybe taking you to a safe house is the best plan. Just think about it."

She glared at him. "I don't want to go, and I can take care of myself. I proved that today. I want to see this through." She dug in the bag until she retrieved a toothbrush and paste. "What we need to do is put Talon behind bars. Talon is infatuated with me, so my involvement is critical if that supposed data doesn't work."

Trent fumed, letting his anger get the best of him. "Grow the fuck up. You were lucky earlier. Do you honestly think your survival today is because you possess skills that are comparable to that of a trained agent? He's a sadistic killer, and you're a schoolteacher."

"Really, Captain Obvious, that's your big revelation? Here's the kicker. I'm the object of his delusions, and I don't need your permission." She stormed into the bathroom. The door slammed behind her.

Fuck him, that was not how he wanted that conversation to go. Losing his cool and berating her wasn't part of the plan. He'd nearly lost his sanity when visions of what could have happened to her flashed in his head. He huffed out a deep breath and tugged on his hair.

When the bathroom door popped open, he swiveled around. Maggie stashed her items into the bag. She straightened and faced him. "I shouldn't have raised my voice, but here's the thing. The other day, when we talked about what happened with Dalton, you made me face a reality I hadn't thought about until that moment. You could have died that day with Dalton. Then I would have had to bury two men I loved." By the end, her face had softened, but the steel in her voice told him she wasn't backing down.

"Risk surrounds us no matter what. All you're doing is robbing yourself of your time with those you care about. Let me ask you one more thing, and then I'll drop it for now. Do you believe that if you had pushed Dalton away to minimize your risk, it would have prevented his death?"

She opened her mouth before snapping it shut. Her eyes narrowed, but she crawled under the covers instead of answering him. He stood there waiting. When only silence greeted him, he forced himself to prepare for bed. When he finished in the bathroom, he slid into his side and stared at the ceiling. His head swirled with ugly memories until he drifted into a fitful sleep.

"Do you have eyes on the shooter?" he hollered at Dalton.

"No! I think up in rafters. It's a fucking trap." He groaned, anguish tainting his every word. "Too late for me," he rasped out. "Did you call for backup? We're all alone here."

The calm voice of the operator filled his ears, "Nine-one-one. What's your emergency?"

"This is FBI Agent Trent Jacobs. I have one unidentified man presumed dead and an agent down. Send a bus and backup. Leaving line open to trace." He tossed the phone to the ground.

Slurred words whispered in his ear, "Promise me...you'll look after Maggie...keep her safe. You're the only one...don't trust...Moo..."

Trent jackknifed up in bed, sweat coating his body. He remembered another snippet. They weren't *alone* in the warehouse—he heard a second set of footsteps.

"Trent, what's wrong?" Maggie asked, her voice full of concern. She sat upright in bed, her hand cool against his warmed skin.

"I didn't mean to wake you."

"It's okay, did you have a nightmare? You were mumbling and breathing so hard." Her worry was genuine and heartfelt.

"Sort of, but I actually zeroed in on something I previously missed."

"What?" she asked in a guarded tone.

"Trust me, and don't worry about it now. Go back to sleep."

She hesitated for a minute before she rolled back over. It wasn't long before her breathing evened out.

First thing tomorrow, he'd call Noah to share his revelation and suspicion. He also needed Dalton's phone records for the week of his death to see if there were any calls to or from Ben. Noah would be pissed if his theory was correct, but he trusted him to keep this between them until he could verify his hunch.

THE BIG METAL CLOCK in the room filled the empty space with the metallic sweep of the second hand. Maggie's mood had worsened with each passing second. A huge hole had opened up in her heart and swallowed her whole. Her nerves had overtaken her while she alternated between bouncing her leg and twirling a section of hair around her finger. Last night, Trent presented a valid point—he knew the enemy better and she wasn't a trained agent.

Finally, the door opened, and Noah, Guzman, and Trent walked in. The three had stepped out to meet with the bureau's forensics team that had taken over the crime scene at the hotel. That didn't bother her because she'd heard enough to supply her nightmares for a lifetime. Trent used the next several minutes to review the latest developments. The bright fluorescent lighting in the small conference room highlighted the tension and exhaustion etched on everyone's faces.

"Sorry for the delay, Maggie," Guzman said as he sat. "I can't believe a stuffed animal concealed a flash drive all this time. It's about damned time we retrieved the data your brother gave his life for. Noah already has his team working on decrypting the individual files since we don't have the cipher. At some point, because I believe in my team, we'll be able to authenticate what is on that drive. My only concern is that the intelligence might be outdated."

That was a sucker punch to Maggie's gut. She hadn't thought about the information being time-sensitive. The door to the meeting room swung wide, and this time, three people she'd never seen before walked into the room.

"Perfect timing," Guzman said as he motioned for the group to enter. "These agents will be accompanying you and Trent to Mill Creek. Please meet Tina, Paul, and Robert. The other agent is Ben, who is already working at the crime scene with Trent's deputy."

"Nice to meet everyone." Maggie nodded at them.

"Maggie." Noah handed her a velvet jewelry pouch. "Inside is a pair of butterfly earrings. Each one has a GPS tracker inside. You can activate and deactivate it by pressing on the head." He demonstrated how to operate them.

She took the box and removed the earrings. "So, this is how you'll track me if I'm taken."

He sat up and turned his laptop around to show her the screen. "Put them on and activate the signal. I'll show you how it works. Since most women fiddle with their earrings occasionally, that motion will seem normal."

Trent turned toward Maggie. "The important part to remember is you can turn them on and off as needed because if you're taken, Talon's men will probably scan you and your belongings to see if you have any bugs or trackers."

Her stomach somersaulted with dread. "Can they get wet?"

Noah smiled and winked. "Good one, and yes, they can be fully submerged up to twenty-five feet. Also, your entire security detail, including Trent, will have access to this program."

Maggie nodded, not thrilled that she'd be the goldfish in the glass bowl. The next hour went by slowly as they covered the basics of moving and working with her security detail. She and Trent would be given an encrypted phone to relay the day's plans. Then, the team would be able to cover them organically while alternating coverage so patterns and faces wouldn't become obvious.

It didn't escape her notice that she'd been reminded at least ten different times during the last hour to activate the GPS tracker so the agents could monitor her every move. Guzman and Noah planned to work out of the Boise office for now. Noah had been tasked with reviewing satellite imagery of Mill Creek and the surrounding forest areas. The goal was to see if anything that wouldn't be normal traffic stood out.

Guzman leaned forward and folded his hand on the conference table. "We successfully stopped the shipment to South Sudan so I know we have Talon's attention. That said, there's no guarantee he'll act. Maggie, the plan will be to have you accessible to see if we can draw Talon out in the meantime. When we validate the data and if it's his account records, we'll seize his money and shut down his operations. At that point, we'll pull you out and move you to a safe house."

"But he would go free?" Maggie asked, her tone sharp.

"Yes, that's correct, but Falcon wouldn't be able to operate, and there is always a chance we'd capture him at a later date. Cases don't always end perfectly. Sometimes we have to take good enough."

Maggie bounced her gaze from person to person in the room. No one but her seemed to find that answer appalling.

Trent rocked back in his chair. "Are there any objections to me letting my deputies know we'll have undercover agents in town? That way, we can send my team out to surveil any areas we deem noteworthy. They can find anything with coordinates, and it'll look like normal route checks. They know this area well and can identify normal activity versus abnormal."

Guzman turned his attention to Trent. "No, that way, if the shit hits the fan, you can mobilize your team faster because they know the area. As a courtesy, I'm also updating the SAC in Salt Lake City."

"Good, that keeps my distant partners happy," Trent said.

"Now, I've got a surprise of my own," Guzman announced, smiling a little on the evil side. "Since we are so close to bringing this fucker down, I've authorized two deep cover assets to destroy one of Talon's operations bases before they disappear permanently. We'll have his full attention between the weapons shipment we intercepted and one of his operations center being destroyed."

"What's the plan to extract Maggie if everything goes to shit?" Trent asked.

"*If*," Guz emphasized, "a helicopter will be on call to pull her out and bring her to me. Once I have her, we'll fly immediately to the safe house."

She wanted to show everyone in the room that she was on board and ready to do her part, even if her insides quivered like gelatin. "All right, we have some bad men to catch."

The next hour was spent reviewing Mill Creek maps and the surrounding area. In between, she'd been updated on how the FBI handled the crime scene with respect to the media. The story the public heard came from the sheriff's office, keeping the bureau's participation a secret. The official story told is that two tourists, who were also staying at the hotel, had an altercation, resulting in one death. The investigation was still active, and the sheriff's office would release more information when available. The few guests who remained at the hotel were moved to the other side of the property, which gave the agents room to operate in the abandoned wing that was cordoned off.

When the meeting concluded, everyone had their assignments. She and Trent were to act normally and resume their activities so that if anyone was watching, their routines would appear normal. She hoped Noah and his team could break that code quickly because the safe house didn't seem so bad. Fear had a way of helping a person evaluate their skills, and she had zero in the kick-ass category.

S INCE RETURNING TO MILL Creek, normal was a relative term. Nothing felt natural, and her acting skills sucked. They had been back in town just over a week, and nothing had happened. Nada.

Clearly, being a third-grade teacher had its challenges and rewards, but this whole let's bring down the big bad guy wasn't the career for her. A door creaked, and she practically jumped out of her skin. She was losing her mind.

Tonight, she had plans to meet Aimee at Two Stepping, to listen to the band and dance. A part of her was looking forward to being out, but the reality of her situation dampened her spirits. The team spent the morning planning the comings and goings to ensure every angle was covered. She also had her bag packed for her other two contingencies where she'd be taken to the safe house—shitstorm or code-breaking. *Yeah, this is all totally normal.*

"Hey, how are you holding up?" Trent asked as he entered their room with a tray of iced teas.

"I detest that question. It's absolutely the worst one to ask someone because the answer is always downplayed or a complete lie," she snapped, disliking the bratty tone in her voice. He didn't deserve her ire, but who else could she vent to?

"Okay. I forgot how tedious the whole lie-in-wait process of an investigation could be. Being sheriff comes with a different set of challenges. It's hard to be on alert twenty-four/seven for the proverbial boogeyman who hasn't shown his head. For what it's worth, you're doing great."

Guilt racked her system. "I'm sorry, I'm just frustrated, and I shouldn't have attacked you."

"Trust me, I understand."

She glanced at the clock on the bedside table. "I better get ready to meet Aimee at Two Stepping." She slipped by him then closed the bathroom door.

Forty minutes later, she emerged freshly showered, her skin soft from her favorite cream, and a light dusting of makeup. Her outside looked good, but her insides were a melty mess of goo. An awkwardness had developed between her and Trent since they returned from meeting with the FBI in Boise. She missed the connection, and warmth, and camaraderie they shared. Solitude didn't hold much appeal, but she was scared of having her heart ripped out and shredded into a million pieces again. The other, what if he kept secrets from her again. Oh man, she rolled her eyes at the irony. Hadn't she just berated Trent for living by the what-*if* philosophy?

He whistled. "You look gorgeous."

The light blue sundress with the embroidered sunflowers on the bottom hugged her curves perfectly. The yellow high heels she wore accented her toned, smooth legs. She fell in love with this dress the day she and Annika had gone shopping. God, what was wrong with her? Maggie wanted to look gorgeous for him. Maybe she needed a timeout herself to get her damn head on straight.

"Thanks, and before you ask me, I'm wearing the butterfly earrings. You don't look so bad yourself," she added the latter hastily.

He'd changed while she was in the bathroom. His jeans molded to his body displaying his muscular legs. The black T-shirt he wore left nothing to the imagination because it fit him like a second skin.

"Aren't you supposed to be my personal protection? Where's a gun hiding?"

Trent barked out a laugh making his eyes twinkle. "That's a loaded question, but I'm always fully loaded for you. My weapon–that's in my ankle holster."

A prickle of awareness rooted low in her abdomen, heating her cheeks from his flirtatious comment. She found herself wishing this was a real date and not a make-believe one where he had to carry a gun because Falcon might make their move. Over the past few days, Trent had been transparent with every update from the FBI regarding her situation, whether it was unpleasant or not. They'd been a tight unit and she couldn't have asked for more from him. He wasn't a perfect man, but he was honest and dependable, and she had blamed him for being human when he'd bared his soul.

Two Stepping was packed tonight. After they arrived, Trent joined Lance and another agent at the bar. She knew they were monitoring the activity around them, but to any patron, it appeared they were engaged in friendly banter. She headed toward the table that Aimee had reserved for them.

She sat, not sure her legs would support her much longer. All this stress was causing her body to tremble. She leaned toward Aimee. "Hey, thank you for getting the email address for the school principal. I submitted my resume. I haven't told Trent yet, so keep this between us."

"That's great news. Now we can make this a regular outing," Aimee said, a smile plastered across her face. "How are you tonight?"

Maggie liked the sound of that and looked forward to moving. "I'm good, all things considered."

The band started their first set at seven-thirty, bringing the crowd's energy to the dance floor. The beat of the drums reverberated against her chest as one of her favorite songs played. As usual, Aimee bounced and swayed to the rhythm of the music in her seat. The girl loved music—that much was obvious, but why she wouldn't dance didn't make any sense to Maggie.

She raised her voice so Aimee could hear her over the music. "Let's dance."

Aimee shook her head. "No, thanks. You go, and I'll watch our table."

Maggie made a big pouty face. One of these days, she would get Aimee to the dance floor. She twisted and shimmied her way toward a group of women who were laughing and enjoying the music. When the first song ended and transitioned to a second and then a third, her stress and anxiety melted away while the music consumed her. Finally, when a slow song started, she thanked the small group for the company and headed back toward Aimee.

A bead of sweat trickled down Maggie's temple. She'd worked up a thirst, so she grabbed her water glass and took a long sip. "That was amazing. I feel so much better."

"Isn't this band good?"

"Yes, and I wish you'd shake your assets with me." Maggie winked.

Aimee shook her head but laughed. Maggie joined her. They were sharing a bit of gossip when a familiar face approached their table.

"Irene, you look amazing," Aimee said then scooted farther into the booth so Irene could sit.

"What are two of the town's most beautiful young ladies doing without dates for the night? Are the men of Mill Creek daft?" she asked disapprovingly as she took a seat.

Maggie smiled at the older woman. Irene certainly had a zest for life. She wore a pink cowboy hat, matching boots, a white and pink-checkered button-down shirt, and a jean skirt that fell below her knees. Her fashion sense fit her perfectly bold and confident. She reminded Maggie of her mother's carefree spirit, and she liked how she seemed to speak her mind.

"I think Aimee needs some dance lessons, or she's just being stubborn. I see her wiggling on the seat every time the music plays." Maggie smiled at Aimee, who scowled at her.

"Oh, I can teach you to dance. My husband, bless his soul, hated to dance but learned because I love to. Music and dancing are good for the soul."

"Maybe another time. I'm more about the music," Aimee answered.

Trent headed over from the bar with two iced teas and handed one to Maggie. "Thought you might be thirsty."

She took the cup and took a large sip. "You read my mind, thank you."

"Hey, Trent," a man said from just behind.

He looked up as the agent from the other day and Lance approached the table. "Glad you could join us. Ben, this is Maggie, Aimee, and Irene."

Maggie exchanged greetings with the others. The next song the band picked was a chart-topper. Once again, the dance floor exploded.

Trent snatched his phone from his pocket and glanced at the screen. "Maggie, I need to take this call. I'll be right over there." He pointed to the front entrance, then excused himself from the group.

When she nodded, he strode off. Her bladder chose that moment to alert her to head toward the restroom. She decided now would be as good a time as any.

"If you'll excuse me, I need to visit the ladies' room before I dance again," Maggie told the group.

"I need to hit the head, so I'll accompany you," Ben announced as he trailed behind her.

Great. Now, bathroom runs have to be monitored.

She navigated through the crowd to the back where the facilities were located. As she turned the corner, she smacked into three large men goofing around in the hallway. Big bodies enveloped her and blocked her view.

"I'll keep the hallway clear for a moment," a familiar voice said from behind her. *Ben Knight.*

A prickle of fear snaked down her spine. *Wait, what's happening? Don't touch me.*

"Sorry, lady," the biggest one said while he managed to back her up against the wall.

She had just regained her footing when the hardness at her back gave away. In its place, a cool rush of air washed over her. Arms wrapped around her body, followed by a sharp prick at her neck.

"Ouch," she bellowed, pushing away from the closest man.

She reached for her neck to see what had caused the pain. A second later, the three men turned and closed a door to a room she hadn't realized she entered. She'd been separated from the bar and anyone who could help her. The loud, pulsing music dulled. The strong smell of cleaning solvents mixed with laundry soap filled her nostrils. *Where the hell am I?*

She turned on her heels, looking for a way out. An instant prickle of foreboding slammed into her. Her chest tightened with the realization that trouble had found her. Big, black dots clouded her vision, and her head was heavy. Sheer panic constricted her air passage, causing a scream to lodge in her throat.

Instead, a pathetic squeak escaped, "Help." She swayed on her feet and collapsed to the floor. The last thing she saw was a pair of black boots.

Fourteen

T RENT PRESSED THE PHONE to one ear and his finger in the other. The *boom-boom-boom* from the bass reverberated against his chest. "Noah, I can't hear you. Repeat what you said."

"Check your phone. I've sent both Dalton's and Knight's records. There are zero calls between Agent Knight and Dalton the entire week. Dalton did not call him on the day of his death. You were right."

Trent cussed under his breath. *Holy shit.* "Ben's the double agent and probably the one who framed Dalton because he had found out." He'd heard two sets of footprints that day. He had to belong to one of them. "You have to tell Guzman about Ben."

Trent twirled on his heels, heading back toward the bar. "That fucker's inside right now. I have to get back to Maggie. We need to get her to the safe house."

"Be careful," Noah warned. "You don't want to tip him off."

Trent blew a strangled breath as he dodged two customers then reached for the door. His cellphone, in his other hand, vibrated with an incoming text. What flashed on the screen chilled his blood and stopped him in his tracks.

"No." Trent dropped his head, and a ragged plea tore from his lips.

He closed his eyes, trying to force the despair of the situation from his mind. This was far from over because Maggie had the trackers, and his woman was smart. They would find her. She just had to fight and survive to give them time to locate and get to her. He flew through the bar to meet the team in the back at the point of egress. When he arrived, the only agent not present was Ben Knight.

Noah called Trent, who answered the first ring. "I know about Maggie, and I'm pulling up satellite footage. Also, we figured out the cipher—it's a treasure trove. It provides the names of Falcon's accountant and operations manager. Guzman is already working with the judge to issue warrants for their arrests."

Trent watched the agents working the scene. He could hear Noah's fingers clacking away on his keyboard. "What about his finances?"

"Hold on a second, Trent." A pause. "I'm back. My team is working the money trail now—private accounts, shell corporation—it's a ton of data. From what we can tell, the best part is that he never changed one password or closed any accounts. Talon's arrogance is going to nail him in the ass. We're working on each one to validate, and seize his funds."

"Trent, we have access to the interior cameras. You want to check out the hallway while I check the outside views?" Tina asked, holding a laptop connected to the feeds.

Trent nodded at her, accepting the proffered PC. "Noah, I've updated my deputies. I need to go."

He put the workstation on the nearest flat surface. The interior camera in the hallway didn't capture much other than three large men and Ben Knight, who were long gone. The men hadn't allowed their faces to be captured, which also didn't surprise Trent. It appeared to be a pretty simple abduction because this feed didn't capture any interruptions or complications that he could see.

"I've got two vehicles, a truck, and van, pulling away from the bar spitting dust. Noah knows and is working the sky to find them," she said, then held up her phone to the team before taking the incoming call.

He had just finished texting his deputies the latest when she conveyed Guzman's directive the moment she disconnected. One agent needed to stay behind to survey the crowd to ensure one of Falcon's men wasn't doing the same. Guzman and Noah would pick up that agent after they landed.

Paul opened a small case containing six communication devices. They'd chosen to use their mobile devices in the bar. Everyone took a small earpiece and popped it into their ear. Tina motioned for Trent to take his, and then she held up four fingers, indicating to use channel four.

He inserted his comms unit after he set the right channel. He raked his fingers through his hair, gripping the short strands until it stung. "Has Maggie activated her tracker?"

"Negative, but I've found the two vehicles. A white van heading eastbound and a white pickup with a toolbox."

Son of a bitch. "That's the same description of the truck that dropped off the dog with the video."

"Okay, team, now that we're all on comms, we can communicate easier." Guzman's voice boomed in Trent's ear. "Agent Knight could be compromised. He is considered armed and dangerous, so arrest on sight and bring in for questioning."

Noah interjected, "I'll send the last coordinates to your phones. I'm going to see if I can continue tracking their movement because they are heading up the mountain

"We'll head toward the last known position, and we'll course correct if needed," Tina supplied. "Trent, you drive."

Paul and Tina followed Trent toward his truck. Robert would stay back as the SAC directed.

In seconds, they were flying down the road. Trent maneuvered the truck until he hit the turnoff for the dirt road. Tina, the agent sitting in the passenger seat, kept relaying their progress to Noah and working on her laptop.

"Six online and active," she reported as she nudged her glasses farther up her nose. "The three of us: Guzman, Noah, and Trent."

Her focus was glued to her cell phone or laptop while her slender fingers flew over the screen's surface nonstop. "Okay, Noah sent updated coordinates. Turn right at the fork in the road up ahead, Trent."

He nodded in her direction, then added for the team's benefit on comms, "The Forest Service maintains these roads. The farther we go, the more isolated the area, and road conditions will deteriorate because it's outside their routine maintenance. Meaning that van couldn't go too far, so I'm betting they'll dump the van and take the truck."

"On it," Noah said. "I'm looking for possible vehicle exchange points or somewhere to stash one out of sight."

Guzman's voice came over the comm devices. "What about places where a small plane or helo could land? They must be looking for or heading to an extraction point."

Trent thought about that question for a minute. "Airplanes, no, but there could be a few spots for a helicopter, especially if Falcon scouted and prepped an area beforehand. *Drones.* The area also has a few abandoned and family-owned mining claims and cabins."

Tina looked up and snapped her fingers. "I highlighted several mines and cabins on my map. I'll send that to Noah now."

"Has Maggie's tracking device come online?" he asked again, his patience running thin as time progressed. Out of the corner of his eyes, he saw Tina shaking hers.

"Noah and Guz's helicopter is landing in Mill Creek. They'll pick up Robert, who's now securing ATVs for us to use," she said.

He cursed and focused on the road ahead of him while he mentally went over this section of the forest. Somewhere out there was Maggie, but where? He hoped to hell it wasn't a makeshift landing zone, or they'd never catch up to her in time.

The next thirty minutes were the longest of his life as they headed toward the location Noah had given. As Trent arrived, the knot in his stomach expanded when he saw the thick grove of pine trees covering the area. Just back from the road, he spied the abandoned van, which he knew wouldn't produce one viable lead. The white truck was gone.

Agent Paul and Trent jumped from the truck. Weapons were drawn and at the ready as they slowly approached the van. The driver and passenger seats were empty, so they headed toward the back. Paul stood with his legs shoulder-length apart and his gun pointed at the two doors. Trent would open one on Paul's signal. When he nodded, Trent clutched the handle and pulled the door wide.

Ben moaned as he clutched his stomach. "Don't shoot, I'm unarmed."

"Put your hands up," Paul commanded. "We have Agent Ben Knight in the back of the van, with two GSWs to his stomach. We need medevac immediately."

Trent jumped in the back and checked Knight for weapons while Paul covered him. "He's clear, no weapons."

Tina appeared with a towel and first aid kit that she tossed to Paul. The agent lifted Ben's shirt and grimaced. "This isn't good, Knight. This is going to hurt like a bitch, but we have to apply pressure to slow down the bleeding."

Knight screamed and let out a string of curses. "Fuck, that hurts."

"What happened back there?" Trent asked.

"I was ambushed—"

Trent had zero empathy for the man who would most likely die of those wounds. Whoever shot Knight wanted to make sure he'd be dead, but in an excruciating way. Gut wounds were brutal.

"Bullshit, you're the dirty agent, and those guys were cleaning house when they shot you. The best thing you can do is tell us the truth. Guzman is already scouring your records and life. We know you set up Dalton. I know you were at the warehouse that day and that he never called you. We have the records to prove it."

He believed what he had said but exaggerated the bulk of the proof for affect.

Paul's gaze shifted to Trent. "And you found the intelligence Dalton had secured. Right at this moment, we're taking down Falcon."

Knight's eyes went wide, and he gasped. "My greatest mistake that day was assuming you were dead. I thought I handled the breach by killing Bart and Dalton. Then, when you arrived at the warehouse, I had to improvise."

"So, you figured you'd paint Dalton and me as dirty agents to cover your tracks by muddling the investigation that day."

"What can I say? Falcon pays better than the government."

The comms came to life with Guzman's voice, "Good work, we have proof that will clear Dalton's name, and it's time to read the Miranda Rights to Mr. Knight. If that piece of shit lives, then I look forward to him rotting in prison."

Trent agreed with Guzman wholeheartedly. He couldn't wait to tell Maggie that Dalton had been cleared. A promise he ended up being able to keep. Paul and Tina photographed the scene and worked on the report while Trent waited impatiently for Guzman, Noah, and Robert to arrive. He had to do something, so he called his team to get their impression regarding possible extraction points or hideouts. He agreed with the SAC that the plan had to be to fly them out of the area so that they would narrow down the possible locations if her tracker didn't come online.

MAGGIE'S HEAD POUNDED FROM a headache of massive proportions that raged against her skull. Her tongue was plastered to the roof of her mouth, like she had eaten cotton. She needed water to quench her thirst and ease the irritation in her throat. Her mind was cloudy as she tried to remember how she got there.

Men's voices penetrated the fog surrounding her brain, but she couldn't quite understand what they were saying. Fear made her skin crawl. What had happened? Everything slammed back into place at that moment, causing her stomach to clench. She'd been kidnapped.

Her eyes snapped open, but she couldn't see anything in the pitch-black room. A soft, lumpy mattress was under her. She inhaled deeply, trying to focus her mind, but she'd made a mistake as her lungs filled with dirt and dust. She tried to stifle a cough, not wanting to draw the attention of her kidnappers. Trent's warning flashed in her mind. *He's a sadistic killer, and you're a schoolteacher.*

He was right. She wasn't trained to handle these types of situations, so no time like the present to figure out her survival strategy.

God, she hoped guardian angels were real because she needed her big brother and parents to watch over her until Trent came to her rescue. The first surge of hope pulsed through her when she remembered the earrings. She clasped her earlobes to ensure she still had them and couldn't hold back the smile when she felt two butterflies. She pressed the small buttons to activate them. Now, she had a fighting chance.

The door to her makeshift prison banged open to reveal the silhouette of a man. Her previous thought escaped her because the boogeyman now stood before her. Tremors washed over her limbs as the big man walked close enough to grip her upper arm.

He hauled her to a standing position, then tugged her into a brightly lit room. The punishing throb of her heart made her head hurt with each pulse. The next thing she knew, the man pushed hard on her shoulders, forcing her to sit on a wooden chair in the middle of the empty room.

"Hello, Margaret King. I must say, you're even lovelier in person," a deep voice announced from somewhere behind her.

Her stomach churned, and she worried she might vomit on the man. That wouldn't be good, but it would be satisfying. A hand tangled in her long hair, causing her to flinch. A moment later, he wrenched her head back until her neck strained against the top of her spine. His blue eyes stared down at her. He surprised her because she wasn't expecting a handsome man, figuring he'd look like a monster.

"I heard you found Dalton's missing data." He released her hair and backed up so they could face each other.

She took in his appearance from head to toe. He wasn't as tall or muscular as the man who dragged her out of the darkened room. That man could have easily played football. This one was shorter but still in good physical shape. He dressed professionally and seemed to like his cologne because he had way too much on.

"Who are you?" Maggie asked.

"Ah, I apologize for the lapse in my manners. The lady would like an introduction." The man looked over her head to someone who stood behind her.

She twisted to find out if another person had entered the room. Ah, it was only Mr. Football. He stood with his feet apart and arms crossed over his large chest. A scowl turned his mouth down.

"That big fellow is my right-hand man, who you should never make angry. He can kill a person in so many fascinating ways. Really quite delightful. But I digress."

She figured the longer she kept him talking the better because it would delay whatever was coming next. "And you? Where are we? What do you planning to do with me? You have to know people are looking for me, right?"

"So many questions. I promise I'll answer each one, but we have some business first."

She tried to suppress the shudder that traveled through her body. God, what business did they have to do?

"What information did you find?"

"Name?" she fired back.

He closed the distance between them and grabbed her jaw with brutal force. She'd have bruises. He thrust her head upward so she could look him in the face. "I don't appreciate your disrespect or tone."

"Asshole," she spat back.

It barely registered that he'd released her jaw because her head snapped to the side from the impact of his backhand. Her mouth filled with the metallic taste of blood.

His mouth twisted into an ugly smile, and he waved a finger in front of her face. "I love your passion. That will keep me on my toes for years to come. You may call me Michael. Now, I do not enjoy hurting you or being disrespectful. I wasn't raised that way. My mother would be horrified to know I hit you. If you persist, though, in pissing me off, I think you'll regret that decision. I have a temper, and that's something you don't want to tempt. Tell me what you found."

She sucked in a shaky breath. "Would your mother like that, you've kidnapped me?"

His smile transformed his face. The handsome and sane-looking man had returned. That just creeped her out even more, if that were possible.

"My mother would not. She was a loving and beautiful woman before my father killed her. He accused her of cheating on him with no proof, and his accusation was incorrect. He took her life because he was a jealous and crazy man. He took my beloved mom away from me, and I never forgave him."

His entire body radiated his pain, and his face hardened into an ugly expression.

"I'm truly sorry. That must have been so hard on you."

"Yes, it was, but I got my revenge. My father was my first kill and probably one of the most satisfying."

Her eyes went wide, and she covered her mouth.

"So, Miss King, or should I say, soon-to-be Mrs. Mason. I've finally found a woman my mother would approve of, and you're Dalton's sister. Certainly, it's a win-win for me, but imagine if he were alive today to know you're mine. We will court and won't marry until you're ready. You will never be able to leave me, and if you try to, I'll have to lock you away. Just know that my patience does have a limit. Now, tell me what information you uncovered."

Hot tears streamed down Maggie's face. Why hadn't she forgiven Trent? He was the man she wanted to marry. Deciding that upsetting Michael wouldn't be in her best interest, she answered his question, "A flash drive, but I've given it to the FBI. I don't know what's on it, and it was encrypted."

"Waltzer, take her back to the room and prepare her," Michael said.

A cold sweat covered her body, and her blood rushed through her veins. What the hell did that mean?

The big man, Waltzer, escorted her back into the bedroom. "Remove your jewelry and shoes and place them here, " he said, pointing to a spot on the floor.

She did as he asked, hoping she wouldn't accidentally turn off the tracking devices when she removed the earrings. *Please don't ask for my clothes.*

He nodded when she complied. "Turn around and put your hands behind your back." A piece of rope wound around her wrists at the small of her back, securing them in place. He secured the other end to the headboard when he finished tying it tight.

She heard his heavy footsteps retreat then the door snicked, sealing her into the darkened room again. He'd given her enough length to move around a little, so she sat on the edge of the bed and cried. If Trent didn't find her quickly, she worried she'd never see him again.

THE STARS SHINED BRIGHT under the moonless night as Trent waited for updates. In any other circumstance, he'd loved to lie next to Maggie in the bed of his truck while they searched for various constellations. She would have enjoyed the view, and he would have found several interesting ways to enjoy both the twinkling lights and her luscious curves.

He'd happily give up his future to get her back safe and sound. The crunching of tires over the rocks and dirt combined with the grind of metal against metal reached his ears. Finally, the rest of the team had made it to their location.

Before the truck stopped completely, the passenger door flew open, and Noah hopped out with his laptop in hand. "Maggie's tracker's active. I'm pinging her location now. Coordinates have been sent to your phones."

No words had ever sounded sweeter to Trent's ears. Noah stood next to Trent, placing his laptop on the tailgate. A burst of restless energy surged through Trent and with it, a prickle of hope. The entire team assembled around Noah. The wind picked up, rustling the branches on the pine trees, which produced an eerie howling sound. Tina, who still sat cross-legged in the back of the truck, moved items around to weigh down the paper maps.

"I've cross-checked with a topography map while the satellite repositions to these coordinates. This ridge could accommodate a helicopter landing, and it's a quarter-mile away from this cabin." Noah poked his computer with his index finger.

More chatter burst out as plans and ideas formed. Trent appreciated how this team broke down each task and associated risk as they quickly formulated a strategy. He missed the action of being an agent, but his favorite part had always been analyzing the information to develop and implement that plan. A well-prepared team meant an efficient and successful operation.

Guzman approached the team, clutching a satellite phone. "We've got a green light to proceed. The warrants have been issued. I don't want to squander this opportunity. We have the element of surprise on our side. Our goal—apprehend and arrest as many as we can and secure Maggie. Let's hear your plans."

After several minutes, all information had been shared and the mission tweaked one last time. Since they had to cover a bit of distance, it was agreed upon to use the ATV's until they were about a mile and a half out. The good news was that the heavy winds developing blew in the opposite direction of the cabin, which would help mask the noise from the off-road vehicles. Noah would send up a drone to provide aerial support as they progressed. Each agent busied themselves with grabbing weapons and ammunition and donning tactical vests from a crate that came with Guzman.

"Stay safe, everyone," Guzman commanded as he strapped on his vest and checked his weapons. "Let's bring back Margaret King, and I want those assholes in cuffs."

Noah tossed a set of keys to Trent. "Grab what you need from the crate and put on a vest. I'll ride with you while you drive. You know this area best."

Twenty minutes later, the team arrived at the designated spot, where they would begin their ascent on foot toward the cabin. When the last vehicle parked under the cover of the ponderosa pines, Guzman huddled the group to reiterate the objectives and scope of the operation. After one more comms check, the coordinated two-man teams trekked toward the cabin. The initial strategy was to secure the premises from three sides since the fourth was the ridge. Noah would stay behind to provide communication and aerial support while watching their backs.

Robert approached Noah, who had already opened the black case he had carried with him. The case contained a drone capable of thermal imaging. "Ready to launch?"

He nodded and sent the quadcopter into the air, thumbing the remote. "I'll sweep the forest, then head to the cabin to take a peek."

Trent fell in line behind Guzman, who moved swiftly up the steep terrain. Trent's head swiveled right and left as he surveyed the land, scanning for potential danger. It was the threat of encountering

Talon's men, mercenary soldiers, that worried him. A fight like that could get ugly and stop them from getting to Maggie promptly.

"Not seeing any action in the woods. Now, heading toward the cabin. Tracker stationary," Noah rattled off.

"Stay alert and radio when in place," Robert directed.

Trent's lungs burned as he pushed himself harder and faster up the unstable terrain. Their night vision goggles illuminated their path without lighting up the whole area. The howl of the wind made conversation difficult, and the sway of branches and bushes kept catching his peripheral vision. The temperature dropped even further as the night transitioned into the wee hours of the morning. An occasional movement or sound from nearby animals added to the ominous environment.

"Tracker just went offline. The cabin area is active. I have four men outside, with an unknown number inside. No eyes on Maggie," Noah reported.

Trent cussed under his breath. *Please let her be here and safe.*

He forced a deep breath into his lungs, making himself focus on the here and now. That was the best way to help her. After several tense minutes, he followed Robert behind a big cluster of brambles and knelt beside him. He told his team they were now in position, and no activity was at the rear of the cabin. Of course, they were still too far away to hear specific conversations.

"A fifth has joined the men in the front yard and on the porch. All are heavily armed. One appears to be on a phone, and another is on a computer," Tina said. "Hold on, the fifth man is heading back inside the cabin."

"The money in Falcon's accounts has been seized," Noah said.

"A helicopter is inbound, and it's not ours," Guzman interjected. "ETA fifteen minutes. Things are going to get interesting and really damn quick."

"The four men in front are heading toward the back. They've grabbed bags off of the porch. An educated guess, I think our window has arrived," Tina said.

One shot penetrated the night air, causing the hairs on Trent's neck to prickle. A second later, chaos erupted.

"Move, move, move," Guzman shouted.

Trent snapped up and sprinted toward the back of the house. Chaos erupted, making it difficult to hear the comm chatter. When he reached the wooden structure, he plastered his back against it. Guzman took cover behind a bush just off the corner of the cabin. He dropped to his knees and fired off three shots in rapid succession.

Trent popped out from the corner and squeezed off two rounds, hitting his mark. His heart beat wildly, but his training kept his actions steady. He advanced to peer around the corner. His gaze swept left and right, taking in everything around him.

"Do you have eyes on Maggie?" he rasped out.

"Agent down. Agent down!"

An eternity passed before he heard the next update on the radio. "Negative. Trent, you need to clear the cabin."

A roar of anger shot through his system, focused on taking out whatever threat stood between him and Maggie. There was no room in his head for fear so he locked it down. He pressed his body against the frame outside the front door and knelt. Twisting the knob, he eased the door open to analyze the scene. What he saw almost stopped his heart. A man stood in front of Maggie with a gun aimed at her head.

"Report," Guzman demanded.

Trent ignored him. He inhaled a deep breath, then exhaled slowly, aiming at his target until he'd zeroed in on his shot.

Fifteen

MAGGIE TUGGED AT HER restraints, trying to wiggle her hands free. Her reward for those failed attempts was raw and irritated skin that burned. The thump of footsteps against the wooden floor echoed louder as they approached her door. The only light she had was the thin strip between the floor and the bottom of the door. Her chest tightened more with each passing minute because she knew her time was running short.

The door burst open, the light blinding her again as her eyes struggled to adjust. Waltzer untied her wrists from the headboard but left her hands bound behind her back as he dragged her into the main room.

"Sit," Michael commanded.

Maggie plopped down in the chair placed in the center of the room. No reason to escalate the situation. Calmer heads prevailed. Her father had always used that saying when she and Dalton fought. Please let her rescuers arrive soon.

A wicked knife held in Waltzer's beefy hand flashed in front of her face. When he disappeared behind her and cut off her restraints, she exhaled. The moment she flexed her arms to get the blood flowing, pinpricks of pain danced along her arms up to her shoulder.

She stretched her arms over her head then removed a few wayward strands of hair from her face. She didn't want to miss one moment of her horror show. She stifled the laugh caught in her throat at that ridiculous thought. She'd actually preferred the other room, even with the restraints, now that she was sitting alone with Michael. God, she was losing it.

"We need to get rolling. The sun will be up soon," Waltzer said before he disappeared out the front door.

Michael approached Maggie until his legs pressed against her knees. A chill vibrated down her body at his blatant invasion of her personal space.

"Where are you taking me?" she asked, trying to add some sand back into her rapidly depleting hourglass if she could get him to talk.

"To my home, of course. You'll be safe there and free to roam about the house and grounds. You'll be comfortable at my estate, and you won't be a prisoner there."

"You said we won't marry until I'm ready. What if it takes me a very long time?"

"I'm not going to force you, but I will be courting you. I'm a gentleman, and we'll take as much time as you need."

Maggie drew in a shuddering gasp. This man was delusional. At the end of the day, she'd be his prisoner even if she weren't wearing handcuffs or locked behind a door.

Michael grabbed a lock of her hair, twisting it around his hand. Her scalp prickled from the tension, and she worried he might kiss her. Without warning, he pulled her head to the side and plunged a needle into her neck. "Your hair is so silky and smooth. Don't worry, when you wake up, we'll be on the plane heading home."

A rush of warmth traveled down her spine. Her vision blurred, and her head went fuzzy. Not this again. She couldn't pass out. How would she report back to Trent everything she learned or heard while she was with this horrible person—when he found her, and he would find her.

Waltzer slammed the front door. "What the fuck, Talon? Have you lost your goddamn mind? I've just heard from a pal of mine that you hired a rival, who failed to try and kidnap her a few days ago."

Holy shit! Michael was Talon. She'd assumed but hadn't known for certain until this moment.

Michael whirled around to face him. "You made it clear you disagreed with my interest in Margaret. Since I'm the boss, and not you, I found someone who didn't have a problem with my order."

"Well, that guy f-f-failed." Maggie slurred her words a little from the drug in her system. "I'm just s- s- saying…It seems Mr. Scarypants over th-there m-m-may have been the better choice."

Waltzer made a noise in the back of his throat. His eyes narrowed into tiny slits. "I never thought I would see the day that your erratic behavior and lapse in judgment would cost you everything. The difference between us is I'm loyal to my team and won't put them at risk for your stupidity."

The *whoop-whoop* of the helicopter getting closer made it hard to hear. Maggie tried to keep her eyes open.

Waltzer smiled at Talon while he removed his gun from a holster buckled at the front of his shirt. He aimed it at Michael. "Your accountant just left a frantic message that most of your accounts show zero balance. It seems that the agent did get the goods. Maybe you should have changed the passwords. Since you can't pay for my services, consider this my resignation. I warned you about arrogance."

Waltzer walked backward, keeping his eyes on Talon as he exited the cabin.

"Fuck," Talon roared, reaching for his gun and firing a round into the ceiling.

Her body shook from fear, now it was just her and Talon and he was beyond pissed. Once again, she pried her eyes open to see him pointing a gun at her head. *I guess the wedding is off.*

Guilt swamped her system when she realized she'd never be able to tell Trent how she felt—that she did want forever with him. Her eyelids snapped shut like a steel door closing. The muscles in her body stopped working. She tried to move but failed as her mind floated into the black abyss.

"CLOSE YOUR EYES, MAGGIE. Now!" Trent hollered. Her head rolled to the side then bounced straight down with her body as she hit the floor.

The man pivoted on his feet, aiming his weapon at Trent. The second he faced him squarely, Trent fired his gun.. His trajectory was up, and he hit the man in the forehead with one shot.

Trent darted to Maggie and swept her into his arms so he could hold her body, but her legs were still on the ground.

"I have Maggie. She's alive but unconscious. We need to get her to a hospital," Trent said. "Hey, I'm here. You're going to be fine," he whispered into her ear.

Tina came up alongside him. "I need to snap some photos of the area and Maggie. I found this syringe. Let me dust it for prints. Afterward, I'll put it in an evidence bag so the hospital can test the substance they injected in her."

"We apprehended Falcon's helicopter," Noah said. "Two men have been taken into custody. The paramedics should be landing up there in five minutes."

Robert entered the cabin and surveyed the scene. "Who's this guy?"

"I don't recognize him, but I hope this is Talon. When Maggie wakes up, she might be able to tell us if they used names. I'm pretty sure the other men were Falcon's mercenary team." Trent carefully removed his arms to lay Maggie on her back to catalog every bruise, scrape, and cut he found.

"I've got you, baby," he said, holding her hand.

"I'm guessing the men who escaped won't show up at a clinic or hospital to seek treatment for a gunshot wound. I know I tagged one," Robert said as he slipped on gloves to help process the scene for evidence.

"Since they are likely to know medical centers have to report a GSW, I'm sure they have a doctor or clinic on their payroll who's off the grid to fix their wounds," Trent replied, rubbing his thumb across the back of Maggie's hand.

Guzman walked toward the group, raising his voice to be heard over the approaching helicopter, "You accompany Maggie to the hospital. Let us know how she's doing and when she wakes. We'll need to get her statement." He squeezed Trent's shoulder. "I'll also need your weapon and formal statement."

He nodded. He knew the drill. After removing the clip, he emptied the chamber before he placed both in an evidence bag.

Guzman thumbed the comms unit. "Anyone have eyes on Noah? He's not responding. Trent, I'll see you at the hospital after we wrap up everything here. Keep us posted."

W HITE HALLWAYS AND THE smell of antiseptic that permeated the walls of every hospital never seemed to change. A flood of memories poured into his mind. He sat waiting for an update on Maggie. Every minute without an update seemed like an hour's worth of time. He'd tried calling Guzman to see if they had an update on Noah. He was concerned about his friend. It wasn't like him to not check in, but maybe his comms unit had failed.

"Mr. Jacobs, Ms. King's been transferred to a room, and she's asking for you." A nurse approached with a warm smile on her face. "If you'll follow me, I'll take you back."

He shot to his feet. "Yes, thanks."

He wanted to ask how she was doing but knew better than to waste his breath. He'd been waiting for two hours without a word. His apprehension skyrocketed when he entered the door into Maggie's private room. Her face was pale, with bruises marring the delicate flesh around her jaw. She looked uncomfortable, and that scared him the most.

"Hey, baby, how are you feeling?" He moved to the side of the bed and, with care, clutched her hand. He had to be connected to her in some way. He didn't want to overstep or hurt her, but her soft skin pressed against his grounded him.

A tear fell before she placed her hand on top of his. "I was so scared. I-I thought I would never see you again."

"Me too, but you were damn brave. I will always be here for you."

Her lip quivered, and she whispered in a rough, throaty voice, "That's what gave me hope. I knew you'd find me. I'm so sorry...I should have listened to my brother and called you to help handle his arrangements, and maybe you would have figured all this out sooner.

Trent couldn't stand the distance. He had to hold her until he felt her heartbeat against his own. He turned, sat on the hospital bed, and put his arm around her. "No, you can't blame yourself. You taught me that, and the only people to blame are those who kidnapped you which includes Agent Ben Knight. He was the dirty agent and killed Dalton. He even confessed that he planted the evidence, so Dalton's name has been cleared."

"That's great. Does Guzman know?"

"Yes, he heard the whole confession."

"How are you feeling?"

She snuggled deeper into his embrace. When she sat back, Trent reluctantly let her go but refused to stop touching her. Instead, he laced their fingers together.

"I'm fine, other than being drugged twice and a few bruises. Oh, and I rubbed my wrists raw, trying to get out of the bindings."

Trent's jaw clenched. "Every one of those fuckers should be dead for hurting you."

A man in his early thirties wearing a white coat entered the room. "Good morning, I'm Doctor Thazle. I have some updates to share. Are you okay with me proceeding, or should your friend wait outside?"

Trent hated being called a friend. He would prefer to be her husband.

Maggie extended her hand. "This is Trent Jacobs, and it's fine. As long as it's good news, that ends with me being discharged."

The doctor gave Trent's hand a brisk shake, then he returned his attention to Maggie. "I'll end the suspense. No discharge. I want you to stay overnight as a precaution. If all goes well, which I assume will be the case, you'll be released tomorrow morning. Other than the cuts and bruises, you're in good health. The toxicology report came back on the syringe sample. You were injected with a large dose of lorazepam, but that shouldn't cause any lasting effects other than some sleepiness. Do you have any questions for me?"

"No, thanks, Doctor," she answered and smiled. When the doctor left, she pouted and huffed. "Damn, I wanted to go home and take a shower."

He winked at her. "I could always give you a sponge bath."

Her laugh eased some of his tension, but he still needed to debrief her on what had happened. "We have to prepare an official statement, so are you ready to tell me what you witnessed? I'll relay this information to Guzman, so you don't have to repeat it. He might have additional questions later, but we can get the initial reporting over and out of the way."

When she agreed, he activated a voice memo app on his phone to record everything. He had her state her name and birthdate for the record. Then, he conducted the interview for Guzman, which he'd forward to him afterward.

"Agent Knight escorted me to the bathroom, then I'm positive I heard him say, 'I'll block the hallway.' Three large men circled me in the hallway. The next thing I knew, I felt a prick in my neck and awakened in a cabin."

When she finished, Trent could barely sit still. She'd actually met Talon and his right-hand man, Waltzer. "Would you look at a picture to identify him?"

"If I have to. I don't really want to see him again. He told me how his father killed his mother. Then he killed this father. I think he said it was his first kill. He wanted to marry me and considered me some kind of trophy because I was Dalton's sister. His real name is Michael Mason."

Trent showed her the picture of Talon on his phone, relieved when she nodded to confirm that he was the man he'd shot.

Trent filled in the gaps for her. "I killed Talon. Ben Knight died after we found him from two gunshots to the stomach. In total, three men were injured, but they escaped with the other three men who were at the cabin. Those men are gone for good or, as we call them, ghosts in the night."

"Is everyone else okay?"

"Noah hasn't checked in, but the team is looking for him. Paul took a round in his thigh, a through and through, so he'll heal quickly."

"Good, I'm relieved no one was seriously injured, and I hope we hear good news about Noah. Oh, I also learned that Waltzer wasn't behind my first attempted kidnapping. He and Talon fought about it right before he resigned."

"That's interesting, but you need to rest. Do you mind if I call Guzman and update him on everything you just told me?"

"No, but don't leave. I don't want to be alone."

"I'm not going anywhere. You're stuck with me tonight."

Trent rang Guzman, who answered this time on the first ring.

"Everything okay with Maggie, Trent?" Guzman asked the *whoop, whoop* of helicopter blades in the background.

"Yes, the doctor's keeping her overnight for observation, but she should be released tomorrow. Any news on Noah?"

"Yes, he's going to be fine. He took a round high in his chest on his right side. Missed everything important, but his lung collapsed. He's in surgery now, but the doctors assure me the prognosis is good."

"What happened?"

"The men who fled backtracked and ran into his position. One of the men took his comms so they could hear all our updates. Noah said they could have easily killed him but didn't."

"Okay, how long will he be here?"

"I don't know yet. I'll have him contact you once he's awake so you can talk to him. Let Maggie know we seized all of Falcon's money that we know about, and we arrested his accountant and operations manager. I'm sure a few more will be arrested in the next few days. Murder and treason charges should motivate one of them to flip and give us more in exchange for clemency."

When Trent disconnected the call, he turned and winked at Maggie. "This has been a good day."

"Wow, that's great news. So, is this over? Can life go back to normal?" she asked with a yawn.

He wanted to say no, she had to stay with him, but that would be a lie. "Yes, your life can resume without tails and babysitters, as you called them."

She smiled at him, her eyes drooping. "Trent, we need to talk."

He pressed his finger to her lips when she tried to continue. "Not tonight, you're exhausted. Sleep now. We can tackle whatever you want tomorrow. The important thing is we're both safe."

Her smile faded with her expression. When her breathing evened, he sank into the chair. Sleep would help her heal the most. The woman he loved was next to him, albeit in a hospital bed, banged up, but alive.

MAGGIE AWAKENED TO A dark room and grimaced. The soft sounds of Trent's snores comforted her while she rested and listened. She'd slept on and off throughout the night, enduring the hourly nurse visits to check vitals as they completed their rounds. A subtle scent of flowers drifted to her nose. At some point, someone had dropped off a beautiful arrangement.

The morning flew by as she prepared for her discharge. The doctor had signed off, and Maggie had just finished reviewing the paperwork with the nurse.

Trent had volunteered to get her some clothing so she didn't have to wear scrubs. Now, all that separated her from freedom was a wheelchair and an escort to the curb. She refused lunch when the trays were delivered. She wanted to eat real food and be ready to roll as soon as her chariot arrived. A person could only take the smell of antiseptic for so long.

He insisted on lifting her into the front seat and fastening her seatbelt. When the truck hit the highway heading toward Mill Creek, she took a deep breath. She rolled down the window and inhaled the warm, pine-laced breeze. The blue sky, dotted with puffy white clouds, made her smile because yesterday she didn't know if she'd ever see such a sight again.

She couldn't wait to eat; she was starving and already knew what she wanted for dinner right after she took a long, hot shower. "I forgot to ask you—who brought the beautiful flowers?"

"Guzman did when he stopped in to check on you before he flew back to DC."

Maggie groaned. "I don't even remember that. Please send a text to thank him. The arrangement is beautiful. How's Noah?"

"Will do. He's doing well and will be discharged within a day or two. Then, once he's cleared, he'll return to DC. I'm going to meet him for lunch before he leaves. I want to see him off. I also want to thank him for his help in keeping a particular woman who is precious to me safe. I owe him greatly, and I'll pay whatever price he names." Trent smiled.

That statement shouldn't make her insides quiver, but it did. He was honorable, noble, and loyal; a very potent combination. For the rest of the ride, she used the time to gather her thoughts. She had to tell him she forgave him and that he was right—pushing him or Dalton away wouldn't have kept them safe. She'd made her decision. It might not always be easy, but she didn't want to live without Trent.

Trent turned onto a street right before the hotel.

"Where are we going?"

He glanced at her and grinned. "I'm taking you home. No more hotels because my roof is finished."

Happy energy zapped through her system. When they arrived home, he insisted on carrying her to his bedroom and placing her down on the center of the bed.

"I thought a bath might feel good," he said. "While you're soaking, I'll head into town and get some food. What would you like?"

"No." She knelt on the bed and held out her hand. When he accepted hers, she tugged him onto the bed. "Circle of Secrets," she said.

He followed her and grasped her hands. "Okay, I'm ready."

"I need to get this off my chest. I forgive you, Trent. I was mad at you for your omission, but mostly for cutting me out of your life. Not forgiving you was my anger talking. Just don't do that again. We have to be able to communicate. If something happens to you, I want to support you. We must promise each other that withdrawing isn't the right way to handle our problems. I love you. You were right. Pushing away those you love only robs you of the time you have with them. It doesn't protect them. Here, I made you face your fears but hid from mine. I'll always be worried that the worst might happen—that's my baggage, but I can't stop living my life."

"Not telling you about any of it felt wrong, but that's part of the job. Keeping the news about me from you was selfish, and I made the wrong decision. My biggest regret is that I should have checked in on you before, during, and after Dalton's funeral. There is no excuse for that. I can promise you I won't push you away again." Trent's expression was soft and earnest.

She squeezed his hand. "It took us a little bit, but we figured it out in the end."

"Earning redemption for my errors and being able to avenge Dalton's death was a gift I never thought I'd receive. I don't know that I deserve you, but I do love you."

"I know, just like I might freak out if you take an unnecessary risk. I'm pretty sure old habits and fears die hard."

"Well, let's agree to retire you from being a junior agent. Once is enough for me to last a lifetime."

"I love you, Trent Jacobs."

"I love you, too. What are your plans now? Will you be heading back to Dallas? My life is here since I'm the sheriff, but I'm willing to try a long-distance relationship if that's what you want."

Maggie shook her head and smiled. "Dallas hasn't felt like my home for a while, and now that creepy people put bugs in my apartment, I'm done with it. Actually, I plan to move to Mill Creek. My boyfriend is here, and the food is amazing, and I've met some really nice people. It seems like a perfect place to start a new chapter of my life."

She loved how Trent's smile widened. "I see, and what are you planning to do here because twiddling your thumbs has never been your thing. Can you work remotely?"

"Yes, I could if I wanted to continue being a freight auditor. Although, I'm ready to teach again. I discovered through the grapevine that Mill Creek Elementary has an opening for a fourth-grade teacher. Aimee helped me update my resume and got the principal's email address, so I applied. I emailed it while we were fighting crime and defeating bad guys."

"You are my superhero. And that news just made my life because I like having you in it twenty-four-seven."

She beamed a smile at him. "So, I guess we're an item."

Trent's snort of laughter made her giggle. "Hell yes, we are, and I'll even love you when you're old and gassy."

Maggie's laughter zipped through their small room. Every unspoken feeling sizzled deep inside, making her giddy. "Well, I'll love you when you have no hair and big ears."

He hauled her into his arms. The fear of what could have happened melted away, leaving behind all the dreams she had for their future. She and Trent had a lifetime of memories to make, and that started tonight. Life didn't come with a guarantee, but she could pledge her love to Trent and enjoy every moment they had together. Her family might not be there to be a part of this new chapter, but she knew they watched from above.

Dear Reader:
Thank you for reading *Trent's Redemption*.
Are you ready for Clarke and Aimee's story? Let the saga continue in *Hidden Identities*.
Turn the page for a sneak peek.
XO-Bailey

Enjoy this sneak peek of

HIDDEN IDENTITIES

Book 2 in the Mill Creek Mystique romantic suspense series

One

THE PULSE FROM THE beat of the music vibrated down Aimee Lang's spine as endorphins flooded her body. Memories of dancing with her father filled her head while lyrics from a popular western song echoed through her ears. She shimmied against the vinyl seat of the booth, longing to join her friends who were on the dance floor.

Friday Fresh was her favorite event at Two Stepping Bar and Grill because they showcased local bands the second Friday of every month. Listening to up-and-coming performers of all types ranked high on her list of favorites, a cathartic experience allowing her to support artists who took risks to share their love of music.

She loved music almost as much as she enjoyed making up stupid little moves and dances. Her father had shared his eclectic love of music with her, and together they'd danced their way through life. To most, their moves had been pathetic, perhaps even silly, but to them, choreographed masterpieces.

A giggle escaped her lips until the warmth encircled Aimee's heart from those memories began fading. When would she stop torturing herself by remembering the past? That life had ended; now she had to focus on the present.

A prickle of awareness washed over her body. Aimee inhaled, moving her neck from side to side. Her gaze scanned the crowd until she saw the hulking man with all his muscles who appeared to be casually leaning against the wall, listening to the band. Clarke Dragoon was anything but casual and pushed all her buttons, from his overbearing personality to his rugged good looks. He'd won over the residents of Mill Creek when he'd helped her friend, Margaret "Maggie" King, out of a perilous situation not long ago, but Aimee had to keep her distance, even if it grew harder every day. Since she couldn't trust her decision-making skills toward men, it was easier to avoid romantic entanglements altogether. She would not make the same mistake twice.

What she wanted more than anything else was to break a damn sweat on the dance floor. To stop observing from the sidelines while everyone else got to enjoy their life—but that was the point. Now, her job was to embrace a new existence and not fall into any norms of the past.

Warm air circled around her body from all the activity surrounding her. Maybe she could allow herself an hour, an amalgam of her old and new self. How much trouble could that cause? That thought rolled around in her head while her heart beat against her chest in excitement. Who would even know?

"You okay, Aimee?" Maggie asked, a frown marring her face, but concern radiated from the depths of her big green eyes.

Aimee hated all the secrets, but that burden would squarely sit on her shoulders until she died. "I'm fine, just tired from a long week."

"I don't know about you ladies, but I'm parched from shaking my derrière," Irene quipped as she approached the table.

Laughter erupted around Aimee at Irene's comment. That woman had a heart of gold, but that didn't mean this petite woman in her late fifties with those beautiful blue eyes and long white hair was a pushover. Neither was Maggie. She fought for the people she loved, but her charm came from her subtlety. There was no doubt Aimee had been lucky in the friendship department since moving to Mill Creek. Both women were fun, loyal, and loving. The burden of not being able to tell them the whole truth weighed on her, but she'd made an agreement that which couldn't be altered. Her lungs constricted with that knowledge.

Maggie headed toward the dance floor. "Oh, I love this song."

Her declaration interrupted Aimee's maudlin thoughts.

"It's time to throw caution to the wind. Dance on wood instead of the vinyl on your seat. You're not fooling anyone," Irene added, extending her hand to Aimee.

Holy smokes. There were times like this when she really thought Irene possessed the ability to read minds. Yes, Aimee wanted to dance, and again, what harm would come from it? It's not like she had a signature move that would give away her identity. She made a snap decision after scanning the surrounding area. Her body vibrated with excitement.

Aimee slapped her hand into Irene's and smiled. "You're right, but only one dance."

Irene's grip closed around her hand, pulling her closer to Maggie. "And at least two encores."

Maggie's pleasure lit up her face when she saw Aimee. "Crap, now I owe Irene twenty dollars."

"What?" Aimee stopped moving, her gaze going back and forth between her friends. "You bet on this?"

"Of course we did. You practically forced our hands with your stubbornness," Irene said, shaking her shoulders to the beat.

"You're both incorrigible," Aimee replied with a laugh. She threw her hands in the air and twirled to the beat.

Before long, her cheeks strained from the size of her smile. She felt alive. The three laughed and danced through another song before the band slowed it down to a familiar love ballad. A slight twinge of longing pinched Aimee's heart as she watched Trent Jacobs, the town's sheriff and her boss, navigate his way through the couples gathered on the dance floor toward his fiancée, Maggie. Those two were a perfect pairing, and Aimee didn't begrudge their merriment. They made each other insanely happy. It was the fact that her dream of love, family, and a picket fence would never happen.

Trent slid Maggie against his body and gave his assistant his best puppy-dog face. "I know it's ladies' night, Aimee, but I need this dance, then she's all yours."

"If it keeps you smiling at work, dance twice," Aimee replied.

He winked at her before twirling Maggie farther into the mass of dancers.

A hand snagged Aimee's arm, halting her exit from the dance floor. "Don't leave now, hot stuff. I need a close-up after watching your sweet performance," a man she hadn't seen before said while he tugged her closer. His breath smelled like stale beer, and his brown eyes were dilated. His fingers dug into the tender flesh of her upper arm, making her wince. "Curvy and plump."

She jerked her arm back to try to break free of his grasp. "Take your hand off me right now. I'm not interested."

"Don't play hard to get." He tugged her against his body.

Aimee's ire erupted at this man's barbaric behavior. She'd never been a pushover, but a sense of *déjà vu* assaulted her. There was no way she'd allow herself to be trapped or powerless again. Straightening her spine, she placed her hands on his stomach and shoved herself backward and out of his embrace. "I said—"

"You nitwitted Neanderthal, no means no!" Irene barked from behind her.

Aimee turned away from the man and looped her arm through Irene's. "Thanks for having my back. What a jerk."

"Anytime, dear," Irene said before she turned to give that man one last glare. "He needs a serious attitude adjustment and lessons on how to be a gentleman."

Once they reached the booth, Irene ordered three water bottles from their waitress. Aimee took a seat and fanned herself with her hand. She'd forgotten how much energy she burned when dancing.

A familiar deep voice caused her to look up. "Do you want me to remove the trash you bagged?" Clarke motioned toward the jerk who watched her from across the room.

"No, it's handled. Besides, I think Irene scared the crap out of him." She appreciated that he'd asked her instead of making a scene.

Clarke nodded and headed back toward the group of men he'd just left.

When the band finished the ballad, they announced a fifteen-minute break.

"I love slow songs," Maggie purred as she approached the table, her cheeks rosy and her eyes bright.

"That's because you and lover boy engaged in dancing foreplay," Irene announced like a host of a wildlife show on television.

Aimee burst out laughing at Irene's reply, especially when Maggie's mouth popped open and her eyes went huge.

She slid into the booth next to Irene. "Oh my God, at least Trent didn't hear you. You'd embarrass the poor man."

"What? I'm old, not dead," Irene said, before twisting off the cap to her water the waitress had delivered.

"Ladies, I'd like to introduce my friend, Noah. Noah, this is Irene, and you should remember Aimee," Trent said as the two stood in front of their table.

Noah extended his hand to each woman. "Irene, Aimee."

"Noah, it's so good to see you again. When did you get into town?" Maggie asked before hopping out of the booth to give him a hug.

"A little while ago. I sent Trent a text to let him know I'd arrived, and he told me to meet him here."

"Let me get you a beer, buddy," Trent said, getting the server's attention.

"Well, at least you're willing to come to the table, unlike our friend who prefers the shadows." Irene pointed to Clarke—who lingered in the background chatting with Lance Charles, Trent's deputy sheriff—and waved them both over.

"Irene, he's a good man. Maybe he's just overwhelmed by your constant critique of him," Maggie admonished.

Irene raised an eyebrow. "Oh hush, it builds character."

"Sorry, we only allow her out every so often," Aimee said as her cheeks tightened into a slight smile.

Irene turned her attention toward Noah. "You, honey, are easy on the eyes. Are you single? Visiting for a little R and R?" she asked, waggling her eyebrows.

Noah's cheeks reddened, but he recovered, rolling with the punches as he said, "Wow, that's quite a welcome. It seems I made the right choice in moving to Mill Creek. All this lovely female attention will be good for my soul."

Everyone laughed except Trent, who grumbled at Irene. "Be nice, or you're going to chase away all the eligible bachelors."

Maggie's eyes widened briefly before her eyebrows drew together, concern written all over her face. "Don't get me wrong, having you here permanently is awesome, but are you okay? Did you retire from the FBI?"

Lance and Clarke joined the group in time to hear Maggie's question. Everyone turned their heads back to Noah, as the group waited on his answer.

Noah shook his head. "Nope, too young for retirement, but my boss, Special Agent in Charge Tim Guzman, offered me a new assignment. I start in a few weeks. The best part is I can live wherever I want, provided there's an FBI office close, which means Boise fits that requirement."

Trent slapped his friend on the back. "Hot damn, that's great news. Welcome to Mill Creek, man. I'll give you the official tour of the area tomorrow."

"Perfect, and a real estate agent," Noah added.

"I guess it's up to me to get the conversation back on track before we all smack backs and celebrate. Right or left? And do you even know how to throw a ball?" Clarke asked.

The waitress delivered a new round of beer and drinks to the table. Trent handed one to Noah and snagged one for himself. "To friends and new beginnings," he declared, raising his beer and clanking each glass and bottle. "Don't worry, Clarke, Noah will pick up your shortcomings."

The guitarist started to play a riff, signaling they were back and interrupting the banter between the men.

"That's our cue to leave. Enjoy the dancing, ladies," Trent said to the group. He pressed a kiss to Maggie's lips before guiding Noah, Lance, and Clarke toward the bar.

"Let's dance," Maggie sang out, grabbing Irene's hand and holding one out to Aimee.

Aimee declined with a wave. "I'm going to head home early. I've got a terrible headache starting, and I'm exhausted."

Maggie grasped Aimee's hand. "Do you need anything? I can have Trent take you home."

"No, I'm good, and I'm not leaving this second. Go dance," Aimee replied, shooing her friends to the dance floor. "Besides, it's Mill Creek, not some big city," she tacked on, not wanting to have an escort as her friends headed toward the crowd.

Aimee sat and listened to a few more songs before making her exit. When she reached the big front doors, she turned to say goodnight to the bouncer and exited. The cool, damp air from fall wrapped around her heated body, carrying with it a subtle scent of pine and rain. Mountain living appealed to her, especially the gorgeous views of the stars at night. Tonight was darker than normal since the stars were hidden behind a thick blanket of clouds.

Droplets of water dotted the sidewalk, which caused Aimee to alter her route by taking the shortcut through the alleyway between the bar and Knotty Pine Tree. She paused briefly at the opening of the narrow passage to look and listen because being drenched, cold, and taking the long route held zero appeal. Bright lights illuminated each end but left the middle section darker. No noises or movement caught her eye, so she squelched her concerns and strode down the pathway.

Around the halfway mark, she heard male voices and laughter in front of her, but the big metal trash bin blocked her view. She slowed as she approached the square object. Beyond the metal structure were three men, and the one in the center was the jerk from the bar. The beat of her heart quickened and caused a rush of blood to pound in her ears. Like a slot machine landing all sevens, her brain registered the mistake she'd made. Now, being cold and wet a little longer didn't seem like the worst choice. Decision made, she propelled her feet to move with purpose and would ignore anything they said.

"My luck has improved tonight," Jerk-o announced to his friends. He stepped directly in front of her, blocking her path.

Refusing to show this idiot any fear, she forced steel into her words and gave him a piece of her mind. "Get out of my way. I already told you no, and nothing has changed—" The words abruptly stopped as her breath whooshed out of her mouth when he yanked her against his chest and into his arms.

"She's that girl I told you guys about earlier. All I want from you is to finish our dance."

Aimee struggled against his grasp. "You're upsetting me. Just let me go. I don't want to dance."

He pressed his face next to her ear and whispered, "Come on, don't embarrass me in front of my friends. Besides, who wants to go home alone?"

Aimee's eyes widened at this creep's gall. She jerked her knee up, disheartened when she narrowly missed his groin. He'd sidestepped her attack and shoved her backward. In a flash, she twisted her body to miss the wooden pallets stacked off to the side but landed hard on her hands and knees. Her skin burned from the asphalt and rocks that tore her flesh.

"Stupid bitch," Jerk Face spat out as he moved toward her. "I told you, I only want a fucking dance. What's your problem?"

To her surprise, instead of being attacked, all she heard were the pounding of footsteps as the three men retreated. Aimee grimaced as she lifted her body from the ground, her knees raw and bleeding. Her white tropical knit skirt and long-sleeved T-shirt did little to protect her skin from the ground or the elements. Her legs trembled, threatening to give out, so instead of ending up back on the ground, she sat down on the stacked skids. When she looked up, a hulking form headed in her direction. *Clarke.* Taking a moment to catch her breath, she flashed back to the night she loathed.

She'd escaped. Had pushed her body as hard as she could toward the big gate that separated the house from the road. The sound of a single gunshot echoed through the air. Aimee's breath caught in her throat while fear crawled up her neck. Her footsteps lumbered as she struggled to stay upright. Seconds later, her face slammed into the newly laid turf; a mixture of grass and dirt infused her senses while her knees dug into the soft ground. In the distance, a flicker of red, blue, and white lights caught her attention, a beacon of hope encouraging her to keep fighting—to keep moving forward.

A deep voice bellowed out her name a second before strong arms hefted her body off the ground. Her memory faded as warmth infused her body. Clarke cradled her to his chest. Tears streamed down Aimee's face and bit into her cheeks from the cold air that funneled through the corridor. The adrenaline that had coursed through her body moments ago retreated, leaving her limbs heavy and her eyes drooping from exhaustion.

"I've got you, you're safe now," he crooned, sitting on the same spot she'd just occupied.

He supported her in his arms as if she were precious to him. This strong, virile man with his bald head, numerous tattoos, and blunt attitude could be so soft and caring. So many people misunderstood him. They lumped him into different categories due to his appearance or his motorcycle. Human nature seemed to gravitate toward making judgments without seeking facts or details in many situations. Something she, too, was guilty of doing when she'd first met him.

"I know," she replied, content to stay in his arms for a little longer while she soaked up his body heat and tightened her resolve.

"Can I see the damage?" he asked, his dark brown eyes angled down to assess her.

When she nodded her consent, he kept her anchored against his body with one hand while he used the other to lift each leg and inspect her knees. After he finished, he tilted her head up with his index finger so he could see her face. His movements were gentle. His brows were drawn together while he studied her. The clenching of his jaw was his only sign of anger. A deep, sudden intake of breath shifted her in his arms.

"I'm sorry, I should've insisted on taking out that trash earlier. That man, he was the one from the bar earlier, right? I'm guessing the other two were his friends?" He exhaled a deep breath and the sincerity of his gesture caught her off guard. The warmth of his breath feathered across her skin.

She nodded. "He wanted to finish his dance, and when I tried to knee him where it counts, he shoved me to dodge my attempt."

Clarke's smile transformed his face. "I like a fighter. I'm just sorry he avoided your knee. He deserved that and much more."

"I don't want to excuse his behavior because it sucked, but I don't think he meant for me to get hurt. I think he's just an obstinate pig."

"So, I guess that leaves me with the 'what the hell were you thinking?' when you broke what I'd call rule number three."

"What are you babbling about? What's rule three?"

"You know, rule one: stranger danger. Rule two: don't jump in front of moving vehicles, and rule three: avoid dark alleyways when alone. No, scratch that, every damn time."

Aimee pushed out of his arms and stood. "Your timing was perfect. Now I need to get home. I appreciate your concern, but I don't need a lecture."

"I'd beg to argue; however, I'll give you a pass tonight if you promise I can walk you home to clean and bandage those knees. That'll satisfy the protective side of me. I'll call Trent on the way so you can file an assault and battery report on that dickwad."

Aimee panicked. A police report would be the exact opposite of what she was supposed to be doing—lying low. That certainly did not live up to blending into her newly crafted identity. She could practically hear the US Marshal in charge of her protective detail reinforcing, ad nauseam, the importance of staying in the background and embracing her new identity. She hadn't seen that loser before, so he had to be a tourist, which meant the odds of seeing him again would be slim. The thought of letting him go stung, but she had other concerns.

She thrust her hand against the impenetrable wall of Clarke's body and stopped him from standing. "You can walk me home and help me with my knees. I'm not filing a report because of a stupid decision."

Clarke's brow lifted. "Run that past me again? What he did was wrong on so many levels."

"Yes, he overstepped. I'm not going to ruin his life because he made an ass out of himself. I know you don't understand, but it's my decision." She turned and took one step down the alley and winced. Her knees hurt from the movement.

"You're right, and for the record, I don't agree with your decision. Let me give you a boost to your place."

Did this man miss anything? She winced shaking out her hand. Her world went sideways for a second time tonight. In a flash, his strong arms slid around her body, hoisting up against his chest. Damn him, she liked how she felt in his arms.

She directed him toward her place on Main Street above one of the stores. It wasn't much, but it was all she needed now. After he ascended the stairs in the back of the hardware and feed store, she removed her keys from her pocket and laid them in his outstretched palm. She expected him to put her down, instead he easily held her and unlocked the door in one fluid motion.

Once inside, she flipped the light switch on the wall by the door and pointed to the sofa. He hesitated momentarily before depositing her on the center cushion.

"Where's your first aid kit?" he asked. His gaze roamed the small living area.

"Bathroom under the sink, and the washcloth on the towel rack is clean."

She took the opportunity to study his powerful, muscular frame as he moved to get her supplies. He had to be at least six feet five inches tall and weigh over two hundred pounds.

Even at his size, his motions were efficient and graceful. He was comfortable in his own skin. His presence took up most of the free space in this tiny studio.

When he returned, he squatted in front of her and examined her wounded knees. Carefully, he wiped away the dried blood, added antibiotic ointment, and applied several bandages.

When he finished, he looked up and watched her for a few seconds. "Do you have any frozen vegetables in the freezer? That'll help with the bruising."

"Uh, no, I have a tray of ice, though."

He nodded and made his way toward the kitchen. When he returned with ice wrapped in a towel, he instructed her to alternate icing each knee. "I know a thing or two about icing injuries. This'll help keep the swelling and bruising down."

She wondered what type of injuries he'd sustained, but the words stuck on her tongue. "Thanks, Clarke."

He took a seat on sofa and ran his gaze over her body. Her skin tingled under his intense scrutiny. "I've got be honest, I'm pissed at myself for not taking care of that douche earlier. I also wish your knee would've had him singing soprano. Are you okay?"

"I'm fine, really," Aimee replied, then shifted the bag of ice to her other knee.

"How long have you lived here? Are you still unpacking?"

That question threw her off balance and wasn't what she'd expected him to say next. "No, I decided to purge a lot of things from my life when I moved here. When this space became available, I jumped at the opportunity. The location is prefect. It's easy to clean, and Daniel and Lana have placed me in charge of security for their Hardware and Feed Store."

His eyebrows scrunched together. "What does that mean?"

"I'm kidding, it's our joke," Aimee replied on a stifled yawn. "I'm sorry, it's not the company. I'm exhausted."

"Understood. I'll head out so you can rest." He pulled out his cellphone. "Give me your number so I can call you. Then, you'll have mine. If you need anything, don't hesitate to use it."

She hedged for a moment, then relented. Having friends helped her blend in and build her new life, but she still controlled what she shared and how close she allowed anyone to get. She called out her numbers while he diligently typed the information into his phone. Seconds later, her phone vibrated, so she answered his call before adding his data to her contact list.

"Good night, Aimee." Clarke said. "Lock the door after me," he added after he crossed the threshold and closed the door behind him.

His concern and thoughtfulness about her safety caused a spot deep inside her chest to expand. Knowing she had support mattered to her.

It was nice to have a few people you could count on from time to time. Loneliness sucked and could overwhelm a person.

That thought made her stomach flutter with hope, until her mind caught up and stomped on that bubble until it burst. She didn't deserve a do-over with her life. She was alone for a reason.

Two

CLARKE DRAGOON HOVERED HIS mouse over the camera icon on his monitor's display before clicking it. A ritual that was ingrained in him, not that he'd expected to find anything amiss on his footage. When you had more enemies than friends, you learned to put in safeguards. His thoughts turned to the day his mother's sister, Elizabeth Pickle, had informed him she was giving him her house. That had been right before she'd been diagnosed with Alzheimer's, well before she'd moved into a long-term care facility.

His aunt enjoyed life to its fullest, and being a flight attendant had allowed her to travel the world. His mother had always teased her sister since she had these wild thoughts zipping through her head that typically ended with a streak of paranoia. Now, Elizabeth lived in Boise at a memory care facility. This past June, he'd decided it was time to move into her home, but he'd kept her name on the deed. He liked the mountain setting and the small town of Mill Creek.

Getting used to nosy residents took patience, but the bomb shelter his aunt had built into the basement during the original construction trumped any negative. Those layers of protection provided a buffer between his personal and work life.

Over the last four months, he'd been occupied with renovating his new home. He was proud of his accomplishments, from the updated kitchen, bathrooms, new roof and windows, to the fresh coats of paint inside and out. The bomb shelter, which he now called his command center, had been perfectly constructed from the beginning. It had its own ventilation system, air filtration, reinforced walls, and an emergency exit, which saved him a good deal of cash. *God, I love my aunt.*

All he had to do was transform the shelter's interior into a wonderland. He'd worked with an electrician to rig the space for all his high-tech gadgets, which included a secured area with a biometric lock that housed his weapons locker, medical supplies, bug-out gear, food, and other gadgets he'd acquired.

Frustration still pulsed through his system, even after his two-mile run earlier. He could blame it on a sleepless night, but his culprit had bright hazel eyes with curves and a killer smile. Aimee's adamance about not pressing charges and reporting last night's incident bothered him. That asshole deserved to be prosecuted to the fullest extent of the law. It made him itch to run into the bastard so he could educate him on the proper way to treat women.

He finished reviewing his surveillance footage and started to cycle through each individual camera feed. He rubbed his eyes with the heels of his hands and let out a deep breath. Why hadn't he taken care of that bastard when he'd seen him being handsy with Aimee on the dance floor? The world didn't need men who acted like that, and Clarke had a real problem with anyone who victimized women, children, and animals. Had that douchebag threatened Aimee, making her afraid to defy him? No, she wouldn't allow that, she had too much pride.

There was also the disturbing fact that her home had zero personal items--no mementos, photographs, or magazines. Hell, she didn't even have food in the freezer. Not that it was wrong either way, but most people at least had a frozen meal or something. If he hadn't known better, it looked like a hotel instead of her home. The place she'd lived for the last ten months was barren.

He clicked on the next camera and did a double take at the screen. *What the hell is my neighbor doing?* He shot out of his chair, ascended the stairs, and exited his house, rushing toward Irene, who clung to the top rung of a ladder. "What the hell, Irene? Are you trying to kill yourself?" Clarke asked in a stern tone, shielding his eyes from the sun as he looked up at her.

"Good grief! Didn't your father teach you that you shouldn't startle a person while they're on a ladder? What does it look like I'm doing, my hair?" she shot right back at him as he looked up at her.

He had to give it to her, she was determined. She redefined "busy-body," but her mind worked like a race car. He'd never admit to this out loud, but she had a heart of gold. Her cantankerous spirit was another matter altogether. A Mill Creek lifer, she protected everyone and everything she cared about, right down to the books at the library where she worked.

He grabbed a hold of the ladder to steady it. "Get down, right this minute. I don't want you to kill yourself. I'd be the number-one suspect."

"If the brooding shoe fits, Mr. Dragoon. Besides, you'd be lonely without all my attention. Oh, and who would complain to the sheriff regarding your insane need to walk and inspect your property? What's the rock count this week?" she asked, while she worked her way down each rung.

Clarke smiled and rubbed his head. He stepped back to make room for her when she got to the bottom step. Once she was clear, he climbed up to inspect the section of gutter that had held her attention. After several minutes, he identified the problem. "These gutters need to be cleaned out," he said, then moved closer to the sagging section.

She folded her arms over her breasts and huffed. "Thanks, Captain Obvious, I had that much figured out."

"Stubborn woman," he muttered under his breath. "Okay, this section separated from the weight of all these wet leaves and debris. One clamp from the hardware store should solve the problem. This fix and a clean out should take about three hours, more or less."

Irene held Clarke's gaze. "You're offering to help? That could ruin your bad boy reputation."

He cocked his head at the small woman. "That's a risk I'm willing to take. Stay away from that ladder. I'll be back in a bit."

Irene called out to his retreating form, "Keep the receipt. I'll pay you back."

C LARKE GUIDED HIS MOTORCYCLE into a parking space outside the diner to catch an early lunch. He planned to call Aimee after he ate to see if he could bring her food.

Mill Creek might be a quaint, small town, but it had some amazing restaurants. The town's architecture appealed to him with the mix of wood, brick, and siding. He loved the long wood-planked sidewalks on Main Street, complete with horse hitching posts. Pretty much each building had its own look and style, which made it unique but showed personality. The residents were good-hearted and loyal, even if the gossip mill worked overtime.

He glanced at his phone when he received the text message alert and grimaced. The psychologist he'd been dodging for the last two weeks had now resorted to messaging him. He knew it was procedure, but it irked him to have a shrink digging into his personal space. Clarke was confident he could discern if he were having a mental breakdown or losing his shit. He didn't need a therapist to sugarcoat it and ask repeatedly, "Tell me how that makes you feel." His psychological fitness evaluation would have to wait.

He'd return the call after he finished his mandatory leave. That last assignment had been a clusterfuck and would haunt him forever. By his calculation, he had just over a week left to figure out what the hell had him all twisted up. He enjoyed his time off. Now, he poured his energy into home improvement projects. It'd been a nice change of pace to let his guard down some and not sleep with one eye open. His aunt's home had now been converted into his primary residence, and he liked the idea that he'd lain down roots. Not sure why that appealed to him, but it did.

Mentally, he complied his to-do list for after lunch. Since the forecast had called for more rain on Sunday, the gutters became a top priority. Hoping to see Aimee put a smile on his face. He wanted to verify that she was doing all right from last night. Also, he wanted to see if she'd change her mind and press charges.

The chimes above Knotty Pine Tree's door jingled as he moved over the threshold. He'd looked forward to Saturday's special all week long. The owners, Peter and Sally, were masters in the kitchen, but Sally's fried chicken and fixings were legendary. Clarke planned to order two servings—one for now, and the second for dinner later.

When his vision adjusted to the interior lighting, he scanned the restaurant for an open booth. He'd taken no more than three steps before his feet stopped dead in their tracks. *What the hell?* Disbelief slammed into him while his hands curled into fists at his side. His body coiled tight, ready to strike. Clarke was torn momentarily over confronting that very same dickwad from last night who'd just finished speaking to Aimee sitting in a booth in the diner. Or follow him outside and let his fists do the talking. Although he'd love to hunt that man down and make him pay, he chose Aimee over revenge.

AIMEE DIDN'T HAVE TO turn her head to confirm what her body already knew. She'd sensed Clarke's presence the moment he entered the diner. She turned to greet him as he approached the table. His eyes were drawn together, and a scowl stretched across his face.

"What the ever-loving hell is going on? Is that thug harassing you?" Clarke asked in a deep, low voice she hoped didn't carry to other tables.

She motioned for him to sit and waited for him to fold his large frame into the booth. His dark brown orbs scanned and cataloged every minute detail. The man missed nothing and had her at the center of his attention. There was no point in holding anything back. He'd dig until he found out what he wanted to know. The sooner she could put this behind her, the better.

Aimee pinned him with a look. "I'm not entirely sure. He approached my table and uttered an apology then left. I didn't say one word to him. I'm not sure if he saw you and left or if that was all he wanted to do."

"I think you need to tell Trent. I don't buy it."

"As I said last night, it's over. Hopefully, that's the last time I'll see him. I'm pretty sure he's a visitor, since I haven't seen him around before last night."

Clarke put his elbows on the table and exhaled. "I don't agree, but I'll respect your decision. Something is off with that man. Promise me, if he *just appears* again, you'll let me know immediately. If that happens, then you should report all of it to Trent."

Her insides churned with indecision because a part of her agreed with him. That man should be held accountable for his actions. People can't force others to do things against their will. He'd scared her half to death last night. The problem was, she'd made a promise when she'd entered the Witness Security Program to embrace her new identity—to live in the shadows and blend in. A police report and potential court hearing were the opposite of that pledge. A simple fact that she couldn't divulge to Clarke or anyone in her life, which meant keeping secrets. *God, why did I take that damn alley last night?*

"I'll promise to let you know," she said, turning her attention toward the menu on the table.

Those words she meant, but she knew he didn't miss her sidestep about reporting the incident. The glimpse of disappointment that flickered in his gaze bothered her. Hopefully, she'd never see that man again, and this would be a moot point. This whole WITSEC thing sucked, but she couldn't go back and undo the past. A lesson she'd mastered in her life.

A waitress stopped by their table with a pad of paper and pencil at the ready. "You two ready to order?"

Aimee closed the menu. "The special and a slice of apple pie. To go, please."

The waitress jotted down her notes and turned her attention to Clarke.

"I'll have the same, but with two specials."

The waitress smiled and winked at Clarke, who seemed oblivious to her flirting. His entire attention was directed at Aimee. "How are you feeling today?"

Pursing her lips, she took a quick survey of her body. "I'm good."

"Whoa, slow down, all those details are overwhelming me, sweetheart."

"My knees are a little sore, but nothing I can't handle," she said, ignoring his arrogance.

She glanced past him to look out the window then snapped her head further to the right. Dark plumes of smoke stained the air surrounding the hardware store and her studio. The deep wail of sirens and horns from the firetrucks reached her ears moments before she saw the streaks of red metal pass the diner. People walking down Main Street either stopped to stare or hurriedly moved toward the frenzy. She grabbed her purse and zipped out of the booth. Determination and anxiety fueled her steps as she ran toward her home. *Please don't let the fire destroy that box.*

"Aimee, wait!" Clarke hollered at her retreating form, but she kept running full speed toward the disaster.

Hidden Identities, Book 2 in the Mill Creek Mystique romantic suspense series is out now.

BOOKS BY BAILEY THOMAS

ROMANTIC SUSPENSE

Mill Creek Mystique Series

Watch for the next book in the series
Kane's Reckoning

CONTEMPORARY ROMANCE

Torrent of Hearts us also available in the
Pack Your Bags short story collection

As an only child, Bailey Thomas' active imagination and adventurous nature always kept her busy. Now, she channels those creative powers into storytelling.

Living in the Southwest, Bailey splits her time between crafting heartfelt stories and indulging in her favorite pastimes—whether it's devouring books, marathoning shows, or catching a game.

Life is too short, so Bailey tries to live by her motto of finding adventures that make you smile. She loves to hear from her readers. You can find and connect with her at the links below.

Website/Blog:
baileythomasauthor.com
Instagram
instagram.com/Author_BaileyThomas
BookBub
bookbub.com/authors/bailey-thomas

ACKNOWLEDGEMENTS

I'm so fortunate to have the best readers in the world; none of this would be possible without you. Please leave a review. They are a tremendous help to the author and other readers looking for their next book. Also, don't forget to sign up for my newsletter or follow me on social media to stay updated on book news and events.

Thank you to A Fabulous Productions for creating the stunning print and eBook layouts and outstanding marketing support. You've made everything more manageable and taught me so much.

Lastly, to my Vicki Jean, who has always believed in me, thank you for always wanting me in your life. I love you to the moon and back!